Sparkelicious

LIBBY FLOYD

ISBN: 0985847638
ISBN-13: 978-0-9858476-30

DEDICATION

Sparkelicious is dedicated to my mom, for her undeniable belief in me, to my father for watching over me every day from above, to my husband, for his love and support, to the Minnesota winters for forcing me to escape the cold through my writing and to the South for its incredible charm and beauty.

Chapter One

Laney Montgomery checked her diamond studded Technomarine watch, swept her blonde, shoulder length hair into an *I Dream of Jeannie* up do and dressed for the evening. She had plans to meet her mom and two sisters at seven for dinner at The Lazy Goat, her favorite new dining spot since arriving in the cozy Southern town of Greenville, South Carolina. Laney had quickly become addicted to the Tapas bar's bohemian chic atmosphere, rare wine offerings and delectable menu.

The Goat, as the locals called it, was connected to The Drake, a swanky new hotel, where she was staying. The hotel showcased beautiful views of the Reedy River from its ten glorious floors of Fleetwood glass. It had a big city feel, impeccably designed with the sophistication of New York and the trendiness of L.A. *Rather surprising for a small Southern town that'd grown up around textile mills,* she thought.

Laney had left the sleepy little town behind fourteen years ago. Even though she had moved to the City of Angels, she often reminisced about her idyllic upbringing in Greenville. She had missed so many family events over the years and could never get those moments back. She remembered her hometown as being so small, so boring, which was the reason she left. But now, Greenville wasn't quite so lethargic anymore. It was vibrant and alive.

Laney admired its new found hipness: the downtown main street abuzz with coffee shops, European bistros, sushi bars and quaint boutiques. All of the stores and shops were just a short walk away from The Drake, which Laney loved, because no one walked anywhere in L.A.

It had been six months since she'd seen her mom and sisters when they all came out west for a visit on her birthday, staying at her posh Hollywood Hills home. And Laney had only returned twice to Greenville in the last five years; when her father died; and when her mother remarried. She found it way too difficult to go home without her father being there.

Laney had become a very successful fashion designer, making a name for herself in Hollywood. Her "Sparkelicious" clothing line had become the *it* attire amongst all of the popular up and coming ingénues in the movie biz. The paparazzi photographed many of them wearing the blingy comfy clothes in the local coffee shops, or on their way to power meetings. And seeing as every day appeared to be casual Friday in L.A., her Sparkelicious brand had become de rigueur of Tinseltown.

After ten years of hard work, Laney's fashion degree at the University of South Carolina had finally paid off. She was a talented designer, but her sheer determination to succeed and marketing smarts was the driving force that had made the line a sensation. No one could ever say otherwise. And Laney had been that way her entire life. She'd worked tirelessly in her dad's restaurant all through high school, instilling a strong work ethic in her.

Blonde, trim and tan, Laney was a walking advertisement for her Sparkelicious brand. She'd managed to almost reach the ripe old California age of shhhhh…four zero…without the aid of Botox, Restalyne or lipo. The sunny, healthy California lifestyle suited her well and she still had a very striking, youthful look considering she was *milf* age. Laney loved the outdoors and enjoyed her long walks along Santa Monica Beach and up in the Hollywood Hills.

Laney had been happily married to Thomas Morgan for nine years. He was a film director from across the pond and twelve years her senior. She'd met Thomas on a shoot for a TV commercial when she first arrived in L.A. and was working as a fashion buyer for Macy's. Laney Montgomery had fallen hook, line and sinker. His intelligence, humor and charm combined with his offbeat good looks and smooth British accent made a big impression on her. He was unlike any other man that she'd ever met, and he sure wasn't like any of the conservative Southern boys she'd dated. He was edgy and exciting. She was crazy about Thomas and their age difference had never been an issue…until recently.

The last few months had been rough on their marriage. Thomas had needed emergency surgery for a thrashed appendix and was hospitalized at Cedar-Sinai for a couple of days. Although the surgery was a little more than minor, Thomas had made it much more of a big deal and was milking it for all it was worth. He acted as if he was entitled to order Laney around once he was home from the hospital. Since the surgery, Thomas just wasn't the same. While he'd made a full recovery physically, mentally his once vibrant spirit was replaced with an irritable grouchiness she'd never witnessed before. Laney understood his frustrations with suddenly being taken ill, and feeling his age, but she didn't understand his newly adopted negativity. She gladly played nurse 24/7, but no matter how much she did for Thomas, he didn't seem the slightest bit appreciative. All the same, she remained sympathetic to his health crisis in every way and did everything she could to get him back on his feet.

Yes, she'd been the good wife, never complaining about his tireless demands, but lately she was beginning to feel that they were growing apart. Laney wondered if Thomas would ever be the same sweet, romantic man she'd fallen in love with. She often thought about their special times together; those halcyon days traveling through Europe along the French Riviera and the Amalfi coast. And she missed her husband's thoughtful nature. During the "honeymoon period" of their marriage, whenever Laney had a long tiring day at work, he'd have a candlelit home cooked gourmet meal and a bottle of French wine waiting for her. Dinner was often followed by a soothing foot massage to further ease her stresses of the day. But what Laney missed most of all was their explosive sex life. It was beyond amazing. She had never felt that kind of connection with any man until she met Thomas. "Mr. Tough Act to Follow," she liked to call him. But post surgery their sex life was pretty much nonexistent. No, this wasn't the same Thomas Morgan she'd married.

While Laney constantly worried about his well-being, over time she began to feel that she needed to take a step back and take care of herself again. It was exhausting running her fashion business from home and caring for a demanding husband.

The trip to South Carolina was a much needed break. Laney was hesitant about leaving Thomas behind, but much to her surprise he insisted that she go. She finally accepted the plain fact that it would be an ideal time for her to see her family and be free of her L.A. responsibilities for a couple of weeks. Well, she wouldn't be completely free of them all; she would stay in constant phone contact with her star clients, just in case of any emergency.

It was a magical Southern summer night. The sun was setting like molasses in the sky. Humidity wrapped around Laney's body like a hot damp blanket as she walked the short distance through the open crosswalk from The Drake Hotel to the entrance of The Lazy Goat. Laney smiled as she passed the young hostess and walked down the mahogany staircase that led into the trendy downstairs bar.

It was crowded with hip Greenville-ites and the atmosphere was upbeat. The last orange glows of sun peeked through the walls of glass that overlooked the Reedy River. Laney found a solitary barstool at the end of the long, contemporary concrete bar and took in the stunning view.

Thanks to her Sparkelicious baby pink hoodie outfit, the extremely cute bartender noticed her right away. "What can I get you?" he asked in a sprightly tone.

"I'll take a glass of Brunelli, please," Laney shot back with a smile.

The bartender nodded, as if to say he agreed with her wine selection. "Coming right up," he announced. Within moments he returned with Laney's favorite red vino – an Italian red from the famous Brunelli vineyard. "Here ya go." He placed the glass down on the bar in front of her, while topping up the customer's glass with more beer beside her.

"Thanks." Laney smiled and lifted the glass to her nose and breathed in the fruity bouquet. She swirled the wine around in her glass and then sipped it. As she savored the bold taste, memories of her vacation in Tuscany with Thomas immediately came back to her.

Her mother, Sophie, and two sisters, Missy and Bridgett, were nowhere in sight. Unlike Laney, punctuality was never their strong suit so she idled her time people watching. She glanced at the bartender as he worked the bar like Tom Cruise in the movie *Cocktails*. He knew how to pour a mean drink and was an excellent multi-tasker. He appeared to be a young stud in his mid-twenties, maybe pushing thirty. It was hard for Laney to tell. Either way, she couldn't help but admire his dashing good looks. His wavy jet black hair and chiseled features were definitely striking. And due to his model-like build and height, she also noticed that he wore his faded jeans and black t-shirt awfully well. With her fashion background, she was always looking at people from a designer's standpoint, or at least, that's what she was telling herself right now, and he definitely had a catwalk kind of appeal.

"So, how do you like the Brunelli?" He asked, stirring two cosmos from a couple feet away.

"It's my favorite," Laney beamed. "I discovered it in Siena. A little restaurant just off the Piazza del Campo served it. I love it."

He dried a wet beer mug with his white towel and gazed into her deep blue eyes. "Really? I love Siena."

Laney caressed the stem of her wine glass. "You've been there?" She was definitely intrigued.

The bartender slung his towel over his shoulder. "Oh yeah, a couple of times. I love traveling and I love great wine. The Brunelli's my favorite red wine too. I have a glass every night after work. There's no need to go all the way to Italy when we serve it right here in Greenville."

Laney was impressed with his sophistication. "It's a small world isn't it?" She wanted to talk more about Italy with him, but she could see that he had other customers vying for his attention. "Well, I guess we both have great taste, don't we?" Laney chirped, then found herself thinking, *What'd I just say? I must look ridiculously ancient and married.* The guy was gorgeous and she could easily pass for his much older sister. Still, she was flattered by his flirtatious attention.

"I guess, we do, ma'am."

Ma'am? Ouch. That hurt.

Before Laney had a chance to feel like a middle-aged soccer mom, he extended his hand and smiled. "I'm Matt, your downstairs bartender."

"Are all of the bartenders in Greenville as cute as you?" Laney surprised herself with that quip. "I'm sorry, don't know where that came from," she mumbled with embarrassment, before introducing herself. "Hi. I'm Laney, I'm visiting from the City of Angels, but I'm originally from here," she said politely with her soft Southern lilt, shaking Matt's strong masculine hand in return.

"Nice to meet you, Laney from the City of Angels," Matt echoed charmingly, his eyes meeting hers without wavering.

Laney touched her blonde hair and felt a moment of shyness. After being married to Thomas for so many years, she had forgotten how to be flirted with.

"Nice to meet you too, downstairs bartender." She raised her glass and took another sip. Laney was starting to really enjoy herself.

"I think I saw you in here late last night, at the upstairs bar." Matt topped up her glass and shot her a boyish grin.

Now Laney felt like a barfly, and that she definitely wasn't. "Oh, yeah, I stopped in around ten after my flight."

"Thought so," he said, pouring more wine for the couple beside her. "I could never forget a face like yours."

She blushed at his compliment. *Or was it a compliment?* She wondered, doubting herself as she looked at Matt's perfect wrinkle free face. Her days as a teenage beauty queen seemed like a gazillion years ago. Laney wished she had the same unabashed confidence as she did back then. Life in Hollywood had made her more aware of her age. But no other man had really flirted so blazingly with her since Thomas, and she wasn't sure how to respond.

Matt noticed her flushed cheeks. "You're very beautiful. I'm sorry if I embarrassed you."

"Oh, wow, I mean, you didn't. Thank you." Laney was now sounding more like a bumbling idiot than a successful businesswoman. *He must be a player*, she thought, taking in a gathering of cute twenty-something females sitting at the opposite end of the bar, clearly in awe of him. Oddly, he seemed not to notice them. He seemed more like a celebrity than a bartender. She felt her face flush again as she nervously sipped her wine, hoping that her family would arrive soon. Personal compliments weren't something that she was used to getting. Her husband hadn't given her one in so long, she didn't know how to accept them. And almost all of the men she encountered in the fashion industry were gay.

"Well, it's true," Matt said softly before reacting to the waitress asking for more cosmos for table ten. "If you need anything, I won't be far away." He glided down the bar in a silly dance move. Laney couldn't help but laugh.

"Hi, honey," came the familiar soft Southern drawl from behind her. Her mom, Sophie, was dressed from head to toe in black sequins, looking every bit like a former Miss America right out of the fifties. Sophie was always overdressed and very glamorous. She looked pretty damn fabulous for a woman in her mid-seventies, especially considering she'd never had any form of cosmetic surgery. Mind you, she didn't need to.

"Honey, stand up. Let me look at you. You're looking a little thin. Are you eating?" Sophie continued her head-to-toe evaluation of her youngest daughter's svelte physique before Laney had even had a chance to blurt out a hello. "You're not doing some newfangled Hollywood diet, now are you?"

This was the standard greeting every time Laney saw her mom, perennially assessing and judging her. Sophie meant well, but she wasn't known for her diplomacy. She still saw Laney as her "perfect" little beauty queen, stuck in high school; and her stage mother ways always came out in spades whenever Laney visited home. As the baby of the family, Laney was destined to be treated as so, no matter how successful she was in L.A.

Laney was determined to not let her mom get to her on her first full night in town. She took another sip of wine, relaxed back on her barstool and let the alcohol kick in.

"Mom, hi, I'm eating. I'm fine," Laney replied with a hint of embarrassment in her voice as she noticed Matt ease dropping from behind the bar, with a grin on his handsome face. The Montgomerys weren't a touchy-feely family and Sophie certainly wasn't one to ever give out a hug. She had grown up on a farm, the youngest girl of seven kids, and always felt ignored by her parents. It wasn't that they didn't love her, but by the time she was born, her parents were exhausted from working overtime to keep food on the table for their large family. Sophie was left to take care of both herself and her baby brother, Eddie. She had to grow up fast and began working in the five and dime store by the age of thirteen. Sophie would often say, "The dogs got more attention than I did."

On the other hand, Laney had adopted more of the open California way; she wrapped her arms around her mom and gave her a big affectionate hug.

"Oh honey, don't be so dramatic," Sophie moaned, feeling claustrophobic as Laney pulled her tighter. She took a step back and patted her big bonnet of blonde hair to make sure it was still in place.

"Honey, you've gone and gotten all Hollywood on me now. But I have to say, you do look good. At least the California sunshine seems to be working for you. But don't get too much. You'll get those wrinkles right here…" she pointed to the little crinkles above her lips,

"...and you don't want those."

Normally, Laney would be ready to scream by now. Her mother's obsession with appearances drove her nuts, but she knew her mom meant well. Instead, she bit her tongue and went with a compliment.

"Mom, you look gorgeous and so 'Sparkelicious' as usual. And, as much as I miss South Carolina, California living is still fantastic."

Sophie smiled affectionately at her daughter. She was very proud of Laney's achievements. But she was obviously irked that Laney had decided to stay at The Drake Hotel and not with her on this trip. But she wasn't going to come out and say it in so many words. She would just make little digs to ensure Laney was aware of the fact.

"I spruced up the guest bedroom room just in case your fancy hotel room isn't up to your standards." Laney tried to snag Matt's attention to get her mom a drink. "How much do they charge a night, anyway?" Sophie asked.

"Chillax, Mom. I can afford it."

Relaxing wasn't something that either one of them were good at doing together or separately. Tonight however, Laney was going to make sure that they both found a way to loosen up, for her own sake. It was her vacation and for once she was going to have a good time on her terms without having to deal with everyone else's stress. But so far, she would need more than one glass of wine to take the edge off.

Matt came over with empathy in his eyes for Laney carrying the opened bottle of Brunelli. It seemed he could sense her stress level had just shot up a notch or two. Laney ordered her mom's favorite cocktail: a martini with extra olives, hoping that Sophie would let her hair down for a while.

Greenville was a cosmopolitan Southern town, yet still small. Sophie had to keep her wits about her when she was out, or she would be the talk around the church service on Sunday. Laney had begun to realize she came from a family that talked a lot but, in truth, said very little. Her family never really opened up about their true feelings. It was almost always small talk.

Sophie told her who had died and who was sick, and rambled on about a bunch of people that Laney didn't know; and she was starting to drift off. Laney was hoping to get some real quality time with her mom but it wasn't looking or sounding particularly auspicious. Maybe after Sophie had her second martini, they could talk about how they were both really doing and what was really going on, but for now, Laney indulged her mom.

Fortunately, just when Sophie was about to tell Laney about her next-door neighbor's lingering sciatica, Missy appeared. *In the nick of time*, Laney sighed inwardly.

Missy was the oldest of the three Montgomery girls; divorced, conservative, pretty, extremely corporate, in construction sales and a Cum Laude grad. She had never dyed her dirty blonde hair in her forty-six years, and she didn't care about the fact that she carried an thirty extra pounds on her petite frame, all of which Laney found rather refreshing. Missy was real, yet not one to ruffle any feathers, a peacekeeper. She didn't like confrontation; she just wanted everyone to get along.

"L.A. Laney," Missy screamed from across the bar. She had called Laney that since she moved to the West Coast. "Love you, mean it. I've missed you," Missy said clinking her glass of rum and Coke she'd brought down from the upstairs bar. She looked like a contestant on the show, *What Not To Wear*, proudly decked out in her brand new indigo denim jeans and white Adidas tennis shoes from Costco. The baby blue eye shadow that she'd worn since the seventies highlighted her light blue eyes.

They toasted being together again, and crossed their fingers for middle sister, Bridgett, to arrive in a timely manner. They weren't sure she was even going to show up. Bridgett was rapidly becoming the black sheep of the family.

The last time Laney had heard from Bridgett was six months ago, via text message on her cell phone. It read: "Met someone, getting a divorce." Laney didn't think that she could be serious. How could Bridgett throw away her twenty-two year marriage to Mitch? Laney had hoped to talk some sense into her and sent a text back saying to please call her, but Bridgett never did.

Bridgett had abandoned her four kids, her eight thousand square foot home with a luxurious Travertine-tiled bathroom suite with imported European fixtures. And she had given up what most women would die for: a man who loved her no matter what she did, and even promised to forgive her for her affair. But no one had really been able to get through to Bridgett.

As the three of them waited for Bridgett to appear, the talk was mainly centered around Sophie's hectic social calendar with her somewhat new, yet older doddery husband; she rarely let the ground stand still beneath her.

Matt played the attentive bartender and kept the drinks flowing. He also kept his eye on Laney as she talked about her life in L.A. and recent events. He seemed intrigued with her independent glamorous life on the West Coast.

Missy knocked back her second rum and Coke while Sophie gave in and had a very watered down martini. Matt emptied the bottle of Brunelli into Laney's glass and she savored every sip of it. Since her hotel was adjacent to the bar, she could really let loose tonight. Besides, the night was young and The Lazy Goat was rocking.

Sophie spied one of her affluent friends across the room and tottered off to say hello just as Bridgett appeared from the staircase behind the bar; and she wasn't alone. Laney felt her heart beat a little faster; her mom was going to freak out.

She took a deep breath, nudged Missy with her elbow, and whispered, "Bridgett's here, and she's with *him*." No one knew what her boyfriend's real name was. Missy had only heard Bridgett call him by his nickname, Maverick.

Missy tensed up. "Mom's going to kill her for bringing him. We have to do something before they get over here."

No one had met the guy responsible for wrecking Bridgett's domestic situation; and Sophie sure wouldn't be ready to meet him right here, right now.

"I'll intercept them. Go get mom and take her to the bathroom," Laney said. "That way you can warn her that he's with her."

"I'm not going to tell her. You tell her," Missy protested, folding her arms. Yes, she was the oldest, but she was tired of putting out all of the latest family fires. She had tried everything to keep Bridgett's marriage together, had called several meetings with her and Mitch, but Bridgett was way too stubborn.

Bridgett had just turned forty-three, was athletically built, attractive with long brown hair. She was every bit a Cougar on the prowl who had captured her young prey and Bridgett showed no regrets about landing a still married member of the male species. Of course, Sophie found the affair embarrassing as Greenville still had the small town mentality and news traveled fast. Bridgett's failings were causing too many glances and whispered words whenever Sophie attended social events, and she did not like that at all.

While Laney and Missy argued over who should do what, it was too late. Sophie spotted Bridgett with the home wrecker and now she was on the move.

"Crap! Mom's glaring at Bridgett and heading toward them." Laney threw her hands up as she watched the reflections of Sophie's sequins dance across the ceiling.

"What shall we do?" Missy gasped.

"Chug your drink for luck, and beat her over there. Let's go!" Laney said, slugging down the last of the Brunelli and darting to the staircase.

Laney arrived first and planted herself in front of Bridgett, gave her a big smile and a bear hug. "Bridge, hey, you made it." Laney hugged her tighter, whispering in her ear. "Mom's not going to be too happy about this, so get ready."

Bridgett looked dumbfounded. "What's Mom's problem?" In her mind, she hadn't done anything wrong. She was happy so everyone should be happy for her.

But Bridgett had shut everyone that loved her out of her secret life. She had rarely phoned any family members over the last year, so her affair had been a surprise to everyone, including her husband, Mitch. But to Bridgett, if anyone was in the wrong, it was Sophie. Her own mom had pretty much disowned her as far as she was concerned, refusing to hear Bridgett's side of things.

The truth was, Bridgett had turned her life and everyone else's upside down. She had become the Kim Kardashian of Greenville and she liked the attention it brought her. Her small town, tabloid affair was giving her a thrill. Sophie, on the other hand, wanted her outlawed from the family.

Now the shit was about to hit the fan. "I'm sure it will all be fine, Bridge. Don't worry, just be cool," Laney said, hoping to reassure her sister as Sophie was waylaid by another one of her friends and was forced to stop and say hello. Missy positioned herself behind Laney like a good soldier keeping guard.

Bridgett swung her arm around her tall, boyishly handsome male companion with the beer belly. "This is Maverick, y'all," she announced loudly and proudly. He smiled like a shy teen.

"Hey," he said in a sheepish Southern drawl. His voice had more of a hint of Forrest Gump than the sound of a rough and tough name like Maverick. But Bridgett just looked at him adoringly.

"His real name is Chase. You can call him that. He's been dying to meet both-a y'all." Chase nodded in agreement.

Missy and Laney looked at each other in disbelief, both wondering how Bridgett could have left Mitch for this character? The new guy had to have some redeeming qualities, though the bright red number ten football jersey he was wearing certainly wasn't one of them. Still, they had to give Chase a chance. And however unlikely, they hoped that their mom would too.

They both sensed Sophie moving into the kill zone and turned to cool off their mom. But they were too late, Sophie was making a fast beeline in their direction.

"So glad you decided to join us." Sophie said sarcastically, slicing through Laney and Missy like a star halfback through a weak defensive line. "So...is this whatisname?"

Rather than let Bridgett spit out some pithy response, Laney jumped in. "This is Chase," she said, smiling adoringly at him.

"Chase?" Sophie sized him up. "I thought it was Mav-Reek."

"That's just his nickname, Mom," Bridgett chimed in, still oblivious that this was a bad time to introduce her mom to her boyfriend.

"Well, pity you hitched your wagon to his horse," Sophie said under her breath.

Chase looked confused; like he didn't know what in the hell was going on; too slow to figure out Sophie's dig. He opened his arms like a big bear, lurched forward, and hugged Sophie…a huge no-no. She rarely hugged her own girls much less a guy who had broken up her daughter's marriage. Sophie struggled free, took a huge step back and touched the side of her hair to make sure it was still in place. She glared into Chase's wide, childlike eyes.

Laney and Missy braced themselves. Sophie raised her hand in the air, as if she was going to smack Chase square in the face. Instead, she slid it to her hip and produced a fake smile.

"Well, nice to meet you, I guess." Sophie was using every possible ounce of restraint. She knew almost everyone in The Lazy Goat, and they all knew good and well what was going on. There was no way she was going to create any sort of scene. Bridgett's impending divorce due to her affair had already spread like wildfire through the Greenville gossip mill. And it made the "About Town" section of *Talk Magazine*, Greenville's small town equivalent to the *National Enquirer*.

Sophie adored attention, but not this kind. Her social standing had been downgraded by this embarrassing event. And her heart was hurting as well. She had already lost her baby to the City of Angels. Now she had lost her middle child to a half-wit. This yokel was hijacking Bridgett's common sense and Sophie didn't trust him as far as she could throw him.

Laney watched her mom like a hawk for fear that Sophie might do something she'd regret. Her own problems seemed paltry by comparison. She knew now, more than ever, why she was needed at home.

Matt had been keeping watchful eye on Laney and her family. "Everything okay over here, girls?" he asked Laney, holding up the bottle of Brunelli.

"Things are better now," Laney said with a forced smile.

"Because, I'm here?" Matt smiled boyishly.

Laney didn't know what to say. The flirting was fun but she was a married woman. Still, Matt was cute and she couldn't resist playing his little game.

"No, because more vino has arrived," she said coyly.

"Oh, that cut deep," Matt laughed, filling her glass with more red wine. He took Sophie's empty martini glass, then returned to the bar after she declined another.

The noise in The Lazy Goat was getting louder, now jam packed with the coolest and hippest people in Greenville. Laney and Missy were trying to talk over the din. Bridgett and Sophie had drifted a few feet away and were engaged in an intense conversation. The second Laney turned her back to them to ask Missy a question, she heard a high-pitched scream. She spun around to see Bridgett had given Sophie a shove, like a mini Hulk Hogan. Sophie stumbled backwards into a passing restaurant patron, who thankfully stopped her from falling. The wine he carried, however, spilled all over the front of his jacket.

"Oh my God!" Laney shouted to Missy.

The crowd in The Lazy Goat went silent. You could hear a pin drop. All eyes were on Sophie and Bridgett.

Laney and Missy dashed over to the staircase where Sophie was now collecting herself and apologizing profusely to the man for ruining his swanky blazer.

Bridgett stood beside Chase, sobbing. He tried his best to calm her down but to no avail. Hoping to make amends with his future mother-in-law, he tapped Sophie on the shoulder and held out his hand to her, as if to apologize for his girlfriend's behavior.

Sophie refused it and snarled, "I'd rather shake hands with a crook, thank you."

Chase backed away like a frightened puppy.

"Mom, are you okay?" Laney helped straighten up her mom's sequin jacket, looking her over to make sure she was okay. "What in the hell happened?" Laney turned to Bridgett and shot her a sharp look. Missy stood in front of Bridgett like a guard to keep her separated from Sophie.

"I think your sister knows exactly what happened," Sophie spat, attempting to put her hair back into place. "I'm a mess now, thanks to you," she seethed at Bridgett. "But then, you've made a mess out of your life since meeting…this character."

Bridgett crossed her arms and wiped her tears in a huff, too upset to speak. Even now, she didn't understand the pain that she had put her mom or her sisters through. She had hurt so many people in her life but still she acted the victim. Her midlife crisis had been a crisis to everyone but her.

Laney had so wanted this to be a happy reunion and now it was turning into a really bad idea. There were way too many unresolved feelings, and too many things had been left unsaid. She just wanted her family back. If only her father were around to make peace. He wouldn't have stood for any of Bridgett's nonsense.

Laney held Sophie's right hand and guided her toward Bridgett. She grabbed Bridgett's left hand and said, "It's time to put the past behind and make up."

More tears streamed down Bridgett's face. "I just want you to love me," she railed at her mom, her bottom lip quivering as she spoke. Bridgett's constant insecurities once again assailed her. She had been the apple of her dad's eye and the star athlete. But it was Sophie's love that she had always wanted. As the middle child, she felt left out. Bridgett always believed that Sophie favored Laney because of her beauty pageants and fashion smarts, and Missy because of her brains, over her, which wasn't true. She never felt pretty enough or smart enough and it still tore her up inside. Even now, Bridgett desperately craved her mom's approval.

Sophie turned away and didn't respond. Bridgett had disappeared from her life for almost a year. She couldn't just forgive her now. Besides, Bridgett had just embarrassed her in front of practically all of Greenville.

Laney was caught up in the middle. In so many ways, she couldn't blame her mom for refusing to forgive her sister, but she also couldn't help but feel sorry for Bridgett. She was blatantly acting out as a cry for help, and didn't know how to verbally ask for it.

Chase stood there like a bump on a log, absently rubbing

Bridgett's back. He finally took a stance. "Bridge, why don't you say you're sorry? I think you should apologize to your mom. You love her and she loves you," he coaxed her in his childishly endearing way.

So, there is something sweet about him, Laney thought. She could now understand her sister's attraction to him. Mitch was often cold and distant during their twenty-year marriage. At least Chase was being present and attentive, which was what Bridgett had always needed in a relationship.

Bridgett turned toward the stairs, ready to leave. "I deserve the apology," she said looking back at Sophie. "Come on." She gestured to Chase in a huff, marching up the stairs. Chase held his head down and followed her like an obedient puppy dog.

Laney shook her head as she watched her sister disappear. She took her mom's hand and put her arm around Missy. The three of them stood there in silent disbelief as the unspoken question hovered in the air…Now what?

Chapter Two

Laney now wasn't sure she'd made the right decision to stay at The Drake. She felt selfish leaving her mom after all of the drama with Bridgett. But Sophie had insisted that she keep her reservation, so Laney finally obliged her. She retired, guilt ridden to the plush grand king suite perched above the rolling hills of the Blue Ridge Mountains in the heart of downtown, hoping to finally relax and calm her racing thoughts. She was dead tired as she crawled into bed and wrapped herself in the 1000 thread count Egyptian cotton sheets. But even with the surrounds of luxury, she couldn't shut her mind off from the evening and tossed and turned all night. The next morning, she awoke weary-eyed to the sun peeking through the small opening of the thick satin curtains.

Laney hoped that her second day of vacation would be better. But unfortunately last night's family theatrics was still weighing heavily on her mind. Laney slipped into the silk robe draped across the foot of her king sized bed, and put on a fresh pot of gourmet coffee. While she waited for her coffee to brew, she collected the USA Today outside her door and flipped through the sections of the paper as light jazz piped through the television speakers. It was a gorgeous Southern day. She swung open the sliding glass doors that led to the balcony and felt the warm sunshine on her face.

She retrieved her iPhone from her purse to call Thomas, and then remembered it was three hours earlier in California. Even though he was an early riser, she decided she would call him later. Laney was finally reveling in a little peace and quiet. She wasn't ready for any chaos yet. Her iPhone messages could also wait.

She poured herself a fresh cup of java and savored it as she sat in the lounge chair on the balcony and took in the fresh Southern air and the city sights and sounds. Greenville certainly wasn't the biggest place on the planet, but from the tenth floor of The Drake it certainly looked impressive. She was happy to be home even though her family seemed to be falling apart. She would get to the bottom of all of it but for now, this was her time and she needed it.

She had a day of pampering planned. She was meeting Sophie for lunch on the river and then heading to the River Place Spa. It had been years since she had treated herself to a spa day and she thought that her mom could use a day of coddling too. She had booked the mother/daughter spa package and had hoped that Missy could join them, but she was too swamped at work. For the time being, inviting Bridgett to anything was out of the question.

Laney combed through the Lifestyle section of the paper, tilted her head back and closed her eyes allowing the heat of the sun to kiss her face. She opened her eyes and gazed out at the amazing city scenery. Unable to resist it, she stood up, leaned over the balcony and looked down at the riverfront below. It was teeming with busybodies. Business people walked to work, while enthusiastic joggers ran along the river's path, passing mom and pop retail stores and artist commissioned lofts.

As she took in all of the festivities, Laney heard a faint, familiar voice yelling up at her from the riverfront walk, ten stories below.

It was Matt, the bartender, in his running gear, holding a cup of Starbuck's coffee in his hand.

"Hey? Come have coffee with me," he shouted.

How did he know it was me? And more importantly, why would he be interested in me? He should be hanging out with girls his own age, she thought, looking down at him.

Laney didn't know how to respond. She pulled her robe tighter so as not to give Matt or anyone else walking below a peepshow. "I'm not dressed," she yelled down, feeling like Juliet talking to her Romeo.

"Well, then get dressed. I'll buy," he hollered back up to her. Although sweaty from his run, Matt was looking quite attractive in his stylish black running shorts. And Laney could tell that he wasn't about to give up on her.

"Oh, okay," she called down, cupping her mouth with her hands, "give me a few minutes." But now, she was feeling a bit ridiculous and like a very mature, over-the-hill Juliet.

"Great. I'll just be sitting here," he smiled, pointing to the bench behind him.

Laney scrambled to get ready. Like a whirling dervish, she tossed her robe onto the bed and pulled her fuchsia Sparkelicious hoodie, tank top and matching shorts out of her suitcase. She quickly dressed, washed her face, brushed her teeth and rinsed with mint mouthwash.

She tied her blonde hair back into a low ponytail, picked up her matching Sparkelicious baseball cap off of the modern black work desk, and pulled it over her head. Since living in L.A., Laney had adopted the casual California dress style and she wasn't as concerned as she used to be about looking picture perfect all of the time. Ten years ago she would have never have gone out in public without a full face of makeup and big hair. Now she kept it simple, applying her favorite light pink Chanel lip gloss and dusted a hint of baby pink blush and bronzer to her cheeks.

She checked herself one last time in the mirror over the small bar that led out to her hotel door and gave herself a brisk smile. *Looking pretty damn good for a woman about to turn forty.*

Laney walked down the cascading slate stairs outside of The Lazy Goat that stood in front of the entrance of The Drake and saw Matt sitting peacefully on the bench overlooking the Reedy River. She approached him from behind.

"Not a bad view," Laney said, startling him.

"God, you scared me." Matt turned and held his empty coffee cup to his chest. "You were fast."

"I'm pretty low maintenance—thank God for baseball caps," Laney smiled, touching her pink hat. She had her husband lurking in the back of her brain. She was still debating whether or not she'd made the right decision in meeting Matt for coffee.

"You're Southern. You can't be that low maintenance," Matt chuckled.

"I'm more of a California girl now," Laney assured him.

"Well, either way, you look fantastic." Matt's perceptive eyes were now appreciating Laney's impressive figure.

"Yeah, right," Laney blushed, tugging at her ponytail. "I need some caffeine. I can smell Starbuck's from here."

"You're good, California Girl. Follow me." Matt said, heading toward the distinctive forest green and white Starbuck's signage on the corner. Laney followed. While Matt was certainly the rugged kind, Laney couldn't help but notice he had a somewhat refined look about him even in his jogging clothes.

After ordering her usual cinnamon dolce latte, Matt insisted on paying.

"No, I got it," Laney said, holding out her credit card.

"I told you I was treating. Put your plastic away." He slipped a twenty into the cashier's hand.

Laney was used to paying for pretty much everything. Her husband almost never had cash or his wallet on him when they went out. And that was fine. She enjoyed the sense of control it gave her.

It's just a cup of coffee, not a dinner date, so what's the harm? She told herself, though feeling guiltier by the minute, with Thomas still on her mind.

Laney and Matt talked like old friends who hadn't seen each other in years, while they waited for their coffees at the pickup counter. She imagined Matt to be an old soul.

As she and Matt gabbed on, Laney's iPhone rang in her hand,

startling her. She glanced down and saw the incoming call was from Thomas. Laney's face became concerned as she excused herself from Matt, feeling like the bad wife, and walked toward the door, so she could talk with a little more privacy.

"Hello, my dear," Thomas's voice reverberated through the phone, his British accent sounding a bit tired. "Do you miss me?"

"Hi, honey. Of course I do." Laney raised her voice to talk over the coffee crowd.

"I was up all night editing that piece of crap film," he said, sounding like the Grinch who stole Christmas. Thomas hated working on other people's projects. But he needed the money. His own projects were box office poison, so he took whatever work he could get. "Where are you anyway? It's bloody noisy."

"At Starbuck's, but I can talk," Laney said sweetly.

"No, call me when we can actually have a real conversation," Thomas said gruffly and abruptly hung up the phone.

Laney stared down at the phone in disbelief. Her happy mood had now turned sad. Thomas knew how to push her buttons like no one else. His moods were one of the reasons she was taking this break and judging from this conversation, they weren't getting any better.

Matt noticed that she was off the phone and approached her with the two coffees. He held out the cup marked "Laney".

"For you, Madame," he said, in his best French accent, handing it to her.

Laney shot him her best fake smile, hoping he wouldn't notice her change in mood. However, as she took the paper cup from him, she couldn't help but notice his tanned muscular legs and sculpted chest muscles bulging from his tight white tank top. His hair was still damp with perspiration from his five-mile run. He opened the front door for Laney, and led her down the stairs to the bench that overlooked the river.

"I love this view," Laney said, sitting down and sipping her designer coffee. "I really need this right now."

Matt sat down beside her. "Why's that?" He could tell that Laney's mood had shifted, but he didn't want to be too nosey.

"Oh, nothing. Just married life," she sighed.

"You're married?" Matt drew back. He looked down at her left hand and lifted it up for inspection. "Where's the ring?"

"Oh, I don't have one. My husband never gave me one," Laney answered matter-of- factly, then laughed.

"Why not? Is he crazy?" Matt blinked back his disbelief.

"Maybe *I* am. I just never wanted one. We had other things to pay for. It's really not a big deal," she shrugged. "See, I told you I was low maintenance."

"You weren't kidding. I thought every girl wanted a ring." At least all the girls that he knew did.

"Most women I know who got the big rings are now divorced. I've been married for nine years," Laney proudly announced.

"Nine years?" Matt almost choked on his coffee. "You're too young to be married that long."

Laney tugged nervously at the bill on her baseball cap.

"I wish," she said, hoping to leave it at that. She didn't want to tell him that she was reeling toward forty, but then again, why would it matter? She wasn't looking for a date.

"Well, he's a lucky man, California Girl." Matt was smart enough not to ask Laney her age.

"So, what do you do when you're not tending bar?" Laney quickly changed the subject.

"Studying for my master's in architecture," Matt smiled. "The Goat is paying for my eight year plan." His accent was more regional than Southern. She surmised he was well traveled and came from a good upper class family.

"That's fabulous! When do you graduate?"

"Hopefully in the next few months. I've already had some interest," Matt replied with brazen self-confidence.

Laney felt somewhat relieved that he wasn't as young as she'd first thought. He was pushing thirty, she guessed.

"Interest from where?" Laney prodded.

"New York." His eyes twinkled with the thought of the prospect. "But I love it here. I grew up here. My family's here…" Matt's voice trailed off, not wanting to reveal anymore about his Southern roots.

Even though Laney was curious about Matt's family, she respected his privacy and didn't want to pry. "Well, I ran away from Greenville as fast as I could after college. But I sometimes feel like I've missed so much," Laney said wistfully.

Matt could sense the conversation getting heavy and tried to lighten it up. "Well, now you're here. You can enjoy your time with your family."

"You're right. Thanks for reminding me," Laney perked back up, sipping the last of her designer coffee drink.

"So, what about you?" Matt checked out Laney's bright athletic attire. "Are you in the fashion biz or something?"

"You're good too." Laney grinned. "Yep, I'm a fashion designer. I'm wearing me...it's called Sparkelicious."

"Wow! That's so cool. Yeah, I've heard that name. You're pretty hot in Hollywood, aren't you?

"My clothing line's done pretty well." Laney said humbly, not wanting to brag about her accomplishments. She glanced admiringly at Matt as he hung onto her every word. The sun shone on his handsome young face and she couldn't help but be caught up in his exuberance. He had so many new and exciting things at his fingertips. Laney loved his enthusiasm for life.

"I think it's done a little bit better than that!" Matt checked his sport watch and frowned. "Well, California Girl, I'm sorry but I gotta go. I really want to stay and chat more about your amazing life but it's time for me to head to class." He stood up from the bench and stared down at Laney with a hopeful expression. "Maybe I'll see you at The Goat tonight?

Laney glanced up and shot him a cheeky look. "Maybe you will."

Matt bounced on his toes like a professional runner. "And, just an FYI, I'll be tending the upstairs bar tonight."

"You get around don't you?" Laney laughed, standing up to

stretch her legs.

"It's rumored that I do."

"Oh really?" she grinned. "I'd love to have a Brunelli waiting for me, Mr. Architect."

Laney held out her hand to say goodbye but Matt ignored her polite gesture and leaned in to hug her instead. "I've poured your drinks, so at least we should be on a hug basis."

Laney didn't have time to think. She hung on to her coffee cup as Matt wrapped his strapping arms around her. "Okay." She agreed, going with his affections.

Matt released her from his tender grasp and smiled. "See ya later." He turned and ran toward the jogging trail along the Reedy River.

"Bye." Laney shouted, as Matt sprinted into the distance.

Laney's somber mood was rejuvenated. *Matt's very impressive and pretty mature for his age however old he is, not that I care about that. Well, maybe I do, but it's time to return my husband's call.* She reluctantly speed dialed Thomas's number and waited for him to answer.

To her dismay, his tone was still gruff and he was no happier than he'd been an hour before; displaying annoyance that Laney was away having fun while he was stuck in the house editing. Box office bombs aside, Thomas believed he wasn't getting hired to direct any first-rate projects like he used to largely because Hollywood now favored the young, up and coming directors fresh out of film school. He was becoming more bitter and jaded about getting older. Laney tried to boost his ego and build his confidence but to no avail.

As she listened to Thomas complain, she considered telling him about her friendly "get-together" with Matt. It wasn't a big deal and she usually told him everything, but based on his present vibe, the time wasn't right. She told him about Sophie and Bridgett's drama instead.

"God, that's bloody ridiculous. Bridgett needs to grow up," Thomas snapped.

"I know. It's crazy. There is so much baggage there with her." Laney talked as she headed back to The Drake. Her mom was probably waiting for her in the lobby.

"Are you walking again?" Thomas moaned. "You know I hate it when you talk and walk. All I can hear is you breathing." He demonstrated a heavy panting sound.

Not again, Laney shook her head. She felt like she couldn't do anything right in her husband's eyes. He was such the perfectionist. She didn't want to have another argument over the phone and stopped at the bench outside of the hotel. "I'm sitting down now. Is that better?"

"Yes." Thomas let out an exasperated sigh. "Now, I can hear you and not your breathing pattern."

She checked her watch and interrupted his ongoing lecture. "Honey, I've gotta go. Mom's waiting for me. I'll call you later."

"No, I'll call you. I have lots of work to do and I can't get anything done with you calling me all of the time," he huffed. His British accent now more pompous than ever.

"Okay. That's fine," Laney clenched her teeth and ended the call.

Laney scurried into The Drake. Sophie was waiting impatiently on the sofa, in the lobby, flipping through The Greenville Times.

"Hey, honey. I was getting a little worried about my little Miss Punctual daughter," she grinned, until she noticed Laney's somber expression. "And, where's my little sunshine face?" she said, standing up to examine her daughter further.

"Oh, my smile was replaced by this frown a few seconds ago. My husband drives me crazy," Laney glared miserably down at her phone. But she wasn't going to let his sour mood get to her this time.

"Don't all men drive us crazy?" Sophie put her arm around Laney. "Come on, we're going to be late for our massages. He'll get over his British self soon." Sophie had always been overprotective with Laney and she never really liked Thomas from day one.

Laney produced a broad grin. "Yes, it's our day out. Let's go get pampered." She swung her arm around her mom and they walked through the sliding glass doors of the hotel. They walked two blocks down Main Street to the River Place Spa. They hadn't had a mother-daughter day in years so this was very special. Lunch was arranged after their spa treatments, since they both had a late breakfast.

As they approached the entrance of the spa, Sophie glared curiously at Laney. She could tell that her daughter was hiding something from her. "What's going on with you, honey? Your eyes have a different kind of twinkle about them. It seems like your sad eyes have turned happy a little too fast."

"Whadda ya mean?" Laney spit out a surprise reply as she opened the door to the spa for her mom. *I did enjoy coffee with Matt but is my enthusiasm showing that much? Mom knows me a little too well.*

Sophie walked through the door and gave her a motherly look. "It's just your mom's intuition. But I think something else is going on."

Laney followed behind her, about to respond, but her train of thought was interrupted by the receptionist at the front desk. "Welcome to the River Place Spa." She announced in a calm voice. She checked them in and handed them a locker key. "Your massage therapists will be right out to take you back to the dressing room."

Within minutes, two women appeared from the dark hallway, ready to take them back to change.

Right now, Sophie wanted to talk. She didn't give a crap about the spa appointment at this moment; she had to get more information out of her daughter. "So, aren't you going to answer my question?" She prodded as the two attendants led them down the hall, to the dressing room.

Laney could feel Sophie's tension. She didn't know what the big deal was. "Relax, Mom. This is our day."

They entered the locker room and changed into their chenille robes and slippers. Sophie wasn't going to let up. It was Sophie's dogged determination that got her to the top at the construction company. She wasn't one to take no for an answer. "Something's up, honey, now spill it," She was so frustrated at her daughter's refusal to elaborate that she couldn't even open her locker.

"Mom, here. I'll do it for you." Laney said patiently, punching in the correct code for the locker.

"God, you always drove me crazy as a child, and now you're grown and you still drive me crazy," Sophie tossed her clothes into her personal locker. "You're hiding something."

"Well, I did have a quick cup of coffee with the Goat bartender this morning, but that was it. It was no big deal," Laney declared.

"No big deal? Honey, let me tell you…" Sophie raised her voice.

"Shhh." Laney pointed at the sign, "Quiet Please!" her index finger now pursed up to her lips.

But Sophie couldn't care less. "Honey, I'm your mother, so I'm going to say and do as I well please." She continued without taking a breath, placing her right hand on her full hip. "Do you know who 'Matt the bartender' is?"

"Yes, a bartender who's studying to be an architect," Laney replied, tying her silk robe together.

Sophie slammed her locker shut, disobeying the spa's "Quiet" sign. "Honey, Matt, your little bartender, architect friend is Senator Rigby's son."

"So? What's that have to do with anything?" Laney was now intrigued with the conversation.

"Well, Senator Rigby is about to run for a second term, so I'm just warning you, honey. His opponents are looking for anything and everything on him right now. And that means his family is an easy target too."

Laney pulled her hair up on top of her head and rolled her eyes. "Mom…I just had coffee with the senator's *son*, not with him."

"That's my point, honey. You're a married woman and his son is at least ten years, or maybe even fifteen years younger than you," she answered with a slight dig at her daughter.

Laney sighed, "Thanks Mom. I'm not dead, though. I can still have friends." She wished her mom would stop trying to protect her. She was a grown woman and she didn't do anything wrong.

"Well, honey, I'm sorry, it's true." Sophie sat on the bench wanting Laney's full attention. "Sure, you can have friends, but you've picked the wrong one." Laney got her point and sat down beside her and listened. "Honey, there's a reason they're called politics. Just be careful."

"Mom, thanks for your concern but there's nothing to worry about," Laney reassured her. "I'm a happily married woman living on the opposite coast."

"An even better story for the press, honey." Sophie wisely deemed. "And, dates in the middle of the afternoon can be misconstrued too."

"It wasn't a date, Mom!" Laney affirmed as her masseuse entered the lounge area, ready to take her back for her massage. Laney happily stood up to follow her. "We just sort of…ran into each other, and decided to have coffee." She mumbled back at her mom as she exited the room.

"That's what your sister said too, honey. And look what happened to her." Sophie blurted out, hoping Laney could hear her. Within seconds, the other masseuse appeared and escorted Sophie down the small dark hall behind Laney.

Laney heard her loud and clear. "I'm not Bridgett, Mom," She snapped before walking into the treatment room. "Now, relax and enjoy your massage." She whispered, closing the door behind her.

Sophie took her daughter's advice and silenced her conversation, following her massage therapist into the private room.

After their hour of pampering, Laney and Sophie met in the outdoor courtyard for lunch. They reclined in chase lounges under a cherry red umbrella. Freshly brewed tea and crisp salad wedges with salmon and cucumber awaited them.

Laney was barely functioning after her massage while Sophie was still raring to go. She seemed more stressed than ever about Laney's innocent coffee "date."

"Honey, we're probably being photographed right now," Sophie announced, peering behind the plant like a detective.

"God, Mom. We just had a great massage. Can we just chill for a minute?" Laney rolled her eyes. "I love my husband, end of story."

"Honey, I know that, but *they* don't know that. I'm just telling you to be careful. Only see Matt at The Goat, nowhere else. And even then, play it cool. I just hope it's not too late," she said, nervously grasping her robe and pulling it closer to her full breasts.

"Mom, who's they?" She laughed, sitting up in her lounger. "The Greenville paparazzi? I don't see anyone lurking behind the trees. This whole conversation is ridiculous. We're in South Carolina, not Hollywood."

Sophie continued looking around the courtyard suspiciously. "Don't be naïve, honey," she said in a loud whisper. "This is just a miniature Southern version of L.A."

Laney sipped on her cup of warm lemon tea and changed the subject. "Mom, I'm not stupid...now, let's talk about Bridgett and what happened last night,"

Sophie sat back in her lounge chair and sulked. "As far as I'm concerned, she's not my daughter, so, there's nothing to talk about."

Laney peered over at Sophie; her face was sad and drawn. "Mom, you don't mean that." She reached through the arm rail of the chaise and gently touched her arm to comfort her.

"Oh, yes, I do," Sophie pouted. "Honey, I have never been more serious." She replied, stopping the spa waitress as she lifted the teapot to pour her another cup of tea. "Can I please get a real drink?" Sophie desperately needed something stronger than tea right now.

"Sure," the young girl smiled. "I can get you some white wine."

Sophie grinned. "Well, then, let the party begin. We'll take two chardonnays."

Laney chimed in, slightly embarrassed, "Mom, we're in a spa, not a bar." She was never one to drink during the day and, as far as she knew, neither was her mom.

"Well, heck, how often do I see you, honey? Let's have some fun," Sophie bubbled, sending the waitress on her way.

Sophie had apparently learned to relax a lot more than the last time Laney had seen her. Laney shrugged her shoulders and went along with the plan. Her conversation about Bridgett would have to wait. She hoped that she could learn more about what was really going on from her mom over a glass of wine.

Within minutes, the spa attendant returned with two glasses of Sonoma Cutrer. She placed them on the round table between them.

Sophie immediately grabbed a chilled glass and handed it to Laney; then got her glass and raised it toward hers. "To my number three daughter who has always been my number one."

"Thanks, Mom. Since I'm on vacation, here it goes," Laney replied, trying to justify her afternoon treat.

Sophie savored her second sip "You're acting like an old woman. Here's to us." Charles had apparently loosened her up a lot since they'd gotten married. He was obviously good for her.

"Yes, here's to us and to you, Mom. I've missed you."

Sophie put her glass down on the table. "What did you say, honey?"

"I said, I've missed you, Mom," Laney announced again. A tear trickled down Sophie's cheek. "Honey, I've missed you so much too. It's so nice to hear you say that."

"Mom, don't cry." Laney put her glass down and pressed the small cocktail napkin to her mom's chiseled cheekbone. "I didn't mean to make you cry."

"Oh, honey, these are tears of joy. You have no idea." Sophie took the napkin from Laney and continued to dab her tears.

"Good, I'm really glad that I'm here." Laney smiled, handing her mom a clean napkin.

"Me too."

As Laney comforted her mom, she heard a rustling sound coming from behind the tall bushes that lined the courtyard. "Shh." She whispered to her mom, sitting up in her lounger. "I think I hear something coming from over there." She pointed across the patio.

Sophie perked up. "I hear it too."

Laney stood up, ready to inspect the mysterious sound.

Sophie grabbed her arm and pulled her back down to her chair. "No, honey. Don't you dare go over there."

"Why not? I'm sure it's nothing."

"Nothing but the paparazzi." Sophie assured her.

A cold shiver passed through Laney's body. "Mom, stop...see, whatever it was is gone...probably just a squirrel." She glared at the now silent trees. But Laney couldn't relax. She couldn't help but think that the sound she heard was closer to a person lurking around than a small rodent. She stayed on high alert. Maybe her mom was right, and Greenville was a little L.A. after all?

Chapter Three

Dinner was at eight. Laney was an hour early. A wave of sound came from The Lazy Goat as she entered the doors. The restaurant was bustling with patrons at every table. She walked with poised pageant confidence past the hostess and gave her a polite wave as she headed to the bar. Sophie and Charles were meeting her for dinner and she had some time to kill. She inconspicuously scanned the bar and the restaurant for Matt, but didn't see him. He'd said he would be working tonight. *Maybe he took the night off, after all?* Either way, Laney tried to convince herself that she didn't care if she saw him or not.

Dressed in tight, indigo jeans, a Sparkelicious aquamarine blue tank top with silver sequins, and embellished platinum gray wedge sandals, Laney was the poster child for a "California girl." Her five foot seven-frame, now a couple of inches taller from the sandals, made her even more statuesque and model like. Her long blonde hair was in loose curls and flowed down her tan back. Her angelic blue eyes sparkled in the dim light.

Laney continued with authority to the end of the bar and sat on the stainless steel stool. A tall young bartender turned around in the low light to greet her, and Laney's smile quickly evaporated when she realized that it wasn't Matt. Unable to get her happy factor back,

Laney started to order her usual glass of red wine, and was interrupted by a familiar voice behind her: "California Girl will have a Brunelli, please."

Laney was elated, yet she tried to remain cool. She felt Matt's warm hand on her shoulder. She turned around and he flashed her a warm smile. He slid his hand gently down her arm as he walked back behind the bar, and handed her the room temperature glass of red wine.

"For you, California Girl," his eyes danced from the glow of the candles that lined the bar.

"Why, thank you, Matt the architect-bartender." Her hands brushed the tips of his fingers as she took the glass from him and led it to her lips.

This little flirtation with Matt is so ridiculous, she thought, *but it's kind of fun at the same time. I'm just enjoying life a little*. Her husband had always been a flirt and had lots of so called girl *friends* over the years, so why couldn't she have a friend too?

With another sip, she looked at Matt. There was no doubt that Matt Rigby was gorgeous. He possessed the sexiness of a Chippendale dancer, without knowing it and had the looks of a GQ model. He was a perfect ten. His seductive eyes pierced through hers as he ran his masculine hands through his naturally wavy hair. Unfortunately, her mother was probably right -- she should be careful -- so she composed herself and vowed to act like a married woman should.

"So, how's it taste?" Matt leaned into the bar, waiting for Laney's response like a curious child.

"Fabulous. Just what the doctor ordered." She put the glass down, now feeling the effects of two glasses of wine. While the chardonnay she'd had with her mom was several hours ago, the massage had made her so relaxed, this wine was hitting her faster than she was used to.

"Perfect. Just call me the wine doctor…at your service." He bowed down to Laney like she was a princess, his black apron caressing the top of the counter.

"You're crazy," Laney said with a giggle. Before she could take another sip of wine, her phone beeped. It was a text message from Thomas: "Can you meet for dinner?" Laney was perplexed… *He's in L.A. and I'm in S.C?* She frowned and tried to decipher his text. *Maybe he has surprised me and flown to South Carolina?* Then again, her husband wasn't one to surprise her with anything except the time he bought a new 65" plasma television without discussing the six thousand dollar price tag with her.

On top of that, Thomas hated text messaging. He thought it was for kids. Laney quickly shot him a text back: "I'm here in S.C., so how can we have dinner?"

Now not so relaxed anymore, she took a huge gulp of wine and waited anxiously for Thomas's response.

Within seconds another message appeared from Thomas: "Sorry my dear, didn't have my glasses on. Meant, hope you're having a good dinner. T."

Laney felt relief as she read his text. Thomas was blind as a bat and indeed couldn't see a thing without his glasses. He had probably lost them again.

She placed her iPhone on the bar and looked toward the front door. Sophie and her stepfather, Charles, were slowly making their way through the entrance. Matt was busy serving drinks but kept his eye on Laney.

Jumping to attention, like a soldier on duty, Laney ran over to Charles and clutched his thin right arm. She put her other arm around his back so he wouldn't fall over, and led him to a barstool.

Her mom walked several feet in front of Charles, like she always did, completely oblivious to the fact that her husband was about to lose his balance. Sophie always said, "Oh, he'll be fine, don't worry about him." And Charles usually was, but Laney became his caregiver when she was around. She worried about him and always made sure he was safe from falling.

A man of eighty, Charles had a sharp mind and a quick wit, but his body and his heart were failing him. He had a pacemaker, was extremely frail, and moved slower than molasses. Just like Sophie, Charles loved to socialize and they were one of the most popular senior couples in Greenville.

A once successful political writer, now retired, Charles either knew everyone or they knew him, and he loved that. The two of them were out and about every night, regardless of Charles' condition. He was an upbeat and positive man, just happy to still be alive, despite all of his health issues. He never complained and he never felt bad enough to miss a party. Sophie always said, "I gotta keep him moving!" And she was right. Somehow, Charles kept going, either his pacemaker or his youthful spirit gave him his get up and go. He just kept on going, or rather following Sophie around, like a little puppy dog. They had been married for almost three years and were still like two young lovebirds.

It was sweet at first, and Laney and the girls supported their mom in her decision to marry Charles two years after their father died. But for some reason, his absence had become harder for all of them, especially for Laney. Or at least, she was the only one who had really dealt with her father's death. Even after all of these years, the other two girls had never even been to his grave; and they lived in town. It was the Southern way to not deal with emotions. Laney had grown and changed since living in L.A. She had matured and learned to deal with things head on, even grief and death.

Laney had been to her father's graveside twice. And it seemed that she missed her father even more now than she did when he died. Perhaps the other girls missed him too; for sure they just weren't as vocal about it. Plus, they never got stuck with Charles like she did. They could easily go home after an evening with him, but Laney had always felt obligated to stay at their house. And their house was not the home she grew up in. Sophie had moved into Charles's house when they married so it wasn't home at all to Laney. Yet she knew she'd hurt her mother's feelings if she stayed elsewhere when she came to visit. And being the youngest child, she wanted to please her mom. If she didn't, she felt guilty. Something she still felt at forty.

Laney liked Charles and was happy that her mom had fallen in love again, but bottom line, he wasn't her father, although he tried to be. Or at least, he told her off in ways that her father never did which was worse. They'd had a few standoffs that for her ended in tears and that was the reason that Laney was now staying at The Drake on this trip. She had finally decided to put her feelings first instead of her mom's. Trying to please everyone got Laney nowhere but frustrated. Staying at a nearby hotel was the only solution. And it was working. She now had the *quality* time with her mom she had yearned for.

Matt wiped the bar down with a white cloth and quickly refilled Laney's empty wine glass, then poured Charles a glass of Chianti. Sophie had her regular martini with a splash of lime. Laney toasted with them while secretly wishing that her two sisters were there, too. Missy was coming, but she got called out on assignment, so she had to catch a plane. At least Matt was around. Somehow, he was starting to feel like family.

While Laney politely listened to Charles's political rhetoric, her phone buzzed again. She glanced at it on the bar. It was another text message from her husband: "I'm here, where are you?" Laney was now getting suspicious with a second text from Thomas in less than two hours. He should have located his glasses by now.

She moved her phone over to the votive flame so she could see the screen clearly to text Thomas back. Pretending to engage Charles and laugh at his horrible lingering story, she quickly typed back: "T, you're in CA, I'm in SC. You're now blind AND forgetful!"

She pressed the blue send button and waited impatiently for his response. At fifty-two, his mind was still usually sharp, but now, she was starting to wonder.

Within seconds, Thomas's text came across her phone: "Sorry, Lane, my love, just wishful thinking again, found my glasses…and my brain…too much editing...xxoo, T."

Laney breathed in a sigh of relief and carried on her one-way conversation with her stepfather. Charles's political ramblings were like a never-ending train, and Sophie didn't dare interrupt. She was just happy that he had an audience, which he loved. Luckily for everyone, the hostess did interrupt his one-way debate and seated them at a cozy table for three that looked over the water.

The Tapas menu was a bit confusing for Charles and Sophie so Laney helped them select a variety of items. She loved Tapas bars and found The Lazy Goat to be very similar to the one near her home in the Hollywood Hills. Matt could see her from the bar and gave her a sympathetic smile. He could tell by Laney's face that Charles was boring her to tears with yet another anecdote from his writing days. Sophie had heard his stories a thousand times too, and occasionally enjoyed them, but even her patience was starting to wear think tonight.

"Honey, that's nice, but Laney is only here for a short time," she said trying to send the *no more political talk* hint to Charles. He was a very sensitive man and she tried to be careful in how she handled him and his feelings.

God, she is more patient than I could ever be, but Mom loves him dearly so I'll do my best to be polite to him. And just as Charles was about to get the hint, Laney's phone went off again.

"Still waiting for you," Laney read aloud, her beautiful face making an unattractive, pinched with worry expression.

"I'm sorry, Mom, but I have to take care of this. I think my husband has lost the plot." Laney knew she must have sounded a little paranoid as she stepped away from the table and walked outside to the veranda. She read the message from Thomas again. These texts were now making her extremely suspicious. But this time, she decided not to respond even though her brain was going a mile a minute with worry.

As far as she knew, Thomas had always been faithful to her; now she was questioning their relationship. She nervously hit the close button on her text message. She had to get back to the table and act natural to avoid a barrage of Sophie questions she wasn't prepared to answer. Laney turned around and accidentally jammed her phone into Matt's chest. He had walked out to check on her.

"Sorry, I wasn't looking," Laney spoke into Matt's strong shoulder, her face pressed up against his white cotton shirt.

Matt looked down at her from his 6' 1" height. On reflex, he'd wrapped his arms around her. He quickly let her go. "No, it's my fault. I snuck up on you." He rubbed his chest as Laney nervously backed away from his bulging pecs. "Next time, I'll give you a heads up. You pack a mean iPhone," he said with a whimper, pretending to be wounded.

"Oh, God, did I hurt you?" She instinctively massaged the sore spot with her hand. "I'm so sorry."

"It actually feels pretty good," Matt smiled. "You can attack me with a phone anytime."

"Oh. I'm touching you." She jerked her hand away from his chest. She hadn't touched another man in years and this felt weird.

Matt feigned a disappointed face. "Oh, don't be sorry. I enjoyed it," then showed concern. "I was worried about you."

"Really?" Laney said, in a more relaxed tone. "You're like a bartender, bodyguard and therapist all in one. If I…

"Shhh," Matt held up his hand. "What's that noise?" He surveyed the veranda like a detective.

"What? I didn't hear anything," Laney whispered.

Matt approached the manicured bushes and peered behind them.

He spun around and laughed. "It's just a squirrel."

"Okay... But what did you think it was?"

"Look, I know it's going to sound like I'm paranoid, but lately I've had the creepy feeling that someone is following me. I'm sure it's nothing, though. Probably just been working too many late nights in a row."

"Are you sure you're okay?" Laney pressed, feeling a little paranoid too.

"I'm sure. Now go back in there and enjoy the evening with your family. Your food is probably at the table by now." He took her by the arm and escorted her into the restaurant.

"Okay, thanks again for checking on me." She left Matt at the bar on the way back to her table. She had put aside her husband's weird text messages and could only think about how she had felt, that brief moment, in Matt's arms.

Laney sat back down at the table and her mom gave her a condescending look. "So glad that you could join us again, honey."

"Sorry…dealing with the Brit."

"And Matt…" Sophie raised a critical eyebrow. "Looks like you're a busy girl."

Laney really didn't have to explain herself to her mother. She was an adult now…yet she always felt like she had to. It was the Southern way. "He just wanted to make sure I was okay Mom. That's all."

"And then what, honey?" Sophie glared.

Charles awoke from a short nap in his chair and chimed in, "Yeah, look what happened to your mother and I after one glass of wine." He let loose with a coughing laugh.

"I know, bad luck." Laney said quietly under her breath. Her Scorpion tongue sometimes got the best of her. Charles shot her daggers from behind his thick glasses, though he didn't fully hear what she had said, being deaf in one ear. But he seemed to get the gist. Laney shook her head. "God, Mom, I'm an old married lady. T and I are joined at the hip." But found herself wondering, *What is Thomas really up to while the cat's away*?

It was almost midnight and Sophie was still in a partying mood, but Charles had nodded off again. Sophie stood up and tapped him a good one on the arm. "Time to go, party animal," she shouted in his good ear.

Laney walked them to the front door of The Goat and gave them both a quick hug. She and her mom had indeed gotten closer since her arrival, and she was feeling happy about that. The valet attendant arrived with the car and Laney helped her mom get Charles into the passenger's seat. The car pulled away from the curb and she waved to them as they drove off.

Though it was after midnight, Laney wasn't ready for bed, and retreated to the bar. Matt was cleaning glasses and wiping down the counter top. He saw her coming toward him from a distance.

"Hey, California Girl," he said, slinging a white towel over his shoulder, "Can I get you an after dinner drink?"

"No, I'm okay. I just want to sit here." Laney suddenly felt exhausted.

"Are you sure? I can pour you a fabulous glass of Cognac." Matt held up an expensive Private Reserve.

She thought about it for a second. "Why not? I don't usually drink Cognac, but my hotel's only about twenty feet away." Laney's twinkle was back in her eyes.

Matt poured two petite glasses of Cognac and took off his black apron. He sat one in front of Laney, then walked around the bar and sat beside her. "I hope you don't mind?" He smiled, grabbing his glass of Cognac and raising it toward hers.

Laney was nervous for a second about drinking with Matt, but gave in to his offer. "Not at all. I could use the company. And I promise that I'll keep my phone tucked safely away in my purse." She laughed and patted the side pocket of her bag.

"Good thinking. I promise to make this drink worth your while," he said flirtatiously, his bedroom eyes looking dreamily at hers.

"I'll tell you what, as long as you don't talk about politics, you can stay," she laughed again.

"I do know a little about that topic but I'll stick with architecture." Matt didn't take his eyes off of her.

"Good. Then it's a deal," Laney said, savoring a sip of Cognac. She actually enjoyed the taste. "So, my mom tells me, that you're also a politician's son."

Matt hesitated, then shrugged. "Guilty as charged. Actually that's why I wanted to have a drink with you," He scanned the room. "I wanted to tell you personally about my family genes."

"Are you looking for that person who's following ya?" Laney giggled, "…that paparazzi person?"

"I know we're not in California, but…" Matt continued to check out the corners of the restaurant like Magnum P.I.

"Seriously? It's that bad?" Laney was now feeling quite tipsy from the mixture of wine and Cognac. "Thatz crazy," she said, tilting her head back and taking one more swig. "This's really good stuff. Howz 'bout a-nother?"

"Well, it's getting late and maybe we should get you back to the hotel." He could now see the effects that the alcohol was having on her. And no photographers seemed to be lurking around…so the coast was clear.

"No, I'm fine. I'm…jus, mad at my hush-band. I think he's cheatin' on me." Laney slurred. She was usually a very private person but the Cognac was doing the talking for her.

Matt didn't want to pry…no questions about her marriage. He gently took her arm, thinking it was best for her to get some sleep. "Let me walk you to the hotel," he said pulling her to her feet.

"No, I'm f--ine, my architect-beertender friend. I kin w--alk to my own room," she said sloppily, wobbling toward the front door and then slipping on the hard wood floor. Not missing a beat, Matt rushed to catch her. Laney fell back into his able arms, giggling like a little girl. "You're turnin' inta my Superman. I f--eel like Loiz Lane."

"Well, Superman is taking Lois Lane to her room," Matt said, scooping Laney up and carrying her out the door of The Goat and down the walkway to The Drake.

"Lois? Can you tell me what room you're in so I can get you there safely?" He slid with her into the elevator.

Laney had closed her tired eyes. "Ten f-fifteens," she whispered.

Matt got off on the tenth floor and looked down at Laney's sweet face. She was like an angel. He came to the door marked "1015" at the end of the long corridor and stood Laney on her unstable feet.

"Lois, I need the key," he said softly in her ear.

"My purze…f-ront side pockit." She opened her right eye and indicated her black leather Gucci bag, hanging off her shoulder.

Matt searched the front pocket and found the white credit card style key. He opened the door and led Laney to the bed. He turned back the white down comforter and the sheets, and gently laid her down. He removed her sandals and placed her designer bag on the chair next to the window.

Laney moaned as Matt covered her with the down comforter. "Ah luv him, ya know," she said, hugging her pillow and turning over on her side.

Her comment caught Matt off guard. He looked down at Laney and caressed her hair with his hand. "I know, Lois. And he loves you too. Don't worry. Everything will be fine." Matt wanted desperately to kiss her soft pillow lips, but he leaned down and kissed her forehead instead.

He opened the door to leave and heard Laney sigh, "Sank you, Suberman."

"You're welcome, Lois," he said turning back to her with a smile.

Matt walked down the hall and left The Drake, totally unaware that the *little Hollywood* paparazzi had followed his every move.

Chapter Four

Laney awoke to a loud knock at her hotel room door. Her head throbbed from the effects of the grape and grain. She knew that she shouldn't have mixed the two last night at The Goat but it was too late now. "God, what time is it?" She said aloud, her voice raspy from the alcohol.

She looked sleepily over at the alarm clock on the bedside table and squinted at the bright digits. It was only eight a.m. and way too early for her to get up on her vacation. And she felt like complete hell. She hadn't been this hung over since college. She sure didn't feel like getting out of bed. *It must be maid service at the door*, she thought. But she always put the "Do Not Disturb" sign on the door…or did she this time? Laney tried to remember but right now her brain wasn't working.

Laney wrapped her pillow around her head and ignored the second knock at the door. She rolled over on her side and tried to go back to sleep, but the obnoxious pounding at the door got louder and louder. Then she heard her mom's raised voice calling her name.

Now worried, Laney grabbed her robe from the end of the bed and stumbled to the door. "Mom, I'm coming," she mumbled, hoping Sophie would hear her and calm down.

Laney unlatched the door and opened it. Sophie stood with a copy of the *Greenville Times* in front of her face. "Have you seen the headlines yet, honey?" she said from behind the paper.

"No, Mom. I've been too busy painting my nails," Laney said, barely able to keep her tired, bloodshot eyes open.

"Well, let me read them to you. While you've been sleeping, princess, the presses have been turning," Sophie piped, brushing past Laney. She sat down on the small love seat and put the morning paper down on her lap.

"Mom, please, before you start, I have to have a cup of coffee," Laney turned on the small coffee maker at the bar.

"I think you may need more than coffee in your cup this morning," said Sophie, picking up the paper and giving it a shake.

"Yeah…like more sleep." Laney collected her freshly brewed mug of java and sat down next to her mom. Still barely coherent, she laid her head on the back of the sofa. "Okay, Mom, I'm ready, go for it."

Sophie cleared her throat as if about to recite a Shakespearean soliloquy. "Okay, honey, here it goes, and I quote: 'Married California Fashion Designer Finds Love with Much Younger Senator's Son at The Drake."

Lethargy vanished and Laney was now on alert.

"What the hell?" she hopped to her feet. "Matt walked me to my room and that was it. Nothing happened. God, nothing happened…I swear." Laney began pacing the floor in her white robe. "I'm married…very married," she proclaimed. "Mom, this is crazy." She realized her head was now hurting more than ever.

"Honey, I told you to be careful," Sophie said in her *I told you* so voice.

"Mom, I didn't do anything." Laney rubbed her head, but the pain persisted. "I need to call him," she urgently searched the room for her Gucci handbag. She spied it on the chair by the window, rushed over and dug her cell phone out.

"I don't think that's such a good idea," Sophie warned her. "I would leave your phone *and* the TV off."

"Why?" God, she wasn't in Hollywood, but she now understood

the power of a small town. Ignoring her mom, she turned on her cell phone and switched on the large plasma TV to news channel 4. Laney's phone showed two messages from Thomas, who, despite the three hour time difference, was obviously up before Laney.

"Shit!" Laney shouted, as she held the phone to her ear and listened to her husband's massages. Thomas had already read the news online. His "Laney Montgomery" Google Alerts on his computer had woken him up fast. The other messages were from Missy, Bridgett, local reporters, and Matt, who apologized profusely for getting her into this mess about a thousand times. Now she knew why her mom told her to keep her phone turned off. Laney sat down on the sofa by her mom and held her aching head in both of her hands.

"I need more caffeine," she demanded.

"Honey, you need to fix this," Sophie replied, getting up to pour her another cup.

"Fix this? There's nothing to fix. I came here to get away from all of my stress and now I have even more. My husband is now convinced I'm having an affair, and here I am with the horrible thought that my nine-year marriage may now be over. This is just fabulous," she moaned. "What am I going to do? Thomas will never believe me." And then Laney stopped. "Why wouldn't he believe me? I've always been faithful to him. This is crazy!" she shouted.

For the first time, Sophie didn't know what to say. She absently checked herself in the mirror and took a deep breath. "Oh, honey. Somehow it'll all be fine."

"You're right. It'll be fine. I'll call Thomas and tell him what really happened, and everything will be okay." Laney tried to convince herself as she nervously paced the floor with her iPhone in her hand.

Loud voices boomed from the hotel hallway and another loud knock came at the door. It was Missy and Bridgett. Sophie got up and let them in. She had now forgotten about the bad blood argument between her and Bridgett. Laney's new drama completely overshadowed that one.

"Oh, my God, Laney, have you seen the local news?" Bridgett exclaimed, bursting in the room without even saying hello. She hadn't seen Laney or Sophie since the big scene at The Goat and was acting like it had never happened.

"Bridgett, don't be so brash," Missy snapped, falling in behind her.

"Why not? This is the most exciting news since I had my affair. Now there's a new Kim Kardashian in town!" Bridgett grabbed the remote from the table and pointed it toward the television. She flipped through the channels until she found what she was looking for.

"Thanks Bridge, you always knew how to make me feel better," Laney huffed from the sofa.

"Look! Lane. There you are!" Bridgett shouted like an excited cheerleader as she pointed to the television. "You look amazing. You always photographed so well." She stared at the screen as if she was watching the biggest stars in Hollywood on Entertainment Tonight. "And he's cute, Lane, and young, you cougar you. Look at his body," Bridgett gawked at Matt on television. She was never one to censor her words and today was no exception.

Laney got up and stormed over to the television and grabbed the remote from Bridgett's hand, turning the TV screen to black. "This isn't funny, Bridge. This isn't Hollywood. I didn't do anything wrong. And, I'm not a cougar, like…" She stopped herself in mid-sentence. Laney so wanted to throw this back into Bridgett's face, but she wasn't going to make things worse than they already were. She was above her sister's comments. She sat down on the bed and sighed.

"Well, he's a hottie, Lane." Bridgett continued with her steamy comments in a monotone voice. She never knew when to stop, never listened, and her hearing was very infuriatingly selective.

"Bridge, put a sock in it. This is serious," Missy ordered like a sergeant major. Her college military training was coming in handy.

Sophie slowly rose from the sofa with a concerned look on her face. The girls went silent. She walked over to Laney, sat down beside her on the bed and took her hand. She locked eyes with Bridgett and Missy a few feet away on the sofa. "This is a time for the four of us to band together. We're a family and we need each other," she said sternly but maternally. Sophie turned to Laney. "It's just a stupid gossipy paper. It ain't the Holy Grail. You know what happened and you know the truth, that's all that matters. Thomas loves you and trusts you. It'll be okay, I promise."

"I hope so, Mom. You've always been right." But Laney knew deep down inside that Thomas had a temper, and she was afraid of what he might do or say. She only hoped that their years of complete trust for one another would hold their marriage together.

"Let's leave your sister in peace now, girls." Sophie announced. She kissed Laney on the forehead, stood up and escorted Missy and Bridgett out the door. They wished Laney luck and promised to stay at the Starbucks downstairs just in case she needed them. Laney sat on the bed and collected her thoughts. She dreaded calling Thomas back. She walked to the bathroom mirror and sighed. *I look like complete hell*, she thought. *I gotta do something to make myself feel better*. She quickly washed her face, brushed her hair and put on her Sparkelicious comfy clothes, which always gave her a sense of strength and security; and that was another thing that she desperately needed right now.

Thomas was an Internet news hound. He had obviously read the article on the AP wire before Laney was even close to waking up. Thomas always told her that so many things happened while she was sleeping, and this time he was right. Then again, he was right most of the time. Thomas was a very intuitive, highly intelligent and creative man. He thought more about life after death than life itself, which sometimes brought Laney down. His recent scare in the hospital had made him rethink his life. But Laney couldn't imagine her life without him.

Laney finished her morning routine, bravely picked up her iPhone, went to 'favorites' and scrolled down to 'Thomas.' As she delicately tapped her finger on his name, there was another knock at the door.

"Now who?" Laney moaned, walking to the door and quickly ending the call. She looked through the peephole and saw a tall man, dressed in a black hoodie with his eyes hidden behind a pair of dark sunglasses. He was holding about fifty newspapers in his hands.

"Matt? Is that you?" she called out.

"Yes, hurry. Please open the door," he grumbled.

Laney opened the door and snickered at Matt's crazy get-up. He looked like a bad rapper. "Are those souvenirs for me?"

Matt wasn't in the mood to joke. He put the down the papers and sat on the loveseat, finally revealing his face and eyes from underneath his garb. "I know that I shouldn't be here, but I just wanted to make sure that you're okay." He breathed heavily as if he'd been running…from the paparazzi.

"Well, besides my reputation and my marriage being on the line, I'm fine." Laney shrugged.

"I'm sorry," Matt replied. "I hoped this wouldn't happen, but it did. I tried to be so careful."

Laney stared out at the view of the river and then glanced back at Matt on the sofa. "It's not your fault. It's mine. I had too much to drink, you helped me out and then *boom*, we're in the paper."

Matt walked over to Laney standing at the window, grabbed her hand and led her over to the sofa; his youthful face looked more mature than usual. His usually, cleanly shaven face had grown a bit of stubble over night. He looked like a young George Clooney, stern and concerned.

Laney became nervous and began twisting her hair around her finger.

"None of this is your fault. I really like you, California Girl," Matt smiled. "My father is calling the editor right now and setting the record straight. They should publish an apology in the paper tomorrow."

Laney frowned." So, does your father do all of your dirty work for you?"

"No." Matt blanched. "But he's the reason we're in this mess.

Everyone's out to get him and the best way to do that is by hurting his family." Matt took the strand of hair from Laney's hand and delicately set it free.

Laney's heart raced. Matt was more confidant and dashing than ever. Her cheeks turned a bright pink. She couldn't take her eyes off of him. *Snap out of it,* she ordered herself. *I have a marriage to repair.* But before she could respond to Matt, a loud beep came from her phone. It was another strange text from Thomas. It read: "Meet me for brunch later today. T."

The baby pink in her cheeks were now red with furry. This was becoming ridiculous. *Is my husband really loosing it? Or is this a way to get me to call him back?* It had been two hours since he had called her and he wasn't the kind of man to keep waiting. The English never waited for anyone.

"That bastard." Laney said out loud, standing up and marching across the room.

"What? Is there another bastard in the room besides me?" Matt raised his eyebrows.

"I'm sorry. I'm talking about my husband. I've got to call him back," Laney responded in a snippety tone, not wanting to reveal anymore than she already had to Matt about her marriage.

Matt took the hint and promptly got up to leave. "California Girl…I hope everything turns out the way you want it to. And again, I'm sorry," he said, heading for the door.

Laney followed behind him. "I'm sure it'll all be fine."

Matt stopped at the door and locked eyes with Laney. "If you need a friend, you know where I am."

"Thanks. Just keep the paparazzi away." Laney smiled as Matt opened the door to leave.

She closed the door behind her, grasped her phone in her sweaty palm, walked out onto the balcony and took in the view of the river. Laney hoped it would help her relax, but she was way too uptight. She was running every crazy scenario in her head. Was her husband having an affair…going blind and just dialing the wrong number?

Was he trying to make her jealous? She had to get down to the bottom of it. Laney dreaded this call because Thomas was so good at twisting situations. He had a lot to explain…but so did she.

Laney took a couple of deep breaths and called Thomas. On the fourth ring, he finally answered. There was no "Hello my dear" or anything like that.

"So, is there something that you need to tell me?" Thomas said in a mock-fatherly tone.

"It's not what you think, Thomas." Laney said. But Thomas remained silent. He was clearly trying to make her feel guilty. But she refused to feel bad for something that she didn't do. "I did nothing wrong," she snapped.

Thomas cleared his throat. "Well, from the looks of those pictures, I'd say you were having quite a lot of fun last night. What am I to think, Lane?" he said in a harsh tone. His British temper was heating up.

"I know it looks bad, but I promise you, all the guy did was bring me back to my hotel room, because I drank a little too much wine," she insisted.

"Back to your room? Who is this kid any way?" Thomas growled. "I thought I could trust you."

"You can," Laney said without waver. "I've never been unfaithful to you, and I never will be."

The conversation went back and forth for about thirty minutes. Thomas informed her that she was the most self-centered woman that he had ever known, which made her furious, having made so many sacrifices for him. Then he began to manipulate the situation even more. She rarely won an argument against him in the years they had been married. She knew she was fighting a losing battle no matter how innocent she was. But she just couldn't get those strange texts messages out of her mind.

"Well, maybe it's *you* who can't be trusted," Laney blurted out.

"And what's that supposed to mean? Don't throw this back at me. This is about you, not me. But then again, everything always turns into poor you, doesn't it?" Thomas shouted.

"No it doesn't," Laney said calmly. "And I'm not self-centered. My life has always revolved around you."

"Oh, not the 'poor me' thing again. It's pathetic. I'm the one suffering here, not you. But it always comes back to poor little ol' Laney," Thomas seethed.

Laney couldn't hold back the tears and they streamed down her face. She was not self-centered and Thomas knew it. She did everything for him. Laney had abandoned most of her friends to be with him 24/7, and even put her fashion business second to dedicate her extra time to him and her marriage. But he always did a superb job of manipulating her and making her feel guilty.

"Well, then what were all those texts that I kept getting from you? Were you really just texting my number by mistake? Or were they meant for someone else?" she demanded, grabbing a tissue.

Thomas hesitated for a brief moment. *What text?* He thought in a panic. *God, did I send another text to Laney by mistake?* He had to cover up the fact that the texts were meant for the young girl he'd met at a casting call for his next film. "I told you, the last time you asked me about this, that I sent you the texts as a little joke. I missed you and just wished that you were here. But I guess that you obviously haven't been missing me." He was back to his usual charming British tone. Thomas actually suspected that Laney was telling him the truth. He wouldn't dare continue to accuse his wife now of being unfaithful when he was actually the guilty one.

It worked. Laney melted. In her mind, Thomas was back to being the sweet man that she loved, adored and trusted. She didn't want to keep accusing him of being unfaithful now and ruin the moment. But a part of her was still very suspicious.

"But three texts, Thom?" she said softly.

God, was it three? Thomas wondered. *Could I be that stupid to send all three to Laney's number?* He was fast losing his eyesight in one eye, so it was possible. Plus, the girl that he'd met did ironically have a name close to "Laney." And her name was stored right above hers. Thomas had to think of something fast.

"Look, I miss you, my dear. Can you blame me for that?" He was now ready to forget the pictures of Laney and Matt in the *Greenville Times.* He had to extract himself from this predicament. Therefore he was willing to let his wife off the hook. Laney had always been the most loyal woman he had ever met. Deep down he knew she was innocent.

"I miss you too. I would never do anything to hurt our marriage, T. You know you can trust me," Laney cried.

"I know. I believe you. Just come home to me soon, my dear." Thomas was just happy that Laney had bought his lies.

Laney was a little stunned and confused at her husband's sudden change of heart. She wiped away her tears, hung up the phone, and breathed a sigh of relief. But those texts were still bothering her. She glanced back down at her phone, pressed the green 'message' button, and read the texts again. She smiled. *Might as well erase them… no need to keep them any more.* But as she lifted her finger to press the 'delete' button, something made Laney stop herself.

Chapter Five

Laney was tired and drained from the events of the day. She threw her unwashed hair up in a high ponytail and checked her face in the mirror. "God, look at me," she frowned, examining her pale face in the light. Her L.A. tan seemed to be fading so she dusted some bronzer and a hint of pink blush to her skin. She lined her plump, full lips with a pink liner and added Chanel Twilight gloss, which gave her lips a shimmer. It was her favorite lip gloss and it always made her look and feel younger.

She threw on her Sparkelicious warm-up suit in midnight coal. The jacket and pants were decorated with silver sequins; it was dressy enough for a night out which her mom should approve of, and not give her any grief.

In L.A. it would have been considered chic. In the South she would be under dressed, but she didn't care. She had learned to do what she wanted to, not what was expected of her. And if her mom said a word, she would be ready.

Laney walked down the busy main street and passed crowds of hip college kids on every block. Greenville wasn't the small town that she remembered as a child. It boasted one of the hottest "new" downtowns in the South and many young people flocked there on weekends. On the corner of Main Street and First Avenue stood the historic Poinsett Hotel. Laney glanced up at the landmark building and felt a warm and fuzzy feeling come over her. So many special memories of her high school days flashed before her as she gazed up at the historic hotel that had hosted most of her teenage proms and sorority dances. Laney had to go inside and reminisce about the fun she had there over twenty years ago.

Greeted at the entrance of the grand hotel by a doorman in a top hat and tails, Laney walked through the revolving glass doors that opened unto an opulent parlor area. She continued up the mahogany staircase to the majestic lobby. Sounds of a baby grand piano filled the air as she glanced around and rehashed all of the beautiful memories that she had experienced there. She felt like a teenager again and she was thrilled to see that the hotel still had its charm and character.

Laney continued through the lobby bar, sat down on the red velvet sofa and just took in the magnificence of the room. It was so glamorous yet still oozed a cozy warmth. She felt like Lauren Bacall, waiting for Bogey to walk in any minute. Laney rested her head on the sofa and her mind drifted back to the eighties. As she relaxed, a table of wealthy revelers interrupted her. They desperately wanted her attention.

"Ma'am, sorry to pry, but my husband says you're the woman in the pictures from the paper today," the overweight lady slurred in a very tipsy voice, her Southern accent turning every two-syllable word into a three. Before Laney could respond, she continued.

"But I told him that you're way too pretty and way too young to be that cougar," she took another sip of wine as her husband glared at Laney with a big grin on his face.

"Well, thank you. But your husband's right," Laney responded, feeling like a cross between a B movie star and Demi Moore.

"See… I told you, honey, it's her," the tongue-tied man whispered from behind his vodka tonic. Satisfied with her answer, the couple went back to their drinks and wished her a good night.

Laney shot them a gracious grin and made a fast escape to the corridor that lead to O's, a chic restaurant a few feet from The Poinsett Hotel. She was now having hot flashes and felt like she was going to throw up. The hot flashes seemed to be happening more often since she returned home. *Probably just from anxiety*, Laney hoped, and not her aging, raging hormones. She wanted to hide in an igloo and cool down.

She reached the restaurant and walked up the flight of stairs that led to the dark cozy loft-style, retro bar. There was a quiet table in the corner where she sat down and ordered a glass of chardonnay from the attentive waiter. *Something cold and alcoholic will do the job*, she thought.

As Laney checked her e-mails on her iPhone, she felt a soft tap on her shoulder. She turned around expecting to see her mom or one of her sisters but instead a handsomely well-dressed, man in his mid-sixties, that she'd never seen before, stood over her and smiled. He was flanked by a tall muscular black man that looked to be his bodyguard.

"Aren't you Laney Montgomery?" The extremely attractive, salt and pepper haired man asked. He was wearing a navy blue business suit and had the look of someone extremely important.

Laney didn't know whether to lie to him or to tell the truth. After her last run-in at the Poinsett Hotel, right now she wanted to hide her identity. She seemed to be turning into a local celebrity again, but this time, not for cutting the ribbon at the new bank as Miss Greenville, but for all the wrong reasons.

One of Laney's long blonde bangs fell across her right eye. She looked at the man, shrugged indifference, and replied, "Yes, I am."

"You are actually more beautiful than your picture," the man said in a flirtatious manner, holding out his right hand. "I'm Senator Rigby. I want to apologize for what happened." He grasped her right hand in a tight politician's grip. "I know that my son really cares about you."

Laney was struck by the senator's charisma and charm; she now knew who Matt had gotten his good looks from. She found herself at a loss for words, unsure how to respond to the senator's statement. She had hoped that Matt really didn't care about her. That's the last thing that she wanted to hear right now.

"Nice to meet you, Senator. I've heard a lot about you." Laney now wished that she had washed her one-day old hair earlier for this. He was an extremely attractive man.

The black Mr. T. like bodyguard stood behind the Senator like an oak tree and surveyed everyone in every part of the room. The senator made a "do you mind?" gesture, then pulled back the lounge chair beside Laney and sat down. A candle flickered on the table in between them.

"You won't have to worry about the press anymore. The editor-in-chief owed me a favor. He called the dogs off Matt. So, if you want to see my son again, you can," he whispered like it was top-secret information.

Laney crossed her arms and sat back in her chair. "Senator, I'm a happily married woman. Matt and I are just friends."

"Well, whatever. My son's a good guy and he's crazy about you. I'll just leave it at that." The bodyguard looked at his watch and gestured to the senator that it was time to leave. He stood up from the table and nodded goodbye.

Now somewhat flattered, Laney didn't know what to say. She took in the senator's words, sat up in her chair and looked up at him as he was about to leave. "Your son is a good guy," Laney said sincerely. "Thanks for saying hello."

The bodyguard led the senator away. One minute he was there and POOF! the next minute he was gone. Laney leaned back in the velveteen chair and thought about Matt for a second before her thoughts turned to her husband. She sipped her chardonnay and heard her mom's voice echoing from the staircase.

Sophie was in full party mode. Dressed in a black sequin dress and black pumps, she arrived at Laney's small quaint table out of breath.

"Honey. Did you see him? Did you see the senator?" she said throwing her hand to her heart. "My God, he's so delicious. I could look at him all day." Sophie turned around hoping to catch one more glimpse at him. "I'm having major hot flashes. I need a fan or something cold on my face. Give me your glass of wine." She placed the chilled crystal on her forehead and continued in a dramatic fashion, drinking the last sips of Laney's wine, "I think I'm going to faint."

"Mom, you'll be okay, I promise," Laney laughed.

"I don't know, honey. Every time I see that man, he does this to me. What's he doing in town anyway? Shouldn't he be in Washington?" Sophie dipped her napkin in Laney's table water and put it to her forehead.

Laney flagged down the waiter and ordered another round of chardonnays for both of them. She felt like she needed one now more than ever.

Sophie continued fanning herself as she turned to Laney. "Well, honey, you're being awfully quiet. Did you see the senator or not?"

The drinks arrived just in time and Laney took a sip of wine before she answered. "Well, actually, Mom, he stopped by my table to say hello."

Sophie gasped. "What? Honey? Stop it. You have to be joking. People always go up to him. He never stops to talk to anyone."

"Well, mom, he introduced himself to me and told me that his son was crazy about me." Laney reached for her Chanel Twinkle gloss on the side of her purse and added some sheen to her lips.

"Just consider yourself lucky, honey. He must really think that you're somethin' special."

"Mom, he's Matt's father. He doesn't care about me. He's protecting his son." Laney nervously brushed her bangs out her eyes. "Anyway, I think my husband's having an affair."

"What?" Sophie spewed her wine across the table. "I never trusted that man… Honey, I warned you about marrying a foreigner."

"Mom. God, he's not an Islamic militant, he's British. And it's not definite, I just have a gut feeling." Laney now regretted bringing the subject up.

Bridgett and Missy appeared at the top of the dimly lit staircase. "Hey," they said in unison, holding drinks in their hands.

"It's like girls in the city," Bridgett giggled in her low cut tank top that showed off her large rack.

Missy was her reserved conservative self, dressed in a black blazer and khakis. "More like *old* gals in the city."

Sophie fired back, "Honey, excuse me. Seventy is the new fifty, you know."

The girls laughed at their mom and her over-the-top gestures, finished their drinks and were escorted downstairs by the hostess for dinner. They were led to a round booth in the back of the restaurant. It was just where Laney wanted to sit, away from everyone. O's was jam-packed. Every table in the house was taken. Sophie knew the owner and they got seated before everyone else on the guest list.

Laney and Sophie sat in the middle of the U-shaped booth, while Bridgett and Missy bookended them. Bridgett scoped out the room and noticed a young couple sitting near the window.

"Lane, I think that's your Matt over there." Bridgett pointed to the front of the restaurant.

"Stop pointing," Missy whispered in her big sister voice. "That's not polite."

God, Laney thought, *the whole reason we came to O's and not The Goat was to avoid Matt.* "First of all, he's not *my Matt*," Laney snapped, stretching her neck out as far as she could to get a better glimpse of the couple. But unfortunately, she could only see the back of the guy's head and couldn't tell if it was him or not.

"Well, he's not your Matt anymore because he's with some cute young thing. I guess he doesn't like cougars after all," Bridgett smirked.

Missy shot Bridgett an *eat shit and die* glance and stamped on her foot under the table. Sophie's daggers came out. She was furious.

"Bridge, you can talk. You're the biggest cougar of all. You left your wonderful husband for a younger man," she said in a pissy tone.

Laney just wanted a peaceful evening. "Mom, let's don't go down that road now," she said with one eye on her mom and the other still glued on the guy at the table.

"Why not, honey?" Sophie insisted. "Now's a good a time as any. It's way over due."

Bridgett jumped up from the table to escape the feud but Missy grabbed her arm. "Sit down, Bridge. You're not going anywhere."

Reluctantly, she fell back into the cushioned seat and pushed her bottom lip out like a sulking child. "Mom, you never loved me."

Oh, here we go again, Laney thought. Bridgett's *always the victim, never taking responsibility for her actions.*

"And what about you, Mom?" Bridgett spat. "You married Charles."

"But honey, I didn't leave your father. He died of a stroke. Do you think I wanted him to die?" Sophie's tone was wounded.

Laney couldn't listen to their attacks on each other any longer. "Can we just get through *one* dinner without an argument?" she begged, turning to her mom like a referee at a sporting event. "What's done is done. Bridgett made her decision. It's her life." She locked eyes with Bridgett. "And Bridge, Mom loves you very much."

Missy hated confrontation. She kept quiet and remained neutral. Sophie glared up at the ceiling with her arms crossed and Bridgett continued to pout, staring down at the floor.

"Now, let's make a toast to all of the cougars," Laney joked, hoping to break the icy mood. She raised her glass. "God, maybe I *am* one?"

Missy, Bridgett and Sophie burst out laughing and tacitly agreed to put their differences aside. "To cougars," they said, raising their glasses in the air and clinging them with Laney's.

The young man and his date got up from the table and headed in the direction of their booth. Bridgett nudged Laney's foot under the table. "Well, cougar, here comes your cub." It *was* Matt and he was advancing toward them.

Laney got butterflies in her stomach. She was actually a little jealous that Matt was with someone else…someone so pretty and young.

Matt recognized Bridgett and approached their table. Then he saw Laney, nestled in beside her. He locked eyes with her. "Well if it isn't the girls," he beamed. He looked impeccable, casually dressed in jeans, a black cable turtleneck sweater, with his hair gelled back, highlighting his handsomely chiseled face. Laney couldn't help but stare back at him.

Matt's date appeared. She stood quietly beside him like a trophy girlfriend. Rather than introducing her, Matt shot Laney a concerned glance. "Hey, California Girl. How ya doing? Feelin' any better?" Everyone at the table was now silent.

Laney nervously tugged on her ponytail. "I'm okay, thanks."

Matt's face showed relief as he held her gaze in his. "Good. I've been worried about you."

The pretty brunette, standing beside Matt, finally broke her silence. "Hey, everyone. I'm Molly…Matt's little sister. I've heard a lot about all of you," she smiled, trying to break the obvious tension between Matt and Laney.

Laney sighed with relief. She was happy to hear that the girl wasn't Matt's girlfriend and gave her a welcoming smile.

Sophie piped in, "I'm sure it was all good."

Not wanting to overstay their welcome, Matt and Molly said their goodbyes and then turned to leave. "Can I call you?" Matt asked Laney politely.

For some reason, he wasn't giving up on her, married and all. But Laney didn't know how to respond.

"Just for a cup of coffee, nothing else," he reassured her. The girls anxiously awaited Laney's response. Her heart said yes, but her head said no.

Chapter Six

A box of Just For Men hair dye, medium ash brown, sat on the black granite countertop in the master bathroom. With his nose pressed up against the mirror, Thomas carefully examined his gray goatee. A large mass of gray hair stared back at him. He then inspected his salt and pepper grey sideburns that were once a natural brown and shook his head in disgust.

Thomas was overcome with desperation. *If I am going to be hanging out with the younger generation tonight in Hollywood, I have to at least appear to look a little younger myself,* he thought. Right now he felt ugly and old. He had dyed the hair on his head for the past ten years and had become a master colorist.

Fed up with his graying facial hair, he grabbed the tube of Just For Men, slathered on the sludgy brown goop and waited impatiently for it to work its five-minute magic. He watched the clock and occasionally checked his beard over in the large mirror. *Not bad for fifty, even though I could stand to lose a few pounds around the waist.* Thomas sure wasn't Joe six-pack, but he made a pledge to himself that he would get rid of the excess weight when his over-50 soccer team started back up in the summer. From a health perspective, Laney worried about his ever-expanding waistline and tried to encourage his weight loss. But Thomas would just grumble profanities at her until she shut-up about it. So, he was still the same, soft around the waist and full of excuses.

Thomas gave himself another pep talk, took a long leisurely shower and rinsed out the hair dye. He grabbed his favorite navy blue chenille robe that hung on the wall and wrapped it around his plump tummy. He checked his freshly colored hair in the mirror and smiled, his famous trademark dimple stared back at him…the dimple that captured attention from almost every woman he met. At a recent Hollywood event, one starlet commented: "I could have a party in his dimple." Thomas loved that story and milked it on every occasion he could, especially when his wife was around.

With an unconventional, heart-shaped face and rosy English cheeks, Thomas looked more like a Frenchman than an Englishman. His complexion was ruddy yet refined. For fifty, he barley had a line on his face, only a few soft lines graced his forehead and framed his eyes.

Thomas held his stainless steel razor in one hand and scissors in another, trimming his freshly dyed brown goatee and sideburns like a manicured lawn. He hadn't been out on the town since before his surgery and realized that this "trying to look younger business" was like a Hollywood production. The maintenance was ridiculous and he now understood why women took so long to get ready.

Thomas had been a faithful man to Laney for the last twelve years. But before meeting her, he hadn't been faithful to anyone. He did love her, but something had changed within himself since he was hospitalized for his emergency appendectomy surgery a few months ago. He claimed to have never had a mid-life crisis, but now it seemed like he was in the throes of one.

He searched for his favorite blue jeans and found them hidden under a stack of unfolded clothes in the laundry basket in the corner of the bedroom.

"There you are, you bastards," Thomas grumbled, snapping up the creased jeans. *No need to iron these babies*, he thought. As a filmmaker, he had to look the part, and the scruffy, creative, casual look worked well for him. To finish off his outfit, he threw on a black t-shirt that lay on top of the messy pile of clothes.

It was now five-thirty and he had an hour and a half to get from the Hollywood Hills down to Santa Monica. He was meeting Kara, a wannabe actress he had auditioned for one of his low-budget films. Thomas always had a number of female friends, and it had bothered Laney when they first got married, but over the years she learned that he got bored from working at home a lot, and just wanted the company of a variety of human beings. And Thomas liked beautiful woman, which most of them were. But Laney wasn't threatened by any of them anymore. She was secure with her marriage and with herself. And there had never been a reason not to trust her husband.

But tonight was different. Thomas was really pissed about the pictures he had seen of Matt and Laney, and he was jealous, which was something that he hadn't felt since he and Laney first met. When Thomas got jealous, it wasn't pretty. And ever since he had been sick with his recent appendicitis, he had lost his sex drive, which also bothered him. Therefore, tonight was about proving to himself that he still had it…and about feeding his ego…and secretly getting back at his wife.

Thomas arrived early at The Casa Del Mar Hotel. His hunter green, weather-beaten Triumph Spitfire came to a screeching halt at the front of the world famous Spanish style hotel. The young valet took his keys and gave him a ticket. Thomas walked to the large bar in the center of the over sized room and instantly felt ancient. The bar was overflowing with many young aspiring actors and a few famous ones. He had to be more than twice the age of everyone there. No one took any notice of him as he tried to find room at the grand oak bar to order a drink. All of the young girls were too busy checking out the hot guys around them. Kara was nowhere in sight. Thomas moved away from the bar crowd and to the back of the luxurious room. The view of the ocean stared him in the face. It was an amazing display for the eyes and one that he never tired of.

It was still light outside. The vast blue water sparkled as the sun set over the horizon. Thomas thought of Laney three thousand miles away and began to miss her. All of a sudden, this date didn't seem like such a good idea. *What was I thinking? I'm fifty and married but my ego is needing to be fed.* He noticed the Santa Monica Pier off to the right in the distance. He was remembering one of their earliest dates, on the pier, when he kissed Laney for the very first time, and he felt a warm breath in his ear.

"Tommy," Kara whispered sexily in his ear, "I'm here." She stood behind him in a pair of washed denim jeans, a black low cut tank top and red stilettos. Her overly processed stick straight blonde hair glowed in the fading sunlight. "What are you looking at?" she asked, stroking her new fake Prada bag and checking her freshly painted nails.

Is she that vapid to not realize that maybe I'm enjoying the beautiful ocean view? Thomas turned and looked at Kara, her Valley girl voice already getting on his nerves.

He tried to act excited to see her, but she was thicker than two short planks, and he was about ready to bail on her. Instead, he gave her a jolly English hug and kissed her on both cheeks. "Hello my dear, good to see you," he said politely, ignoring her lack of observation.

"Isn't this place way cool?" Kara said, indicating the massive Spanish style room. "I've never seen a room decorated like this."

Thomas tried to go with her on this, even though he had been to dinner at Buckingham Palace and had dined with royalty and slept in castles. "Yes, not a bad room. It is quite big, even by American standards."

Kara took his hand and led him to the bar. The bartender saw her coming and had her drink ready at the end of the bar when she arrived. He knew her from another bar in the Valley that he used to work in, where she was a regular.

Kara picked up her margarita and took a sip. "Tommy, whaddya wanna drink?" Her voice already sounded a little tipsy. She had obviously been to a couple of other bars before meeting Thomas. "I know the bartender. I'll set ya up," she winked.

"A merlot would be lovely," Thomas replied.

The bartender handed Thomas a glass of merlot and Kara whisked him away to a cozy table with two comfy leather chairs in the back of the room that overlooked the youthful crowd. Thomas downed his merlot and ordered another from the waitress while Kara had two more margaritas. The only thing that Kara wanted to talk about was the movie business. She had no interest in anything else.

"So, Tommy…kin I star in your nex' film?" Kara slurred, getting drunker by the second. She kissed Thomas's neck and whispered sweet nothings in his ear. He wasn't that turned on, but he felt wanted and needed; something that he hadn't felt in a long time.

"Maybe so, my dear," Thomas replied, knowing good and well this girl couldn't act to save her life and that he didn't have a script for her to even star in. Kara moaned, kissed his neck, then put her lips to his. He didn't want to kiss her back but he couldn't help it. He was surprised he liked it. But Thomas was getting tipsy and Kara's drunken giggling was getting out of hand. It was probably time to leave while he was still half sober. He took Kara's hand and led her outside to the valet stand. She stumbled as she tried to walk arm and arm with Thomas to the car. He put his arm around her, holstered her up and helped her into the front seat.

"Are we goin' ta yer house, Tommy?" Kara asked in a tipsy baby voice, leaning her head back onto the black leather seat.

"I could take you home, if you'd prefer," Thomas offered in a kind voice, giving her the option.

She giggled and replied, "Yer house…yeah."

Thomas arrived at 1200 Laurel Canyon Drive and pulled his compact car into the garage. He looked over at Kara sleeping in the passenger's seat and was riddled with guilt. Laney would kill him if she knew what he was doing right now. *I should be ashamed of myself*, he thought. But he was still pissed about the pictures of Laney and Matt on the Internet and couldn't get the images out of his head even though he knew his wife was innocent. However, he was stuck with Kara now and would have to sober her up.

Thomas walked over to the passenger's door and opened it, hoping Kara would awake from the sound, but she sat there snoring. He tapped her on her right shoulder and she whimpered like a baby, "Are we there yet?" reaching her arms out to Thomas for him to carry her.

He lifted her from the sports car and carried her to the side entrance of the updated modern ranch style 1970's home. He opened the door and tripped on Laney's tennis shoes. "Damn it," he exclaimed. She always left them at the back door, but he of course, forgot to pick them up. *This a huge a mistake*, he thought. *Why did I bring this girl home*? But he had gone this far and he couldn't turn back now.

Kara stirred in his arms as Thomas carried her to the den and laid her on the plush, chenille, chocolate brown sofa.

"Wow, this place's hot," she said, her eyes full of excitement as she took in the impressive room. "You've done pretty well fer yourself, haven't you, Tommy?" Kara was thanking her lucky stars that she'd latched on to a famous Hollywood filmmaker. *Maybe now I can have this life*?

Thomas knew that he couldn't take any of the credit for his beautiful home; Laney had bought the house with her fashion success, not his nonexistent movie profits All the same, he said, "No, I haven't done badly at all, now, have I?" He guiltily cleared his throat and proudly glanced around at their possessions. The living area was stunning with walls of glass overlooking the canyons.

Kara, beginning to sober up, got up from the sofa and walked over to the contemporary art that hung on the wall. The piece over the marble fireplace caught her eye. "My God, Tommy, that's a nice one!" She pointed at the red and black abstract. "What's it suppose to be?" Her finger moved toward the painting to touch it.

Thomas leapt like a panther over to the fireplace. "No!" he said loudly, waving his hands in the air to stop her. "If you don't mind, please don't touch the canvas. You'll get your fingerprints on it." He didn't like anyone to touching his precious art.

Kara yanked her hand back. "Sorry…I wasn't gonna hurt it," she said in childish tone.

Thomas stepped between Kara and the painting. "I know that you wouldn't hurt it, but it took me a bloody long time to paint it and I don't want to have to paint another."

"Wow, you painted this? You're amazin'," Kara bubbled with admiration. "You're so talented, Tommy." She took his hand and led him over to the sofa.

Thomas didn't resist and they fell onto the sofa as one. Kara rolled her thin body on top of his. She kissed him passionately and whispered sweet nothings in his ear. Thomas quickly forgot about Kara's lack of brainpower and couldn't help but fall under the spell of her killer body and her kisses. He kissed her back with intense lust, but with little emotion. His heart was with Laney, but his mind was on sex. So, here he was letting this young woman undo his pants and take off his shirt because he felt deprived. Kara's attention did stroke his ego and boost his confidence, which was something he was desperate for since he wasn't a wanted man on the Hollywood scene. And, with Laney away, his needs weren't being met. He wasn't in any hurry to push his ingénue away.

Kara removed her black tank top, pressed her breasts up against his bare chest and moved her hips up and down on his. For a moment, Thomas felt light-headed and dizzy. His lungs tightened up. He clenched his chest and gasped for air, but still couldn't breathe.

Desperate for air, Thomas shoved Kara off of him and mouthed to her for help: "Think I'm having…a heart attack…" he tried to say with barely a sound coming from his mouth.

Kara now understood that something was really wrong. She jumped up off of the sofa and ran for her purse, which she'd dropped on a nearby chair.

"Crap!" she yelled, scrambling for her cell phone, buried somewhere in her purse. "Where are you, stupid phone?" She found it and frantically dialed 911 as she watched Thomas on the sofa, gasping for air and holding onto his throat.

God, he can't die on me, Kara had the selfish thought. Thomas was her only hope if she was going to make it in Hollywood.

The paramedics arrived within minutes. Fortunately, the fire station was only a few miles away from the Hollywood Hills home. And the paramedics had been there before for Thomas's earlier emergency, the burst appendix, so they knew him and the house very well. But Laney had been out at one of the department store's doing a trunk show when it happened.

The emergency crew moved with precision, pulling out a defibrillator and placing two paddles on his chest. After two rounds of electric shocks, Thomas's pale face began to show some signs of color. One of the paramedics gave Kara a thumb's up. Thomas's chest was still tight but he was no longer gasping for air. The paramedic placed an oxygen mask over his face to help stabilize his breathing, and Kara let out a deep sigh.

They placed Thomas on a stretcher and wheeled him out to the ambulance. He was totally out of it. He didn't know where he was or where he was going; his oxygen levels were way down and he was extremely dizzy. Kara followed the paramedics out to the ambulance and looked down at Thomas's poor, helpless face.

He looked up at her from under the oxygen mask and tried to muster up the strength to speak. "Lan-ey," he whispered, his voice muffled. Kara knew exactly whom he was referring to. She knew he was married but didn't care. And she wasn't about to call his wife. She would leave that to the hospital.

As the paramedic closed the ambulance doors, he looked at Kara standing in the drive. "Mrs. Morgan, you can come with him," he said kindly, "but we need to go now."

With no time to explain that she wasn't his wife, Kara hopped in the back with Thomas and sat beside the stretcher. She glanced down at him and smirked. She couldn't wait to tell her friends about this. They would never believe that she almost killed one of the "hottest film directors" in town during sex.

Chapter Seven

Midnight was fast approaching and "the girls" had one more drink before turning in for the evening. Laney said goodbye to her mom and sisters and started her five-minute walk back to The Drake. But, as she walked out onto Main Street, The Poinsett Hotel stood gracefully in front of her like a beacon in the night. It called out to her and she had to go back inside and reminisce once more about her youth. She walked through the revolving doors; a piano played in the distance and became louder as she meandered through the hall, upstairs, to the lobby bar.

The smooth sounds of one of her favorite jazz songs lingered in the air. Laney made her way to the vintage sofa, in the back of the room, sat down, and was greeted by a waitress. She didn't really want another drink, but she placed her order anyway. She leaned her head back on the sofa and closed her eyes as she listened to the beautiful music.

Her thoughts went straight to Thomas. She missed him and wished that he would call her. But Laney knew that if he wanted to talk to her, he would call her in his own time. And then her mind switched to Matt. She thought about how charming and gentle he was—quite the opposite of Thomas, and found it difficult to get him out of her head.

The waitress walked over quietly, trying not to disturb her and sat the tall glass of chardonnay on the antique wooden table. But Laney opened her eyes, thanked her for the wine, and returned to the music.

She was intrigued by the talent of the pianist, and glanced over at the piano in the dark corner. Laney assumed it was the same pianist she'd heard earlier in the evening.

Laney's heart raced as she listened to the young virtuoso play. The candlelight flickered on the piano and lit the man's face. To her amazement, it was someone new. It was "her" Matt, as Bridgett would say. His amazing talent took Laney's breath away. Matt played the Steinway like John Legend, only with more attitude.

Matt brought the song to a power crescendo and ended it with a combination of gusto and sensitivity. The bar erupted with applause. Matt stood up and bowed. Laney watched as a bevy of young women flocked over to him from the corner table. One girl bounced on her toes with excitement, while another clapped her hands like an excited baby seal. Laney frowned as another one of Matt's groupies made no pretext of touching the back of his neck with her hand. *How do I compete with that?* Laney thought. *They're all young enough to be my daughters.*

Matt politely spoke to them and seemed to revel in the attention.

Laney thought there was no reason to say hello. She figured that Matt would have his choice of any of these lovelies - or maybe even take two home with him tonight. She waved to get the waitress's attention, so she could pay her bill and quietly leave.

As Matt thanked the cuties, he picked up a waving motion out of the corner of his eye. At first he thought someone was waving to get his attention; then he realized that a woman on the cozy sofa was trying to hail the waitress. He did a double take and realized it was Laney. Matt quickly said goodbye to the girls, and they returned to their tables with pouty faces.

Matt sat back at down at the piano and adjusted the mike. "I was going to take a break, but I think I'll play one more song. I would like to dedicate it to the beautiful lady over there on the sofa." He glanced in Laney's direction. "This one's for California Girl."

The waitress arrived and Laney politely excused her. She locked eyes with Matt and he flashed her a heart melting smile. Laney reclined back on the sofa, wondering why this young guy was making such a fuss over her. In her mind, she was old and married, and from the looks of things, he could have his pick of the litter. Apparently, there were more sides to Matt than she ever imagined. He began Joe Cocker's, *You are so Beautiful*, and Laney was overwhelmed with emotion. It was one of her slow dance songs from high school and it brought back so many memories. She used to dance with her first ever boyfriend to it. She felt fifteen again.

Matt finished with a grand flourish and announced this time, indeed a break. He stood, took a slight bow to the applause, and made a hand to head motion as if tipping his "hat" goodnight to the girls. He turned his focus to Laney, waved, and made his way over to her table.

First, his dashing looks and now his incredible musical talent, Laney thought as he approached. A glass of merlot, from the alert waitress greeted him at the table.

Matt plopped himself down beside Laney and planted a gentle kiss on her cheek. Laney wanted to back away but decided to just go with it, feeling she'd allow him at least a little kiss after his musical spectacular.

"So, you are becoming more of a real Superman every day," Laney smiled as she sipped her wine. "You are a man of many hidden talents. And I see you have a lot of fans." She looked over at the girls who were now staring at them.

"If you stuck around long enough, you might find out more about me," he chuckled, ignoring her remark about the young posse of girls. "Music is actually my first love. Architecture, my second."

"Then why not pursue music?"

"Because music never paid the bills. I needed a plan B when I realized that doing a few gigs a year wouldn't keep a roof over my head." Matt shrugged. "Enough about me. What about you? Fashion design was plan B too, wasn't it?" He raised his eyebrows.

Matt hit a nerve. "How'd you know?"

"You look like a singer, not a stuffy fashion designer," he surmised like a Svengali. Laney was now getting a little freaked out. Matt's intuition about her was spot on.

"Yes, I was singer, but I gave it up years ago. I miss it though."

Singing was indeed her first love, she even had her own band when she first moved to Los Angeles, and she had been so close to a record deal. But her dream of becoming a singer had died. Being on the road with the band would have meant little or no time with her new husband. She felt it wouldn't have been fair to him…or to them. So she stuck to her second love, designing clothes, instead. And, as Thomas reminded her, she wasn't making enough money from music to turn it into a full-time career. She sat her glass of wine down and gazed into Matt's eyes.

"Wow. You do seem to have some super powers, Superman." Laney's eyes were filled with sadness and regret. She shook it off and forced a smile. "And what about you? You're a phenomenal pianist."

"Thanks. I'm classically trained, but I decided to have something to fall back on. And, as you can see, I'm pretty good with my hands, so architecture was my other love." Matt moved closer to Laney and caressed her hand. His hand felt warm and comforting against her skin. His touch shot a shiver up her spine.

She removed her hand from his, still intent on keeping it on a friendship only basis. "You shouldn't have given up music, Superman. It's your gift," she said sweetly.

Matt wasn't the least bit phased by Laney's rejection. He took her hand again in his and squeezed it tightly. The candlelight on the table enhanced his chiseled face. He looked like a movie star, gorgeous, and difficult to resist. Matt leaned in to Laney and put his lips to hers.

She was so tempted to kiss him back, but she hadn't kissed another man in twelve years and wasn't going to start now. *I am a loyal loving wife, not a cougar*, she reminded herself. *Besides, why is he giving me all of this attention and not one of those babes in Toyland*? And just as their lips touched, Laney's iPhone rang and she pulled her lips from his.

"I'm sorry…I should get this." She frantically dug into her purse in search of her phone. Deflated, Matt leaned back on the sofa and waited patiently for Laney to answer her phone. He knew he had no right to tell her not to.

Laney found her phone and placed it up against her ear. Her face turned pale as she listened intently to the person on the other end. Matt sat up to attention as he watched her worried expression. In a pinch, Laney ended the call. She jumped up from the sofa and cried, "I have to go, I'm sorry. Thomas has had a heart attack. I have to get to L.A. as soon as possible." Without saying goodbye Laney ran for the door.

"Laney, please, let me help you," Matt called out in desperation. "I'll drive you to the airport…anything." He sprung up and sprinted after her.

Matt flew through the hotel exit, just in time to see Laney yank the taxi door shut, and helplessly watched as it sped off. His Lois Lane was gone and so was his heart.

Chapter Eight

The taxi ride from LAX to Cedar-Sinai hospital seemed longer than the four-hour flight from Atlanta to L.A. Laney sat anxiously in the back seat of the cab, hoping for a call from the hospital with an update on her husband. The thought of losing Thomas was way too painful.

As she thought about Thomas lying helpless in the hospital, her phone rang from her clinched hand. With anticipation, she glanced down at the incoming number. It was Dr. Weston, the leading heart surgeon at Cedar's Sinai.

"Mrs. Morgan?" he asked somberly.

"Yes, this is she," Laney pressed the phone tightly to her ear, fearing the worst because no one ever called her by her married name unless it was usually bad news or pertained to her husband. She was known by Laney Montgomery in her fashion life and had never legally taken Thomas's last name. "How's Thomas?"

"We had to do an emergency bypass surgery."

"What? Surgery?" Laney shrieked. "Why didn't someone call me sooner and tell me?" she demanded. "Oh my God, how is he?"

The doctor remained calm, hoping to ease her mind. "I'm sorry about that. But there was no time. Your husband is responding well to the surgery. He's in recovery and resting."

Laney felt a sense of relief from his words and regained her composure. "Thank you, Dr. Weston. Thanks for letting me know. I'll be there soon."

She said goodbye to Dr. Weston and laid her head back on the headrest and sobbed. *How could I have been so stupid to even look at another man*? She hated herself for being so immature. All she wanted to do was to see her husband and tell him how much she loved him.

The taxi arrived at the hospital and she rode the elevator to the sixth floor. The nurse at reception directed her to room 608. Laney opened the door and began to cry again when she saw Thomas lying so helplessly in the hospital bed. He had so many tubes and wires hooked up to him. He looked more like a robot than a human being.

Laney rushed over to his side and gazed down at his pale face that had grown a slight beard and his goatee was now grey. He resembled more a man of sixty than fifty. His eyes were shut and he looked close to death.

"Honey, I'm here," Laney said quietly, hoping he would open his eyes and look at her. But he just grunted. She took this as a positive sign and spoke to him again. "Honey, it's me." She leaned down and kissed his forehead. But Thomas drifted back to sleep. Obviously, he was still heavenly sedated, but Laney didn't care. She kept talking to him.

"Honey, I'm sorry for not being here for you. I'll never leave your side again," Laney declared, wiping tears from her eyes.

As she spoke to Thomas, she heard a noise coming from the bathroom. "Who's there?" She turned to look behind her.

Must be a nurse, she thought, but no one responded. Laney turned her attention back to her husband, when another thump came from behind the door. She spun around to see the light go off from underneath the doorway. *This is getting spooky*. And then the bathroom went silent.

Laney let go of Thomas's hand and walked over to the bathroom door. She turned the stainless steel handle--it was locked. She jiggled the handle several times but it still wouldn't open. "Is someone locked in there?" Laney called out. There was no answer even though she could hear someone moving around.

Laney was tired of the game. "Okay, I know that someone is in there. I can call security to let me in, or you can open the door yourself…Or, I can knock the door down myself."

Still, there was no response, only the sound of nervous breathing coming from the other side of the door. "Okay, ready or not, here I come," Laney said, lifting her leg up in the air like Lara Croft.

And then she heard the small voice: "No, don't. I'm coming out." The door opened and Kara stood in the doorway, awkwardly shifting her weight from one foot to the other.

"You don't look like a nurse to me." Laney eyed the strange young woman, noting the fake boobs spilling over her low cut halter top.

"Course I'm not," Kara replied coyly in her Valley girl voice. "I'm a friend of Thomas's."

Laney crossed her arms and glared at Kara with daggers. But before she could ask any more questions, a nurse walked in.

"Mrs. Morgan," she said, addressing Kara, holding a pen and a clipboard with several papers in her hand. She didn't even give Laney a second glance.

Now Laney was really annoyed. She couldn't keep her Southern charm under control any longer. "*I'm* Mrs. Morgan." She turned and stood in front of Kara, reaching out her hand to the nurse for the papers.

The nurse was clearly confused. She pulled the papers away from Laney's grasp. "Well…then why did *she* sign the admittance papers?" the nurse asked, pointing at Kara.

"I have no idea. I just flew in from South Carolina. I don't even know who *she* is," Laney fumed.

"Then why is she in here? Is she a relative of your husband's?" the nurse demanded. "And if she signed the papers, then how did we know to contact you?"

Kara stood there in silence, then raised her hand to speak.

"Ladies, excuse me. I found this woman's name and number in Thomas's cell phone. Her name looked important so I wrote it down on the admittance papers and asked the head nurse to call her," she said, smacking a piece of gum.

"Looked important?" Laney said sharply. "I'm his *wife*."

"Thought so," Kara replied, looking down at her fang-like nails and pulling out a fingernail file.

The nurse shook her head in bewilderment. "But, honey, you signed off as 'Mrs. Morgan.' That's against the law." She held up the paper with her signature on it.

Pissed to no end, Laney didn't know what to think. *Is this woman a stalker? A hooker? Who in the hell is she and why is she signing my name*? Laney placed her hands on her hips and glared at Kara, "You signed *my name* on a hospital form?"

"Yeah… It's a long story. Maybe your husband can explain it better when he wakes up," Kara said coolly. She took a step forward and looked Laney over. Kara's hand went to her mouth. "I thought I recognized you…you're that designer…I love your Sparkelicious sweat suits." Kara now sounded like a crazed fan. Before Laney could say anything, Kara continued her love fest for her. "Thomas never told me he was married to someone famous." Kara was even more impressed with Thomas. "And you're really beautiful. I expected you to be way older. You look so much younger in person." She said this just like an immature twenty-three year old.

Laney didn't know whether to thank her for her back handed compliment or to smack her, but she did her best to hold her temper intact. Laney shot her a fake smile and then an *eat shit and die* look. She just wanted to know why this girl was here. And it seemed that this stranger wasn't willing to tell the whole story. Hopefully Thomas would.

Just then, Thomas began to stir in his bed. *You have a lot of questions to answer, buddy-boy*, Laney thought, the first one being, "*Who in the hell is this Valley girl*?"

The nurse quickly left the room to get Dr. Weston. She thought it would be a good time for the doctor to check on his patient.

Thomas slowly opened one of his eyes and then the other to see the two women standing over him. He was groggy, and didn't really know where he was. His eyes focused. First, he recognized Laney's face, and then he saw Kara standing beside her. It was all coming back to him. "Hi," he whispered, his voice scratchy and weak.

"Are you talking to me or her?" Kara piped up.

Thomas didn't know what to say. Being the polite Englishman, he replied. "Both of you."

Laney's sympathy for her husband went out the window. "Who is this girl anyway, *Thomas*?"

She never called him "Thomas" except when she was mad. And he could tell even in his groggy state that she was starting to boil.

Thomas put his hand up to his heart. He looked like he was begging for forgiveness as he mustered up the energy to speak. "That's Kara…" and then he fell back asleep.

"How convenient," Laney shook her head.

Kara walked around to the other side of Thomas's bed and looked Laney in the eyes. "Well, now that you know my name, the cat's out of the bag." She grinned like a schoolgirl.

"But I still don't know *why* you're here."

At this point, Kara didn't really care about Laney's feelings, or about the fact that she was Thomas's wife. She was ready to tell her everything. "Well, I…" she began to say.

Thomas suddenly woke from his not-so-deep sleep. Before Kara could finish her sentence, he finished it for her: "She saved my life."

Laney's mouth fell open. Her thoughts were racing. She was extremely thankful - - if that was the truth - - but she also wondered why Kara was even with her husband at the time.

Before she could find out anything more, the doctor walked in with a confused expression on his face. He didn't know which woman to turn his attention to. And before he could ask who the *real* Mrs. Morgan was, Laney volunteered the information.

"I'm Mrs. Morgan, Doctor Weston. Thanks for taking care of my husband," she said looking at his ID on his green scrubs. She walked over to him and shook his hand. "What's his prognosis?"

Doctor Weston put on a serious face. He scanned the stainless steel chart in his hand and walked over to Thomas's bed. "Well, he seems to be doing really well after the surgery," he said matter-of-factly. "It's a good thing that he got here when he did, or he may not have made it." He glanced over at Kara and gave her a nod of thanks.

"Oh, God? Are you serious?" Laney cried.

Kara sat down in the chair in front of the window and glowed at the doctor's remarks. "Well, I guess it's a good thing that I was around when it happened."

Doctor Weston could feel the tension in the room and wondered, himself, what was going on. He shot Kara a curious look then tried to console Laney. "He's going to be fine, Mrs. Morgan. Your husband should be back to normal within a few months."

"Thank you, doctor," Laney said.

Doctor Weston wanted no part of a three-way Q and A. He abruptly excused himself and left the room; and there was silence.

Laney leaned up against the wall and was overcome with emotion. "I'm sorry," she said to Kara, "but I need to be alone with my husband."

Kara nodded in agreement and strolled to the door. As an afterthought, she looked back at Laney. "Say…I would love one of your fancy sweat suits. Any chance of a special discount?"

Laney's tears turned to coughing laughter. "You're kidding aren't you?"

"No…I really do think they're way cool!"

Laney couldn't believe her nerve. She just wanted the girl to leave. However…because Laney was from the South, and Thomas had said that Kara had saved his life, she replied, "You know what, leave your address and your size with the nurse and I'll just mail you one. It will be a 'thank you.'"

Kara clapped her hands like an excited child. She couldn't believe she was getting a free Sparkelicious outfit from her favorite designer. "Sweet! I'd love a pink one," she said without skipping a beat; then she turned and literally danced out the door.

Laney sighed with relief as Kara left the room. She wasn't in any hurry to ever see that nutty woman again.

Chapter Nine

Thomas was recovering well from his surgery. He had his strength back, had mastered his rehab and was now able to do some light cardio. While his heart was getting stronger every day, Laney and Thomas's marriage was getting weaker. There was definitely something missing between them. A raw, eerie silence now lingered throughout their Hollywood Hills home.

Laney was still very suspicious of Kara. Thomas hadn't fully explained to her why this *strange girl* was with him when he had the heart attack. And since Thomas was recuperating, Laney hadn't pressed the subject with him, nor had he volunteered any more information. But it seemed, the healthier Thomas got, the grumpier he became. She had seen a glimpse of the old fun loving, kindhearted Thomas when he first came home from the hospital, which made Laney hopeful. However, the Thomas she'd fallen in love with was fading away. He now played the helpless patient to the hilt, ordering Laney around like a hired servant…just like the last time he'd been ill.

And while Laney didn't mind taking care of Thomas, she only wished that he showed a little appreciation for some of things that she did for him. She was doing everything she could to make him happy. She even put the expansion of her fashion business on hold so she could be there for him around the clock. But no matter what she did, it wasn't good enough. Thomas was angry, moody and over emotional and Laney didn't know how much more she could take. He was crushing her positive spirit.

She desperately wanted to start designing again, but with all of the stress, there wasn't an ounce of creativity coming from her brain. She thought it best to cancel any appearances for her line until Thomas was fully recovered.

Laney frantically cleaned the black granite counter tops and the stainless steel appliances in the kitchen. She wanted to surprise Thomas with a spotless kitchen when he returned from his rehab session. When Laney heard the garage door close she feverishly ran the cloth over the stovetop one more time. Thomas walked in wearing an old t-shirt and black sweat pants. The tiredness from his rehab showed as he looked around the expansive modern kitchen with a grouchy expression on his face.

"So, what do you think?" Laney stood next to the island and marveled at her sparkling kitchen.

Thomas scowled as he ran his fingers across the surface of the counter top and checked it for dirty marks like he was Mr. Clean. "Bloody hell, Lane. You used the wrong cleaner again, didn't you?"

Laney jumped to attention. *Oh, God, did I really use the wrong one? Or is he just testing me like he loves to do?* "No. I used the one in this drawer." She pulled out the can of marble cleaner wipes.

Thomas was furious. It was the cleaner he told Laney never to use. "What do I always tell you?" His voice sounded more like her father than her husband. "This is my kitchen, not yours."

Laney threw the rag down on the counter, feeling like a reprimanded child and marched out of the kitchen and into the den. "You know, I paid for 'your little kitchen'. I'm just trying to help."

"It always comes back down to money with you, doesn't it?" Thomas said sharply.

Laney stormed back into the kitchen and sparred back. "No it doesn't. But it would be nice to be thanked for something, once in a while."

"Oh, now it's about you again. Everything's always about you." Thomas stood an inch away from Laney's glum face and exclaimed, "I'm the one that had the heart attack."

Thomas's harsh words brought tears to her eyes. Laney knew she was fighting a loosing battle. Her husband was the master of manipulation and knew exactly how to bring her down.

Laney returned to the den, sat down on the sofa, and wiped her teary eyes. "Ouch," she shrieked, as a sharp object jabbed into her right butt cheek. "What in the hell is this?" Laney held up, what looked to be an earring. "It sure isn't mine!"

Thomas's face was bright red. "What? Let me see?" He sprinted over to the sofa, like a marathon runner, not like a man who recently had a heart attack. He knew good and well what his wife had found and whom it belonged to.

Instead of letting Thomas see the earring, Laney held it tightly in her hand and eyed him suspiciously. "Well, it sure isn't yours, either."

Thomas was screwed. He struggled to make something up fast. But before he could defend himself, Laney glared at him, tears streaming down her face. "This is Kara's isn't it?"

Thomas nervously cleared his throat and looked away from her. He couldn't tell his wife the truth. As Laney waited for his explanation, her phone rang. *Whew*, Thomas thought, *saved by the bell.* "Who is it?" he prodded, trying to divert the conversation.

Laney ignored it. "The call can wait."

But the phone continued to ring and Thomas insisted, "It could be important, Lane."

"It's just Missy." Laney said, peering down at the caller ID. "I'm sure it's nothing."

"You never know, Lane. I'll bet it's important. I think you should talk to her," said Thomas, needing time to get himself out of the doghouse.

After a moment of indecision, she answered the phone.

"Charles is dead." Missy said, without even a hello.

Laney's face contorted into anguish. "Oh, my God. What

happened? How's Mom? Can I talk to her?"

"He died in his sleep," Missy went on with deep sadness in her voice. "Mom doesn't want to talk to anyone right now. She asked me to call you. Give her some time, Lane."

Laney and her sister exchanged a few more words then said goodbye.

"Charles died this morning. I have to go home," she quietly declared to Thomas. "The funeral is only three days away and I have to be there for Mom."

"I'll go with you," Thomas said lovingly. He sat down on the sofa beside Laney and put his arm around her. All of a sudden their problems didn't seem so big. Laney now had to help her mom mourn the loss of husband number two.

They sat in silence; Laney clutched the gold hoop earring in her hand. She knew the truth would hurt, but she couldn't wait any longer.

"I need to know what really happened, Thomas." She got up from the sofa and walked to the sliding glass doors that led to the deck; she slid the doors open, walked out into the balmy California air and looked over the handrail. The lights twinkled throughout the canyon.

Thomas was a coward. He just couldn't muster up the courage to tell his wife, whom he'd known for twelve years, that he had an affair, but he owed her some explanation. He walked out onto the deck and stood beside Laney and brushed his shoulder with hers. He turned to Laney and saw the hurt and disappointment in her eyes.

"I'm waiting," she said, with her arms folded, glued to the view.

But Thomas wasn't ready to confess anything to his wife, even though he was disappointed with himself.

"You know I love you…" he whispered, running his hand along her back.

Laney flinched. Thomas felt like a stranger to her now. "But…" she prompted, knowing good and well that he had a lot more to tell her.

Just then, the doorbell rang. Laney jumped.

"Ignore it," Thomas said, pretending valor.

But Laney knew from the look in his eyes that he was calling her bluff and wasting her time. "I have to get it…I've been waiting for a cloth delivery from overseas, and I have to sign for it."

Thomas was relieved. He now had time to make up a good story to tell his wife. Laney left him on the deck and walked through the den to the hall. She opened the door, expecting to see the UPS deliveryman. Instead, Kara stood in the doorway in a model pose, wearing black oversized Chanel sunglasses and the baby pink Sparkelicious outfit that Laney had given her.

"So, whaddya think? Pink's my color, isn't it?" she quipped.

The timing could not be worse, Laney thought. She couldn't believe this girl's gall and gusto. Kara was so obnoxious yet inexplicably likeable at the same time. Besides, she had supposedly saved her husband's life, so Laney felt she had to be somewhat cordial to her. "Yep, it suits you." Laney rolled her eyes at Kara and put on her best sincere face.

"Wow. Thanks." Kara feverishly chewed her gum, pushed Laney out of her way, and barreled through the door and into the hall.

Thomas had become anxious. He couldn't wait any longer for Laney to return to the deck. He walked into the narrow foyer and saw Kara admiring herself in the mirror. He felt beads of sweat begin to drip down his face. He couldn't let her see him. He had to escape. Thomas held his head down, shielded his face, and made a beeline for the kitchen; but it was too late, Kara caught a glimpse of him out of the corner of her eye. *Oh, God, no*, he thought, *please let this be a dream*. But it was his worst nightmare, come to life.

Kara's eyes lit up like saucers. She was ecstatic to see her meal ticket to stardom looking so fit and healthy. "Hey there, Tommy," she called out.

"Kara, is that you?" Thomas was perspiring profusely. He had hoped that he would never see her again, but as he observed her young, svelte body, their steamy and passionate night resonated in his mind. His eyes became fixated on her enormous "double D" boobs.

The thought of touching them again made him horny and her nativity was attractive to him this time.

"Hey, Tommy. You look hot." Kara unzipped her hoodie a little lower and revealed the line of her cleavage to him. All of a sudden her Valley girl voice didn't annoy him so much.

Laney made a sour expression. "Yeah, Tommy, you do," she said sarcastically, shooting daggers at her husband.

Another bead of sweat dripped down his face. He quickly wiped it away with his hand. "Lane, aren't we late?" he asked, winking at her.

Laney wasn't going to bail Thomas out of this one. "No, as a matter of fact, we have all the time in the world."

Kara didn't take the hint at all and walked farther into the house, leaving them to argue it out. Thomas and Laney followed closely behind her. This woman was getting creepier by the second. She made her way over to the sofa and started stuffing her hands in between the cushions.

"Nope, not there…not on that side either," Kara announced, putting her hands on her anorexic hips. "Did you happen to find…?" she asked, without thinking about the repercussions, and began running her fingers underneath the third cushion.

Laney finished Kara's sentence while pulling the trinket out of her pocket and dangling it in the air. "An earring?"

Thomas fought off the urge to slump to the floor. *Why didn't the heart attack just kill me?*

Kara squealed with elation, galloped over to Laney, snatched the earring from her hand and embraced her like they were the best of friends. "Thank God you found it!" she chirped. "They're my favorite earrings of all time."

Laney let loose a devilish grin. "Why would it have been in *my* sofa?"

Kara removed the matching earring from her purse and proceeded to put them both on. "Because we were…"

Thomas shot her daggers and cut Kara off before she could say anything incriminating about him. "W-We were rehearsing that scene in my movie," he stammered.

Laney wanted to believe him. No longer welcomed at the major studios, he did audition and rehearse with a lot of actors at their house. But this time, she wasn't convinced, and she wanted to make him sweat a little more. "You know, Kara, we were just about to open a bottle of red wine. Why don't you stay and have a glass."

Thomas cringed and gave Laney a look of terror, which she ignored. Laney just wanted the truth about Kara; and if her own husband wasn't going to tell her, then maybe Kara would spill the beans after a strong glass of wine.

Kara put her hands in the back pockets of her Sparkelicious comfy pants and thought about Laney's invitation for a second. "That sounds like fun. I'd love a glass of vino."

"Fabulous." *This is all working out perfectly*, Laney thought. She had always been good at keeping her enemies close, and right now, they were all about to become three's company; then again, she second-guessed herself, *Maybe too close for comfort.*

Chapter Ten

Sophie could barely breathe. She was close to hyperventilating. Her beloved Charles was dead and she wanted to die too.

The paramedics had done everything they could to revive Charles, even though he wasn't breathing upon their arrival. The only solace Sophie had was that her dear Charles left this world in peace. He had told Sophie that he wanted to die in his sleep when his time came, and he did. Sophie was glad, at least, that he had gotten his wish. As the county coroner analyzed Charles's cold lifeless body, Sophie excused herself to their master bedroom.

She sat solemnly on their king sized bed, wiped the tears from her swollen, bloodshot eyes and blew her nose. Missy tiptoed into the room, holding another box of Kleenex and sat on the bed beside her. Bridgett followed, with a small black purse in her hand and climbed up onto the other side of the bed.

Bridgett opened her purse and pulled out a small white pill from the side zipper pocket. "Here Mom. I think we both need this." She handed Sophie half of a Xanax, keeping the other half for herself. Missy didn't object and poured Sophie a glass of water from the carafe that sat on the bedside table.

Within seconds, Bridgett's mood grew more somber and she began to sob. She hadn't cried since her father died, but Charles's death was bringing back all of the repressed memories of him. Even Missy, who hadn't expressed much emotion since her pet snake died when she was ten, began to cry. Sophie joined in and all three of them cried together. Sophie was obviously upset from losing Charles, but she also had repressed so many feelings for her first husband, Clayton, that she now missed him more than ever.

"I miss Dad," Bridgett cried, not thinking about how insensitive she was being in not mentioning Charles.

"Me too," Missy said, grabbing the box of Kleenex by the bed and offering them to everyone.

Sophie took a tissue and then wrapped her arms around her girls. "I miss your father terribly, too. And now my dear Charles is also gone." She sobbed uncontrollably. The girls consoled their mom and gave her a big bear hug.

Missy's cell phone buzzed from her pant pocket. She lit up when she saw Laney's name appear on the caller ID.

Laney was definitely more relaxed after a glass of red wine. She'd left Thomas and Kara in the kitchen and excused herself to make the call. As she spoke to Missy, Laney kept her eye on her husband and his ingénue from the hall.

"Hey, L.A. Laney. We miss you." Missy put on her best *happy* voice and sniffled into the phone.

But Laney could tell that Missy had been crying. "Hey, how's Mom?" She was definitely concerned about her mom, but now Laney also worried about her sister. Her astute intuition was kicking in.

Missy took another tissue to her nose and tried to pretend that things were better than expected. "Oh, she's hanging in there."

In the South everything was always peachy which drove Laney crazy. That's partly why she left. But Laney knew better. "Is Mom up for talking? I would really like to talk to her."

Missy handed her phone to her mom.

"Hi, honey," Sophie said, her mood more upbeat from the Xanax. "We miss you."

Laney frowned suspiciously. Something was up. Her mom was

good at hiding her feelings but this was way too unusual. "Mom, hey. How are you holding up?"

"Well, your sister gave me this pill and I'm feeling much better now," Sophie giddily replied.

Ah-ha, Laney thought, *Bridgett is the obvious culprit.* She always had a Xanax on hand. When their father died, Bridgett shared a whole bottle of the pain medication with the entire family, except Laney. She had refused to take one. Laney wanted to feel every last emotion of losing her father, and she did.

"Oh, that's good. That should help you a little," Laney said, now sounding like her mother. She knew there was no point in asking her mom any deep questions right now, which was probably a good thing. "I'll see you tomorrow, Mom. I love you."

Laney hit the "end" button on her iPhone and held it close to her heart. Now she missed her dad more than ever. She walked to the master bedroom and sat on the leather chair next to the expansive window where she watched a deer run through the backyard and down into the canyon. She savored these few seconds of silence.

From the kitchen, Thomas yelled, "Lane!" His voice echoed down the hall.

"I'm coming," she responded. Laney sprinted to the kitchen and found Kara dancing on the massive granite island. She was two sheets to the wind. Kara began singing at the top of her lungs.

"So, what do you suggest we do with her now?" Thomas said smugly in his English accent.

Laney knew from Kara's drunken state that she couldn't drive home. "Let's put her in the guest room. The bed's made up."

Thomas glared at his wife like she was crazy. "What? You want her to stay the night?"

"Yes, I do." Laney firmly answered, ignoring his protest. She took Kara's hand and politely asked her to gently sit down on the granite counter. Instead she landed with a thump on her butt and continued to sing and giggle. Thomas and Laney checked their precious granite surface to make sure it was still in one piece. They helped Kara down from the island and walked her down the long corridor to the cozy guest bedroom at the end of the hall.

Laney pulled back the white down comforter, and without any objection, Kara climbed into the queen sized bed and dropped off to sleep like a baby. Thomas was way too uncomfortable to say a word. He didn't want his mistress around at all. And now she was spending the night.

Chapter Eleven

Two black limos lined the driveway of Sophie and Charles's exclusive home in the gated community of Hampton Hills. Sophie was still in a state of shock. She couldn't face the fact that her husband was gone. She sat somberly on the leopard print chair in the master bathroom and gazed sullenly into the makeup mirror that sat on the marble counter top.

Her unmade face was dispirited, her eyes swollen and puffy from endless crying. For the first time in a long time, she looked all of her seventy plus years. Dark circles encased her teal blue eyes. As the rock and matriarch of the family, Sophie had put on the bravest face that she could for the last two days, but now, with the funeral only an hour away, reality had crept in and her life without Charles felt unbearable.

A bottle of Lancôme creamy beige foundation and a compact of medium tan face powder sat on the counter and awaited to awaken Sophie's dejected face, but she just couldn't muster up the energy to slather it on. It seemed that loosing her second husband was harder than loosing the first.

Charles's death brought her closer to her own mortality and it scared her. *You gotta pull yourself together*, Sophie told herself. *The girls need me to be strong*, she repeated over and over again, but she just couldn't do it. She was depressed and too far gone. A crystal clock sat by the mirror but Sophie took no notice of the passing time. She just wanted to see her dear husband again, not lying lifeless on a stretcher, not in a casket, but sitting in his favorite navy blue chair in the den. The bathroom door opened and Laney quietly walked in, wearing the same black Armani suit she wore to her father's funeral. She had arrived a few hours earlier from L.A. Sophie tried to perk up for daughter. She reached for her comb to touch up her hair and pretended to be putting on her makeup.

"Mom, hi. Are you almost ready?" Laney softly asked, tiptoeing into the bathroom. She knew from her mom's unmade face that she wasn't. And she didn't blame her. But her mom wasn't one to go anywhere sans makeup, no matter what the occasion was, so this wasn't a good sign.

Sophie turned to Laney and cried, "Honey, I can't do this again." Her hand shook as she reached for the bottle of foundation. "I miss him so much."

Laney rushed to her mom's side and kneeled down on the travertine tile floor and wrapped her arms around her. "Mom, I know."

Sophie held tight to Laney and then pulled away from her. "But, I've done this before and I can do it again," she said in a warrior-like tone. And then Sophie doggedly began applying her makeup to her dark olive complexion with unwarranted strength.

But Sophie couldn't fool Laney. She knew that this little breakthrough would disappear when they all got into the limos.

Missy and Bridgett entered the bathroom, both wearing black. "It's time to go, Mom." Missy announced.

"Everyone's waiting," Bridgett softly chimed in.

The girls escorted Sophie down the long, narrow hallway where pictures of her and Charles lined the walls. Sophie looked straight ahead; she couldn't bring herself to look at any of them. She took several deep breaths and then broke down again as they approached the front door. On cue, Bridgett pulled out a Xanax from her purse and Missy ran to the kitchen for a glass of water and returned within seconds.

Bridgett handed the white pill to Sophie with the glass of water. "Mom, this will make you feel better."

Without hesitation, Sophie took the pill from Bridgett's hand and swallowed it. Bridgett and Missy followed their mom, taking half a Xanax each. Bridgett offered one to Laney, but as usual she declined. She didn't handle any kind of drug well, not even Nyquil. Besides, she knew that someone had to be totally on track during this emotional time.

The driver got out of the limo, opened the front door and helped Sophie inside, while Thomas, Chase (aka Maverick) and Missy's leech of a boyfriend, Brody patiently waited in the backseat for the girls. They were all in the lead limo while Charles's two sons; their wives and children rode in the other car. The mortuary had arranged the limos and decided that the entire family should be picked up at Sophie's house so Lake and Carson had reluctantly agreed to the arrangements. On the ride to the Baptist Church, no one said a word. It was the same eerie journey that Sophie and the girls took five years ago when Clayton died.

The limos finally arrived at the massive contemporary Baptist Church and the families were escorted to the front of the stadium-size room and seated in the first three front pews. The service was standing room only, with over one thousand of Charles's closest friends and acquaintances from all over the country. His dearest friends sat near the family. Charles was an exceedingly popular man due to his fame as a political columnist, and was also very well respected. And it showed with so many people there to pay their respects to him and Sophie.

Sophie hardly took any notice of the enormous crowd. She was far too emotional, and just stared, almost comatose, at the long black casket that encased her dear Charles on the enormously cold – looking stage. Clayton's funeral had also been held here. It was bringing back those sad memories of loosing him, too.

Laney and Thomas sat to the right of Sophie, while Bridgett and Chase, Missy and Brody sat on her left side. Charles's two sons sat in the second row behind them. His sons had never been that close to their dad and weren't shedding any tears. Both seemed almost annoyed that they even had to attend their father's funeral. Neither were happy that their father had married Sophie ten years after their mother's death.

Lake, Charles's oldest son, sat with his snooty, uptight wife, Shirley, while Carson sat on the end of the wooden pew alone. His wife and three children had refused to attend the funeral because of Sophie. They had dissed Charles ever since he had stopped giving them an annual check from his substantial retirement account, and they had blamed his marriage to Sophie on that. But it was actually Charles who was fed up with all of their greedy ways.

The preacher finished the eulogy and the choir stood and sang a haunting version of *Amazing Grace*. Sophie grabbed another white handkerchief from her small sequined black purse and blew her nose loudly and wiped her tears. Laney reached for her mom's hand and held it tightly. Even though Charles wasn't her father, she was going to miss him and felt for her mother. His death was taking her back to her own father's funeral and she began to cry. Thomas, who was usually supportive in situations like this, was distant and in his own little world. Laney wanted him to take her hand and tell her it was all going to be okay but he was cold and unavailable.

The preacher asked everyone to stand and gave a touching closing prayer. Afterwards, without any warning, Sophie ran to the pulpit, hurried up the stairs and stood over Charles's black coffin. Laney panicked. She jumped up from the pew to rescue her mom, but Missy grabbed her arm and pulled her back to her seat. Missy felt it best to give their mom some space to grieve. But Laney wasn't so sure. She watched her mom with much anticipation up on the pulpit.

Sophie placed her hands on top of the casket and everyone in the church watched in silence. She leaned down and kissed the end of the coffin where Charles's face would be. "I love you," she whispered.

And then she hit the casket with her hand and yelled, “you bastard, why did you have to leave me?”

With that emotional outburst, Laney, Missy and Bridgett jumped up. They couldn’t watch their mother suffer anymore. They made their way onto the pulpit, consoled her, and escorted her back down the stairs.

Lake and Carson sneered at the stepfamily from the second pew. Both were already thinking ahead to the reading of the will, anxious as to how that scenario was going to play out.

Chapter Twelve

Friends, family and acquaintances, poured into Sophie's beautiful two-story home to pay their respects to her, after the burial at Forest Lawn Cemetery. Bridgett had given Sophie another Xanax after they left the church, and she was much calmer now.

Laney greeted, what seemed to be, the two-hundredth person at the door and was exhausted. Thomas was nowhere to be found. She took a break and searched for him. She peeked into the first guest bedroom on the right side of the hall but he wasn't in there. Next, she walked across the hall and opened the door to the larger guest bedroom and found Thomas sitting on the king size bed.

"What are you doing in here? Laney demanded. "I need your help out there."

Thomas stood up, walked sexily over to Laney, and put his hands on her waist. "I'm waiting for you. Let's do it," he said in his horny English accent.

Laney was appalled. She pushed Thomas away. "What? Now? Are you crazy?" She shot Thomas a hard look. "My stepfather just died and you want to have sex?"

Thomas ignored her comments, moved in closer to her and squeezed her right breast. "God, I love your tits…I want to do it. Come on."

Laney rolled her eyes in disgust. "What in the hell is wrong with you?"

This wasn't the Thomas that she'd fallen in love with years ago. He was different. He wasn't showing any signs of sympathy for her or to her family.

Thomas smirked. "There's nothing wrong with me. I'm a man who wants sex with his wife. Maybe there's something wrong with you."

"Maybe you should call Kara," Laney huffed. "I'm sure she's available."

Thomas ran his hands through his hippy-length, freshly dyed, brown hair. "Well, maybe you're just saving it for Matt."

"Don't even go there, Thomas. I was and still am very loyal to you. You haven't even been man enough to tell me the truth about what happened between you and Kara." Laney believed that Thomas had been unfaithful to her, but she wanted him to admit.

Thomas didn't say a word. The guilty expression on his face along with his silence said it all.

As Laney waited for her husband to confess his affair, there was a knock at the door.

"Lane, are you in there?" Missy asked through the crack in the door. "We need you out here, now."

Laney put on a brave face and opened the door. "What's wrong?"

Thomas sat pouting in the chair by the window with his arms folded.

Missy said with panic in her voice, "Someone just put a 'For Sale' sign in Mom's front yard."

Laney was now all business. "What the hell is going on?"

From the kitchen, they heard Sophie yelling at the top of her lungs, "No one else is going to live in our house but me! It's not for sale!"

Laney and Missy dashed down the hall to the kitchen to see what was going on. Sophie was holding a letter over the stove, flames were just inches away from the white paper.

"Mom, no, wait. Let us read it first," Laney begged. She turned off the gas on the stove while Missy grabbed the letter from her mom's hand.

Missy scanned the letter. It was from Lake and Carson's estate attorney. "Oh my god! It says that Charles left the house to his sons, and that they have the right to sell it."

Sophie laughed and took a sip of her stiff drink. She was now feeling the effects of the alcohol and the Xanax. "You know what? He gave them everything else. Why not give them our house, too. What else do those bastards want? I'm sure they wish that I was dead too, but I'm not."

Sophie peered around the kitchen and into the atrium. "Where are those greedy boys anyway?"

Everyone at the house were either family or very close friends of Sophie's and were well aware of the family feud.

Lake appeared from the living room with Shirley glued to his side.

"Here's one of the bastards now," Sophie said, marching over to him. "You should be ashamed of yourself. Your father loved you very much. You may have never accepted his love, but you're not going to now take everything that he worked so hard for."

Lake looked down his nose at Sophie. "This is business, Sophie. Dad left the house to us. My attorney will be calling you, and in the meantime, that sign stays in the yard."

Sophie moved closer to Lake and put her nose to his. "If you want a fight. I'm in. You're not getting my house or anything else that is in it -- everything belongs to me. Now, get out of MY HOUSE," she yelled into his face. Lake and Shirley hurried out the back door.

Sophie stepped outside with guns blazing and ripped the "For Sale" sign off its hinge. And as Lake's black Lexus tore out of the drive, Sophie winged the sign at his prized car. It ricocheted off the back bumper and fell onto the street.

"Take that!" she yelled. Sophie pulled the bottom of her dress down to her knees, fixed her hair, and headed back into the house, carrying on like nothing had happened.

The girls watched their mom out of the window and applauded her as she walked in the front door. To Sophie's surprise, the entire group of mourners, in the living room and the den, gave her a standing ovation.

"Well, I never," she announced at first shyly, then changed her stride, "Is that the best that all of you can do? More? I need more." She bowed to her friendly admirers, and then raised her hands in the air for more applause. Sophie always loved a crowd, and she was putting on a pretty good show for someone who had just lost their spouse and possibly her home.

She stood up from her third bow and said to her friends in the room, "We need more drinks, don't we?" Her tone was now jolly. "Girls, can we get more wine for everyone please? And I'll take a Cosmo."

Missy's boyfriend, Brody, was already filling everyone's glasses with California Chardonnay and merlot. Laney glared at him, noticing as he surreptitiously made eye contact with a hot looking female guest. She had a sneaky suspicion that Brody was up to his old cheating ways, and was just putting on a show of having reformed. She hoped for Missy's sake that it wasn't true. Bridgett handed Sophie a Cosmo while Missy tucked the attorney's letter into her pocket, and Laney went in search of Thomas again.

Her husband was still in hiding. Laney was fed up with his childish ways. She walked into the atrium and found Thomas sitting in the corner of the glass patio chatting up a young girl. He'd now had way too many drinks.

"Oh, here comes the ole bird," he stage-whispered to the young woman as Laney approached.

"Hi, can you excuse us for a minute?" Laney said politely. The ingénue excused herself and disappeared into the kitchen.

"So…now I'm your old bird?" Laney said, raising her voice.

Thomas got up slowly from the sofa and wobbled like a weeble doll, his eyes were bloodshot from way too much scotch. "My dear, lighten up. You know it's an old English expression. You take yourself way too seriously."

"Oh, I can take a joke, but now isn't the time for one."

Thomas balanced himself on two feet and performed a sloppy salute. "Why can't you loo-zen up like…" he slurred, reeking of alcohol. Before Thomas could finish his sentence, Laney finished it for him.

"Like Kara?"

Everyone in the room turned to look at them.

Thomas responded, "Yeah…like Kara. Why can't you be more like her?"

Laney was fuming. She wanted to hit him. Brody overheard the argument from the kitchen. He burst into the atrium, stood between them, and took Thomas by the arm. "Dude, you need to come with me." He led Thomas down the hall to the guest bedroom. Thomas tried to fight Brody off, but he was too inebriated to resist.

Laney had never liked Brody. He was always eyeballing her like he was imagining what was going on under her clothes; but right now she was relieved that he had come to her rescue. Otherwise, she might have regretted what she did next. Laney dropped into the white high back chair in the atrium and stared out of the window at the garden. The sun was setting and the sky was a tapestry of pink and lavender. Twilight was usually her favorite time of day. But at the moment, she was feeling incredibly sad.

Just as the last of the sun shyly kissed the sky goodnight, she felt a gentle touch on her shoulder. She looked up and there was Matt's kind face to greet her. *His timing is perfect again*, she thought. It had been almost two months since she had seen him and he looked more attractive than ever.

"Hi, California girl," he said sweetly, his striking tall frame towering above her. Matt was dressed in a black Armani suit, a crisp white shirt, and a black and white tie. He could have passed for a top fashion model. His dark hair had grown even longer and the waves in it caught the last glimmer from the sun.

God, he's so gorgeous, Laney thought. She was numb and at a loss for words.

Matt kept talking to break the silence. "I'm sorry that we had to meet again like *this.*" He sat down on the navy blue sofa next to Laney's chair. "I spoke to your mom. I'm so sad for her."

Laney was so happy to see him, but she tried to keep a lid on her emotions. "Thanks for stopping by."

Matt squeezed her right hand and moved closer. "You look amazing. It's so good to see you again."

Laney blushed, pushed her lips together and looked down at the floor. His confidence and maturity was so intimidating. *God, how could I look amazing to him? What could he ever see in me? Does he tell every girl this*? she wondered.

"It's good to see you too," she replied shyly. Her usual self-assured manner had now turned to mush. Matt was driving her crazy. She had already forgotten the disagreement with her husband.

"I know that this isn't really a good place to talk…maybe you could stop by the Goat before you go back to L.A. and we could catch up?" Matt's eyes sparkled in the dim light with a glimmer of hope.

Before Laney could open her mouth to answer him, Thomas appeared in front of them. He was posturing like a bodyguard, eyes glaring.

"You know what, young chap? My wife's busy," still tipsy but his tone was stern. "Why don't you go meet a bird your own age?"

Laney tensed up, her face flush with embarrassment. "Matt, I'm sorry. This is my husband, Thomas… I'm afraid he's had a little too much to drink."

Matt had no interest in an argument with a drunk Englishman. He stood up and reached out to shake Thomas's hand. "Nice to meet you. I've heard a lot about you."

Thomas ignored Matt's outstretched hand. "You know, on second thought," he said, still wobbly on his feet, "how 'bout let's double date. I'll take my new girlfriend Kara and you can have the bloody cougar." He tossed a thumb at Laney and let loose a lopsided grin.

"Thomas, I think that's enough." Laney hopped up from the sofa and looked around the atrium for Brody. Matt fought off the urge to defend her. He knew it would only stir up more trouble if he made a scene.

"You know, I better go. I have to meet someone anyway." Matt touched Laney's arm as Thomas sidled up against her.

Laney didn't want him to go. She needed Matt more than ever. And she wondered who he had to go meet all of a sudden. But she didn't question him, she knew that under the circumstances, it was best that he left. And, the last thing she wanted was to sound like a jealous girlfriend.

Matt nodded to Thomas. "Sir… I mean Thomas. You're a lucky man. Your wife is a great person."

Thomas laughed and got in Matt's face. His breath reeked of scotch, and Matt took a small step back. Thomas sprayed Matt with his saliva as he barked. "Oh, she's so good that you had a fling with her?"

Matt stared Thomas in the eye. "We're friends…period. She loves you."

Thomas lifted his arm in the air, as if ready to throw a punch. But Matt didn't flinch.

By now, Brody had heard the commotion from the other room and raced to break up the fight. He grasped Thomas's cocked arm and began to forcibly escort him back into the guest bedroom. But Thomas had to get in the last word in, like always. He turned around in his drunken stupor and shouted at Matt, "I don't believe a bloody word you said. I saw all I needed to see in the papers. I don't want her any more…the cougar's all yours."

Laney was livid. *My husband's pretty much admitted to an affair, then offended me, and now he's offering me to someone else*…Laney watched Matt disappear out the door as she finished her thought: *a man who I'd bet is already taken*

Chapter Thirteen

Laney awoke to a stream of bright light peeking through the satin curtains. She sneered, covered her eyes and turned over on her right side, away from the light.

"Ouch," she moaned. Her back was killing her. The sofa, in the den, wasn't where she'd planned to sleep, but after Thomas's tirade, and the fact that he passed out cold on the bed, this was the best option. Laney tossed and turned for about thirty more minutes and then looked up at the large wooden clock that hung above the mantel over the fireplace. It was only seven a.m., but she couldn't sleep. She was still too upset with her husband.

She reached for the Visine on the coffee table in front of the sofa; her eyes were red and swollen after crying herself to sleep.

At the end of the sofa was her pink robe. Laney put it on and walked quietly down the hall toward the bedrooms. No one was up but her. She opened the white wooden door to the guest bedroom where Thomas slept.

She tiptoed past the king sized bed and opened up her black suitcase that lay on the floor by the window. Lucky for her, Thomas was still out cold and snoring like a lumberjack. She threw off her robe and quickly put on her running clothes. Walking was Laney's favorite therapy; a two-mile trek to and from the exclusive golf course down the street from her mom's house would help clear her head.

The sun rose over the manicured golf course as she walked the last mile back to her mom's home. Laney was feeling stronger by the second. She arrived at the French provincial home, entered through the front door, and walked through the den past the kitchen.

Sophie, Bridgett and Missy, still dressed in their pajamas, were gathered around the rectangular glass top table in the atrium. They greeted Laney with coffee mugs in their hands. Sophie then pointed to the coffee pot. "Honey? You want some?" she said, sounding like a waitress at The Waffle House. "It's freshly brewed."

"I think I need the whole pot." Laney sighed and collapsed down into the chair next to Missy, tired from her morning trek and lack of sleep. Sophie poured the coffee into a white china cup and handed it to Laney.

They all sipped their coffee and sat in silence at the table, afraid to address the elephant in the room…Thomas and Laney's fate.

Bridgett had enough of the icy quite. She placed her cup down hard on the lace tablecloth. "So cougar, what-cha gonna do now?"

Sophie stepped in to defend her youngest daughter. "Your sister is not a cougar," she snapped; the dark circles under her eyes more pronounced from a night of crying.

Missy chimed in, "You never think before you say anything, do ya, Bridge?"

But Laney began to laugh. "I'm sorry," she giggled. "I've cried so much that I can't cry anymore." And then she began meowing like a cat.

Missy and Bridgett burst out laughing, and soon Sophie joined in.

"Me neither, honey. I'm all dried up now too, I'm sorry, Charles, my love." Sophie said with a belly laugh. It was like old times before their father had died and it felt nice. They were finally a family again.

Thomas stood in the doorway of the atrium with his suitcase in his hand and sat it down loudly on the hardwood floor to get their attention.

The girls were startled by Thomas's sudden appearance, and their laughter was hushed. Laney's heart sank. A cold chill filled the air. Sophie cleared her throat, peered down at his suitcase, and asked, "Son, are you going somewhere?"

Thomas looked scruffy, unshaven with bags under his eyes, as he glared at Laney and said somberly, "I'm going back to L.A. A cab is on its way."

Laney gulped in disbelief. "But we're not supposed to leave until next week." In spite of what had happened, she was hoping she could change his mind.

"I think we all know that it's better if I leave now." Thomas said, emotionless and withdrawn.

Laney stood up from the table and walked over to him. "Why? Can't we talk?"

But Thomas didn't even blink. He picked up his suitcase and turned toward the door. "I don't think there is anything to talk about."

"Is that your cab already?" Laney asked, startled when she heard a horn honk. "I don't want you to go. I love you." She grabbed the back of his coat. He removed her hand from his jacket and walked out the door, not even turning back to say goodbye.

Laney wasn't going to let her husband walk out on her that easily. "Please don't go, honey," she pleaded to him through the screen door as approached the yellow cab.

Thomas got into the cab and shut the door.

Laney watched the cab drive away, then fell to the floor and sobbed.

Chapter Fourteen

It was an early Monday morning. Sophie poured herself another cup of coffee and paced back and forth on the hardwood kitchen floor as she waited impatiently for her attorney to call. She looked flawless for a woman who had just lost her husband. Her hair was perfectly coiffed with fresh soft beige highlights and her face was fully made up. The house was hauntingly silent and she wished one of the girls would wake up soon and keep her company.

Although it been a little over a week since Charles had been laid to rest, Sophie still didn't want to accept the fact that her beloved husband was gone. More importantly, she was now also dealing with the fact that she may soon be homeless. *Loosing my husband AND my home in one week isn't going to happen*, she told herself, preparing to give Lake and Carson the fight of their lives.

The clock struck eight thirty and the phone screamed from the kitchen counter. Sophie put her lipstick-stained cup down and stared at the handheld phone that Charles had often used. That phone hadn't rung since he died. It was his private business number and Sophie couldn't bring herself to have it disconnected. It rang a second time and she hesitantly reached for the receiver. But she just couldn't pick it up. When the phone rang a fourth time, Charles's voice sang eerily through the old dusty answering machine.

Sophie grabbed the phone, angrily disconnected it, and threw it down on the counter. The sound of Charles's sweet voice made her hurt more; but at the same time it was soothing for her to hear. She ran into the den and fell into Charles's favorite navy blue chair; held her head between her hands and cried.

Laney rolled over onto her right side in the king sized bed and wiped her sleepy eyes. The sound of the phone and her mom's cries had woken her up. She walked zombie-like into the den, wearing her pink fleece Victoria's Secret robe that read "Angel" on the back in sequins.

"Mom, are you okay?" Laney asked softly, her eyes still trying to adjust to the light.

"Oh, honey, no. No, I'm not." Sophie bravely admitted, which was something she never did.

Laney kneeled down on the floor in front of the chair where her mom sat, wrapped her arms around her and held her. "Mom, I'm here for you. Everything will be fine."

Sophie continued to cry like a baby, thanking Laney for her support through her tears. But after a few minutes, her tears were all cried out. She sat back in her chair and put on her best *Sophie* face. "Now," she said, looking deep into Laney's eyes, "we have to take care of you. I'll manage. I'll be just fine." Sophie brushed Laney's bangs away from her eyes and held her face in her hands. "You're so beautiful, honey. So young and vibrant."

"You are too, Mom." Laney smiled.

Sophie kissed Laney on the forehead. "Oh, honey, I'm a grandmother, and I've had the two loves of my life."

"Well, I'm a cougar and I thought that I had found my Prince Charming," Laney shrugged.

And then they both began to laugh. "Well, you're one hot cougar," Sophie said with conviction.

"And you're one sexy grandmother," Laney growled.

In the doorway, Missy and Bridgett stood frozen like two exhausted little soldiers. "Is somebody having a party in here?"

Bridgett asked. Her long brown hair was pinned up on top of her head.

"It's a pajama party," Missy exclaimed. She wore one of Brody's old white shirts and a pair of baggy navy blue sweat pants.

Even though the events of the week had been sad, the four women found themselves happier than ever. Laney realized she'd missed so many great years with her mom and sisters. And Sophie had so desperately missed her youngest daughter.

The hours had passed like seconds. It was now late afternoon and the girls had spent the entire day in their pajamas talking about life. It had been a fabulous day and Laney had even forgotten about the fact that her husband had walked out on her--well, almost. He lingered in the back of her mind the entire day. But his drunken outburst had made her so angry, she'd begun to resent him more than miss him.

And Sophie was feeling a bit less morbid and more festive surrounded by her girls.

"Who wants a glass of champagne?" she cheered, getting up from Charles's favorite chair and heading to the kitchen.

Bridgett didn't waste a second. "I want one," she yelled back.

Laney wasn't one to drink during the day, but why ruin the party? "Me too."

"I'm in," Missy confirmed, as she snuggled up next to her younger sister.

"Wonderful," Sophie sang out to her girls from the nearby kitchen, returning with four glasses and a bottle of expensive Cristal champagne on a silver tray. "I've been waiting to open this bottle for a long time," she announced, handing the glasses, one by one, to her daughters, "but there was never a good time…" Sophie peeled off the tin seal over the cork and grinned, "until now."

Laney knew from her mom's forced smile that she was about to break down any minute. She stood up and made a toast. "Here's to the best mom in the world, and to all of us…*the girls*. I've missed y'all," she chanted in her Southern accent.

Sophie turned her glass up to the sky and drank every last drop.

"Now…" she beamed, "that is what I call wonderful champagne."

The girls were all impressed and quite stunned with their mom's newfound drinking skills. She was never one to knock back a glass of champagne or any alcoholic drink like that. Sophie had to be extremely stressed and they knew it.

"Who would like another glass?" Sophie asked, practically galloping back into the kitchen to get another bottle of the bubbly.

As she approached the kitchen, the phone rang again. But this time, she fearlessly picked it up. The girls listened intently from the den.

Sophie's merry voice turned melancholy and then crescendoed to a loud angry tone as she talked to the person on the other end of the phone. "Well, you're wrong. My Charles would never do that," she shouted, pacing up and down the kitchen floor. "Oh, screw off!" she yelled into the receiver and slammed the phone down.

Laney shot Missy and Bridgett a worried look and opened her mouth to speak. But before she could get the words out, Sophie strolled confidently back into the den with a new bottle of less expensive champagne. "Okay, I'm back," she said, refilling their flutes like nothing happened.

"Mom, is everything okay?" Laney blurted out. This time, without any interruption.

Sophie topped up Bridgett's glass. "Oh, that was Lake's idiotic attorney. He said that all of the crap that Lake has been saying to me is all true. Charles signed a new will and the house isn't mine anymore."

"What?" Laney and Missy asked in unison, while Bridgett gulped more champagne.

"I still don't believe it," Laney said aghast.

Sophie sighed with frustration and plopped down into Charles's chair. "Well, he can just go and screw himself right now."

The girls chuckled at their mom's gumption. The champagne had kicked in and she was in top form.

But then Missy became pensive. "Mom, Charles may have signed the will under duress."

Laney added her two cents: "And if he did, then the new will is invalid."

"Yeah, Mom." Bridgett added with a hiccup.

They all gathered around the chair and sat at Sophie's feet.

"Mom, we'll fight this and win," Laney guaranteed her.

Sophie was so thankful for her daughters' support. She raised her glass and cheered, "All for one and one for all." *No matter what happens, Lake won't take my dignity away from me*, she thought. And with her daughters surrounding her, she felt stronger than ever.

With that settled, Bridgett left the room to get dressed. It was eight p.m., her usual party hour. She couldn't sit around in her pajamas any longer. As the wild, middle child, Bridgett loved going out. Within minutes, Bridgett pranced back into the den, wearing her jeans and her favorite tank top that showcased her full bosom and announced her plans. "Okay." "I'm ready for The Goat."

Laney and Missy sat on the floor, still enjoying their pajama and for once, Sophie was relaxing; sitting on the sofa, reading the paper with her eyes half open, exhausted for good reason.

"I'm not going anywhere tonight," Laney exclaimed.

"Me neither," Missy seconded.

Bridgett stood in the middle of the room with her hands on her hips. "Okay…this isn't right. Someone has to come with me." She walked over to the sofa and pulled the paper away from Sophie's face, startling her out of her light slumber, "Mom, what about you?"

Sophie sprung up from the sofa like a cheerleader, quickly shaking off her exhaustion. "I'll go if everyone else does." Sophie was never one to turn down a party invitation even when she was down.

Laney and Missy were then subjected to Bridgett's childish begging. Half-heartedly, Laney gave in first. "Okay, I'll go."

"Me, too." Missy conceded, not wanting to be the lone party pooper.

"Sorry, I changed my mind. I can't go." Laney blurted out, remembering that Matt might be there.

"Why not?" Bridgett protested. "Your husband left you. He's in California, remember?"

"Bridge…" Missy sighed.

Sophie embraced Laney and chimed in, "Oh, it'll be fun, honey. It's no big deal."

Laney hesitated and then caved in to their nagging, "Alright…I'll put some lip gloss on, change, and be ready soon."

Within minutes, Laney reappeared in the den looking like a rock star--or the quintessential California girl, decked out in her black sequin trimmed, Sparkelicious hoodie and matching sequin pants. Laney looked glam, yet comfortable. Her blonde hair was swept up in her signature 'up do', her cheeks glowed from a dusting of baby pink blush, her skin shimmered from her Chanel Starlight bronzer, and her lips glistened with her favorite Twinkle gloss. She could easily pass for a girl in her late twenties than a woman of forty. She cocked her head back, put her hand on her slim hip, and jokingly announced, "The cougar is ready for the Goat."

"Wow, Cougarella, you look hot," Bridgett exclaimed. "Let's get this party started."

The Goat was low key as the girls sauntered in through the glass doors that led to the upstairs bar. There were four seats waiting for them at the counter. Smooth Jazz was piping through the room. There was no bartender in sight. Bridgett stood up and yelled to no one in particular, "Is there a Matt the bartender in the house?"

Laney's heart skipped a beat. "Bridgett, shut up. Don't embarrass me." She hit her sister on the arm. "I'm not here to see Matt."

Bridgett just ignored her like she always did. "Of course you are. I'd be."

"Well, you're not Lane," Missy jumped in, "she's not like you."

Before Sophie could add her two cents, Bridgett got defensive. "And what's that supposed to mean? That she's perfect and I'm not?"

"No, I didn't say that," Missy backed down.

Sophie couldn't hold back any longer. "Yes, Bridgett, that's exactly what your sister meant, and she's right. Lane is perfect…compared to you." Sophie was tired of treading lightly around Bridgett's feelings--or the lack of them.

Laney was horrified, Bridgett had been jealous of her since she was born and now her mom was making things even worse. "Mom, that's not true," she cried.

A bartender appeared from behind the back room door. It wasn't Matt; rather a tall lanky guy with red hair. "I'm Matt's replacement, John."

The girls looked at the bartender with long faces. Laney actually pouted. She was dying to see Matt before she returned to California. "So, where's Matt?" she said, slumping down in her chair.

Before the bartender could respond, Laney heard a familiar voice.

"Be good to these girls, John. They were my best customers." Matt said, placing a hand on Laney's shoulder.

Laney sat frozen like a statue in her chair, unable to respond.

Sophie took the reins: "So, honey, where ya goin'?"

"Home…right now," Matt said with a poker face. He wasn't offering any information on his future. "It's my last night at The Goat," he glanced toward the door, "so I'm out of here."

"Well, you can't leave your best clients on your last night without a toast, now can you?" Sophie manipulatively responded.

Bridgett had been leaning her arms on the granite counter top, her big bottom lip stuck out in a pout, still upset over her mom's comments. But her mood quickly changed when Sophie mentioned a drink and a toast.

Missy and Bridgett were game for Matt's company, but Laney remained silent.

Matt wanted to stay just to be close to Laney one more time, but he knew that it might not be appropriate. "I'll stay under one condition," he replied, gazing into Laney's eyes. "If 'everyone' wants me to stay, then I will."

Sophie tapped Laney's arm and shot her the look that only a mother could give her daughter. Laney needed to be cheered up and

Matt was the perfect potion.

"I want you to stay too," Laney allowed like a meek schoolgirl.

"Okay, the drinks are on me." Matt pulled up stool from the end of the bar, placed it in the middle of the girls and sat down. "John, start pouring." He rattled off everyone's preferred wine.

Sophie moved closer to Matt; her large breasts brushed his arm. She had to find out his plans in her *Sophie-no-holds-barred*, kind of way. "So, give it up, honey…where are you really going?"

Matt wasn't quick to answer. He kept the girls in suspense while John placed the drinks down on the bar. Everyone grabbed their wine of choice. Matt took his glass of merlot and raised it for a toast. "To the most beautiful girls in Greenville."

The girls loved Matt's celebratory toast and clinked their glasses together.

Laney raised her chardonnay to her lips and peered at Matt over the glass. She couldn't stop staring at him. She anxiously awaited his response on his future whereabouts.

Matt locked eyes with Laney. "You know, I don't know where I'm going to go yet. I may open an architectural firm here, or…"

"California," John blurted out from behind the bar. "That's what he told me earlier."

Matt winced and gave John a *shut it* look. He wasn't supposed to say anything to anyone about Matt's possible plans.

Laney's heart fluttered at the news; then she started to panic inside. *God, Matt can't move to California. Thomas and I live there. But then again… L.A. isn't the only city in California, so maybe I'm jumping to conclusions.*

Bridgett couldn't contain herself. "I knew it! I knew it!" she proudly announced.

Laney squirmed in her seat.

Matt felt her discomfort at his possible move to the West Coast and tried to convince everyone he was just kidding. "Oh…I was just throwing out cities last night. I'm not planning to move to California. I'll probably just stay here in South Carolina. It makes more sense."

As John refilled Bridgett's glass, she stood up from her bar stool and put her arm around Matt's shoulder. "It makes no sense to stay here, 'cause my sister lives in…"

Before she could finish her sentence, Missy diplomatically butted in. "Well, wherever you decide to go, we wish you the best."

Laney wanted to throw her arms around Matt and give him a hug. Instead she joined in and agreed with her sister. "Yes, we wish you the best," she proclaimed, sounding like a distant friend.

Sophie sat her glass of wine on the bar with a hard clink for emphasis. "Oh, hell, Matt, go to California. You need to get out of here and spread your wings," she said without holding back, her voice tipsy from the wine. "Plus, for once, Bridgett's right."

Bridgett grinned from ear to ear. Laney popped her mom on the arm, hoping to shut her up. And while everyone was deciding Matt's future, a loud ding rang out of Laney's phone. She took it out of her purse, looked down to see a text from Thomas: "I want a divorce." It read in cold black letters.

This has to be a mistake, she thought. Her face was flush and she began to have hot flashes.

"I have to go," she blurted out, clutching her cell phone in her hand and jumping off her bar stool.

Matt and Missy both rushed to comfort her.

"What is it, Laney?" Missy asked, while Matt wrapped his arm around her trembling body.

The room began to spin and Laney just wanted to run away. "It's nothing. I have to go." She broke free of Matt and ran out of The Goat and was in the lobby of The Drake before she realized that she wasn't staying there. She was staying with her mom.

Sophie, Missy and Bridgett threw their drinks down on the bar and darted to the front door. Matt stayed behind, feeling it best to stay out of the way and give Laney her space.

The girls reached the door and saw Laney sitting on the stone steps that led down to the Reedy River, balling like a baby.

"What is it honey?" Sophie asked as Missy and Bridgett looked on helplessly.

"He wants a divorce, Mom. The bastard wants a divorce," Laney cried.

Sophie placed her hand over her mouth in disbelief. "Honey, what are you talking about?"

Missy and Bridgett stood in silence, trying to grasp the situation.

Laney held up her cell phone and showed them the text from her husband.

Missy and Bridgett both stared down at the text.

While the girls consoled Laney, Matt hesitantly exited the bar. He wasn't sure if he should go and comfort Laney, or hang back and give her some space. Before he could make up his mind, a taxi pulled up in front of The Goat and a gorgeous young blonde hopped out.

Matt made eye contact with her and froze. The girl ran to Matt, threw herself in his arms and planted a soul kiss on his lips. Matt didn't resist. He quickly ushered her into the bar, clearly relieved that Laney didn't see him.

But Bridgett, surreptitiously, out of the corner of her eye, had witnessed the whole thing. *That bastard*, Bridgett thought. *I better tell Laney…*

Instead, Bridgett bit her tongue. For once, Bridgett knew to keep her mouth shut. Laney had enough problems right now and she didn't need one more.

Chapter Fifteen

The yellow taxicab dropped Laney off in front of her beautiful Hollywood Hills home. She was exhausted, emotionally drained and looked like crap. Her eyes were bloodshot from a sleepless night, the blonde highlights in her hair had faded to a dirty blonde, and she had consumed way too many glasses of cheap chardonnay on the plane while sitting in First Class. And she had a headache that settled in for the long haul.

Laney left her black roller bag in the entry hall while she looked over her dreadful self in the massive silver framed mirror that hung on the wall. *God, I can't see my husband looking like this*, she thought. She was here to save her marriage not throw it away.

She opened up her platinum Gucci handbag and pulled out her Channel Twinkle lip gloss and her Mac studio fix powder and bronzer. In record time, she touched up her lips, dusted on some powder and brushed on a ton of bronzer. She ran her fingers through her unwashed hair, pulled it up in a clip and smiled back at herself in the mirror. It was the best she could do for now.

The house was eerie silent. There was no sign of Thomas anywhere. Laney walked through the kitchen to the sitting area, and still no Thomas. He said that he would be there when she arrived, so where was he?

Laney peeked out onto the expansive deck and there he was, sitting in the chase lounge overlooking the canyon. Laney froze. She didn't know how or what to feel at this moment. The man she had loved for most of her adult life was ready to walk away from their life together, and she was about to find out why.

She slung open the sliding glass door, took a deep breath and hoped for the best.

Thomas heard the sound of the door, turned in his chair, and smiled at Laney. "Hi, Lane, how was your flight?"

He seems rather cheerful for a man who wants a divorce, Laney thought.

On the outside, Laney projected calm, confidence, and in control; but deep down inside, she wanted to shake some sense into her husband. "It was great. Maybe one of the best flights ever," she replied, with a slight dig at him. She was too nervous to sit down.

But Thomas didn't flinch at her sarcastic overtone. "Oh, good, glad to hear it." He pulled back a chair for Laney to sit at the glass top table. "I'm having a glass of red wine, which the doctor says is good for my heart. Would you care for one, my dear?" He poured Laney a glass from the bottle that sat on the table, without waiting for her reply.

His aloof persona was driving her insane. "Sure. Why not?" She sat down in the chair beside Thomas. *Is this a meeting about our divorce or a date? Maybe he's changed his mind?*

Laney gulped down the wine and peered at Thomas. He looked rested, fit, tan and extremely handsome – much better than she had seen him look in years. She was still wildly attracted to him even after all of the terrible things he had said to her.

Thomas relaxed back in his chair and gazed out over the canyon. He reached for his glass and tipped it toward Laney's.

"To new beginnings," he said softly, clinging his glass to hers.

What in the hell is going on? Laney was confused but she went along with his hope filled toast. "To new beginnings." She prayed this was a good sign about the fate of their marriage.

The sound of crystal chimed in the air. And then Thomas jumped out of his seat like a hyper five-year-old. "I just can't wait any longer, I have to show you something."

"Okay..." Laney hesitated, "what is it?"

Thomas took her hand, led her into the house, down the hall and toward the garage. Laney began to grow more suspicious.

Thomas threw open the door to the garage with pride, and there sat, a brand new shiny, black Porsche 911.

Laney stood there bewildered. Number one, her husband didn't have the money for a car like this; and number two, he was obviously going through a serious midlife crisis. This was not what she expected.

"So, what do you think, Lane?" Thomas walked over to the black car and kissed the top of the hood, like a proud papa.

Laney looked at Thomas like he was crazy. She threw up her hands in disgust.

"What do I think? Do you really want to know what I think?" she shouted, her voice echoing throughout the garage. "I think this is completely crazy." Laney marched around the car and scolded him like a two-year-old. "And may I ask you how you paid for this, Thomas?"

Oh, no, Thomas thought, Laney only called him "Thomas" when she was seriously angry. "I just took some money out of our joint savings account," he declared with a shrug.

"What?" Laney paced up and down the garage floor, fuming. "That's our retirement money, and it's all from my hard work, not yours!"

"Calm down. You always said that your money was our money," Thomas smiled, caressing the car with his hand.

"Well, right now, it's *my* money." Laney stormed back into the house.

Laney had never known Thomas to be this irresponsible. He seemed to be losing the plot. She marched out onto the deck and poured herself another glass of merlot. Thomas followed.

"It's no big deal, you've got plenty of money left, my dear." He spoke to her like an innocent child, oblivious to what he had done.

Laney gripped the wine glass and did everything in her power not to throw it at him. She walked to the railing of the deck and tried to cool down, but she couldn't. "It *is* a huge deal, Thomas. What's wrong with you? First, you say, you want a divorce, and now you buy a Porsche with our savings?"

Laney leaned her back up against the rail and looked Thomas in the eye. "And how did you get that much money out anyway? They should have asked for both of our signatures."

"Oh, the girl at the bank, she's a friend of mine," Thomas grinned. "She said that my signature would do."

"Oh, perfect, another friend. So, is she your new girlfriend now, or is it the car?"

Laney snapped.

Thomas walked over to Laney. "The car," he purred. "There's no one else." He hoped she couldn't tell that he was lying through his teeth. "I'm the problem. It's just not working for me anymore. We're not the same couple that we used to be…or maybe I'm not the same person since my heart surgery."

Laney tilted her head down and the tears began to flow. Thomas put his arm around her but this time, he couldn't comfort her like he used to do. He felt so distant to her now. Maybe she had changed too. But she was still willing to make it work, and wasn't ready to throw away their nine-year marriage. Divorce just wasn't in her DNA. Her parents were married for almost forty years, so she believed in the institution of marriage. She could even possibly forgive Thomas for "the affair" that he never fully admitted to. "So, what do you want to do? Do you want to just flush our marriage down the drain?"

Thomas turned to Laney, his voice cold. "I have a meeting with my attorney on Monday."

Laney gasped. "You already have an attorney? This is crazy. You're crazy. I don't know who you are any more."

Thomas didn't say a thing. He just stared at her with zero emotion on his face.

Laney fled to the doorway, but before going inside the house, she glared back at her husband. "What in the hell has happened to you?" In an instant she made her firm and final decision. "You know, I wanted to make this work, but I've changed my mind. If you want a fucking divorce, then you can have one." She slammed the door and sped to the master bedroom. She had finally come to her senses and listened to the little voices in her head. Her Scorpio loyalty now out the window.

She entered the bedroom, intending to close the door before Thomas arrived; but it was too late. Within seconds, he was confronting her in the archway of the door.

"You know, you can talk, Miss Perfect," he yelled, putting his hand on the door so she couldn't close it all the way. "You're the one who had the affair."

Laney realized what this was really all about. *Thomas still thinks I slept with Matt, and he's acting out of jealousy.* She couldn't understand why he didn't believe or trust her. "Old Faithful" was her middle name. She stared into Thomas's eyes through the half closed door. "I never cheated on you, and would never ever cheat on you. And you know that."

Thomas knew in his heart that his wife was loyal, but he wanted to argue it out anyway. "Then why was Matt at the funeral?"

"Because he's a friend of my mom's," Laney said through clenched teeth. "You know, this is so stupid." She pushed the door toward him, trying to close it in his face. "Maybe you're the one who shouldn't be trusted." Laney pushed with all of her might as Thomas put his weight on the other side of the door. "Maybe the new Porsche isn't your only girlfriend," Laney egged him on, hoping to finally get the truth from him.

Thomas rolled his eyes, threw his hands up in the air and let go of the door. Laney fell backwards and the door slammed in Thomas's face. But he wasn't about to back down. He flung the door open and stormed into the bedroom. Laney stood by the bed with her arms folded as Thomas ranted on. "You know, here you go again, throwing it back on me. Can't you just take responsibility for your shameless actions?"

From behind her, Laney heard a distant "dinging" sound like a text message on a cell phone. She scanned the room but she didn't see a cell phone anywhere. *Thomas's phone must be in here somewhere*, she thought. She shot daggers at him. "Who would that be?"

Thomas had heard the dinging too, but he played dumb as his eyes combed the room for his phone. "What? I didn't hear anything. You know I'm deaf as a post."

Laney became relentless when she heard the sound again. She looked the room over like a bloodhound. Thomas was now beginning to sweat. He stood in the middle of the room while Laney searched for the mysterious phone.

"Ah-ha!" Laney proclaimed, pulling the iPhone out from underneath the unmade bed. She studied the black text on the screen and then read it out loud: "Where are you Tommy? I'm lonely without you. K."

Laney stoically handed the phone to Thomas. She couldn't cry, scream or argue any more. It was now obvious that her husband was interested in someone else. "Here," she declared, "Kara misses you." Laney shoved the phone into his hand.

Thomas took the phone from Laney and stood guilt ridden in front of her. His affair with Kara was now completely out in the open. Neither one of them said a word. Only their breathing filled the air.

Laney broke the silence. "Well, what are you waiting for, Thomas? Pack your things and get the hell out of my house."

Chapter Sixteen

Sophie entered the glass doors of the high-powered law firm, Easterling and Tate, looking like she was going to another funeral. And in her mind she was. She wore a tight black dress that hit her right above her womanly athletic knees, her golden beige highlighted hair flowed softy around her face and framed her strong jaw line and high cheekbones. She was stunning for a woman closing in on eighty, and even under duress she looked impeccable.

The cheery receptionist greeted Sophie and offered her a cup of coffee, but she declined.

"Do you have something stronger?" Sophie asked, with one eyebrow raised. "Like a vodka tonic?"

The receptionist smiled politely and apologized for their limited selection of beverages.

But when Sophie got a glimpse of Lake and Carson out of the corner of her eye, sitting at the table in the glassed in conference room, she instantly changed her mind. "On second thought, honey. I'll take the strongest cup of coffee that y'all can make, all black, hold the cream and sugar."

Sophie had to keep it together. She hated meeting with those two dreadful boys by herself, but the girls were all tied up with other commitments. Laney was in California, Missy was traveling on business and Bridgett had done her monthly disappearing act and wasn't picking up the phone when she called.

The receptionist swiftly returned with a large red mug full of piping hot coffee. She gestured for Sophie to follow her into the conference room. Sophie took in a deep breath to calm her nerves. She hadn't seen or heard from Lake and Carson since their father's funeral; and there the two of them were, sitting smugly in the middle seats on the far side of the mahogany table. Sophie wanted to ring their necks; instead she gave them a "go screw yourselves" smile, took the mug from the receptionist and sat across from them. No one said a word. Sophie sipped her coffee while Lake checked his Rolex on the minute; and Carson nervously bounced his knee up and down like a child.

The five minutes or so of silence seemed to last for hours. Thankfully, Sophie's attorney, Al Easterling, finally entered the conference room and placed a large black leather briefcase on the table, making a loud thump. Lake and Carson's attorney, Frank Jenkins, followed seconds later and sat next to them with a dour expression.

Before Al began the estate proceedings, he motioned for his assistant to enter the room. She carried a grey conference phone, and placed it in the center of the large table. Lake and Carson scowled while Sophie looked concerned.

Al said to his assistant, "Go ahead and put the girls through, please." He winked at Sophie, which immediately put her at ease; then he stood up. "I needed some witnesses, so I asked your girls to do a conference call. They have provided me with some very interesting information."

The assistant turned the volume up on the phone and the sweet sound of all three of her girls' voices echoed through the speaker. "Hi, mom," they said in unison.

She leaned toward the phone in the middle of the table and cried, "Hi, my babies, miss you. Thanks for being here."

Lake cleared his throat and interrupted the love fest. "Can we please get started?"

Al remained standing, placed his reading glasses on the tip of his nose and began the meeting. "Well, based on the information that I…I mean, we have gathered, the new will was signed when Charles was in the hospital, and was too sick to transfer any documents into his sons' names."

Sophie practically jumped out of her seat. "So, what are you saying, Al?"

Lake angrily repeated the question. "Easterling, what the hell are you trying to say?"

Al ignored Lake and continued, "What I'm saying is, we have proof, which Mr. Jenkins just reviewed in my office, that Charles's new will was signed under complete duress. The house is yours, Sophie."

The girls cheered through the phone and Sophie burst into tears of joy; she wouldn't lose her precious home after all.

Lake hit the table with his fist. "Easterling, that can't be. My father specifically left the house to us."

"Son, I'm sorry. But here are the hospital records and a letter from Charles's doctor stating that your father wasn't in any condition to sign any papers on the day this new will was executed. Case closed," Al declared with another wink at Sophie.

But Lake wasn't through. "Dan, you have to fight this!" he barked at his attorney.

Dan crossed his arms in defeat. "Sorry guys, there is no contest here. It's over."

Without another word, Lake and Carson, got up and stormed out of the conference room. Sophie shunned them as they walked by her and out the door. She never wanted to see or hear from them ever again.

She glanced down at the large conference phone and beamed with joy. "Thank you all for being here for me," she said to the girls nearly hugging the phone.

"We said that we would be there for you, Mom, no matter what,"

Laney replied.

Bridgett blurted out through the speaker, “And she’s not kidding, either. Thomas still wants a divorce.”

Missy jumped in like only a big sister does, “Bridgett, hush. Just hush. Let Lane tell Mom about it.”

Sophie leaned down and spoke directly into the speaker. “Okay, everybody, stop. Lane, what in the hell is going on with that dumb husband of yours?”

“He’s going through with the divorce, and I’m going to give it to him,” Laney’s voice broke up, “Mom, I need…” but Sophie understood the message all too well.

Sophie leaned in closer to the receiver. “Honey, you just hang in there. Don’t you worry, Mom’s on her way. I’ll be on the next plane to L.A.”

Chapter Seventeen

The trip to L.A. came just at the right the time for Sophie; unfortunately it was due to Laney's adversity. She hadn't flown by herself in about twenty years, and was a little anxious. Sophie was happy that Laney wanted her *mom's* emotional support during this troubled time. And, because of Sophie's fear of flying, Laney booked her a First Class ticket from Charlotte to LAX.

Dolled up in her new black sequin jacket from Chico's, black jeans and gunmetal wedges, Sophie took her seat in 2B next to the window. She settled in, placing her black leather oversized tote on the floor and reclined back in her seat. The First Class flight attendant stopped by and offered her a glass of wine before takeoff. Sophie gladly accepted the plastic cup of wine, and thanked the pretty flight attendant in her Southern drawl.

Sophie savored the California white wine, flipped through a fashion magazine, reclined further back in her seat and closed her eyes as the rest of the passengers boarded the plane. It was a full flight so she was doubly happy to be in First Class. As she began to doze off, the sound of a somewhat familiar male voice woke her from her short slumber.

She opened her eyes to see an extremely distinguished older man struggling to lift his large carry-on luggage into the overhead compartment. Within seconds, the flight attendant arrived to help him. As the flight attendant looked closer at the debonair gentleman, she began to blush. He thanked her for her help and glanced down at his seat. Even before he could sit down, another flight attendant rushed over and sweetly offered him a beverage of choice. He requested a chardonnay and settled in his seat.

Sophie gasped, as she looked the man over. *Oh my God, it's him, the gorgeous Senator Rigby.* Matt's famous father was about to sit in 2A, the empty seat next to her. *Oh, dear God, how do I look? Is my mascara running down my face? How is my hair?*

Even though Sophie was still in mourning over Charles, she couldn't stop the rush of emotion that she was feeling. Her heart raced as she frantically grabbed her purse off the floor to check her face. *God, what am I thinking? He wouldn't remember me anyway.*

They had only met, briefly, one time, at a fundraiser and then she last saw him at O's with Laney. Senator Rigby was not only a powerful man but also the best looking seventy-year old man in the state of South Carolina. But before she could add more burgundy gloss to her lips, the Senator glanced over at her and smiled. He seemed to recognize her right away.

The senator sat up in his seat and held his Blackberry in his hand. "Sophie? Sophie Montgomery?" he asked, taking a better glimpse at her.

Sophie dropped her purse to the floor, glanced up from her compact and played dumb.

"Why Senator…Senator Rigby?" she asked, pretending not to notice him until now. "Why, it's so nice to see you. Are you heading to L.A. too?"

"Nope," the senator teased, "heading to Kentucky. Isn't that where you're going?" He let loose with a smile.

Sophie quickly checked her ticket, then realized he was joking. "It says L.A., Senator, are you sure you're on the right plane?" Sophie flirted back, touching her blonde highlighted hair to make sure it was in place.

"My eyes aren't what they used to be," he laughed, pulling his readers out of his coat pocket to tease her even more. "Maybe I should double check my ticket again, too."

The senator reached for his glass of chardonnay. "I don't usually drink, but I'm off the clock right now," taking a sip of his wine, "I have a couple of very needed days off."

Sophie assumed he was speaking of his recent marital problems that she had read about in the papers. But she didn't pry, feeling it wasn't her place to do so.

The plane's engine began to roar and the pilot announced that they were ready for takeoff. Sophie and the senator finished their wine and the flight attendants collected their empty cups.

As the plane reached thirty-eight thousand feet, Sophie griped the armrests tightly and sighed. Senator Rigby touched her hand to calm her down.

"Would you like another glass of wine? I think you need one," he said to her as a flight attendant walked down the First Class aisle with a bottle of wine and a couple of fresh new wine glasses. But she was too nervous to talk.

The senator motioned for the flight attendant. "We'll take two glasses of white wine, please."

The stewardess smiled and placed the glasses on the built-in tray in between their seats.

Sophie let go of the armrests and took a sip of her chilled wine. "Thank you, Senator. I haven't flown alone in years."

He sat back in the large grey seat, ran his hands through his thick, wavy, salt and pepper tipped hair and comforted her. "You're not flying alone. You're flying with me," he said with a twinkle in his sable brown eyes.

Sophie blushed like a little girl and was speechless for once.

The senator quipped, "To be honest, I haven't either. Usually, I have a refrigerator-size bodyguard beside me, not a beautiful woman."

Sophie's felt a rush over her entire body. His comment made her feel special and alive again. Her fear of flying was now behind her. She took another sip of wine and held it up to the Senator for a toast. "To, my flying partner, Senator Rigby…and new adventures."

"Well, Mrs. Montgomery, first of all, please call me Cary. And second, let's toast to new friendships," he said, clinging his glass of wine to hers.

They reclined back in their seats and talked for the duration of the flight, like they were two old friends. Sophie missed Charles's male companionship so much, and talking to Cary made her feel warm, fuzzy, and secure. He wasn't the pompous guy that she had read about in the papers. Rather, he was down to earth and easygoing.

As they drank their third glass of wine, Sophie now felt immensely comfortable with the senator. "So, why are you going to L.A?"

The senator proudly replied, "To see my son."

Sophie's expression was slightly confused as she tried to remember which son lived in L.A. Matt was still in South Carolina, so it couldn't be him. "Which son would that be? Your oldest?"

"No, your daughter's friend, Matthew, who's my youngest," he said, loosening his grey and white tie.

Sophie almost spit out her wine. "What? Matt's in L.A.?"

"Oh, it's no big deal," he shrugged, "he's just test driving the place…just looking around for a few days. He'll probably hate it."

Sophie sat up in her seat and gathered her thoughts. "I think you're wrong. He's going to love it." And then the wine began to do the talking. "Plus, my daughter's getting a divorce." Realizing what she had said, Sophie quickly put her hand over her mouth. "I'm sorry, I didn't mean to tell you that."

Cary put his hand on Sophie's. "I didn't hear a thing. Your secret's safe with me."

The three and a half hour flight ended way too soon for both of them. The plane landed and the senator jotted his private cell phone number down on the back of his business card along with the number of the W Hotel in Westwood. Sophie was surprised at his gesture, and took his information knowing, good and well, that she would probably never speak or see Cary again.

"Enjoy your time with your daughter," he smiled sweetly, collecting his luggage from the overhead compartment.

"I'll try… under the circumstances. Please tell Matt that I said hello," Sophie responded, sad to say goodbye to him.

Sophie exited the plane and watched the senator disappear into a swarm of bustling travelers. It had been a plane ride that she would never forget. She was giddy as she approached the baggage claim area, still thinking about the magical four hours she had spent with the prestigious gentleman.

She glowed as she quickly removed her black suitcase from the conveyor belt at the baggage carousel. Zone B was ahead on the left so she walked through the automatic glass doors to meet Laney, parked right outside of the exit, in her white Mercedes ML 350.

"Hi, honey," Sophie gushed, holding her arms out to Laney for a hug as she approached her from the other side of the SUV. Laney leaned in, embraced her, then turned up her nose.

"Mom! Have you been drinking?" she reprimanded, reeling from the alcohol on her mom's breath. Laney then backtracked, realizing that she was sounding like an old fuddy dud. "Well, if you have, good for you!"

Sophie laughed as she stumbled up into the passenger's seat. "Yes, I have and it was so much fun."

Laney was befuddled as she drove off. "What? On the flight? You hate flying."

Sophie just beamed. "I love flying now."

"Since when, Mom, what's going on? Did Bridgett give you another Xanax?" She shot Sophie a suspicious glance while driving up the entrance ramp to the 405 freeway.

"No, I flew with an angel." Sophie was euphoric as she gazed up to the sky.

Laney griped the steering wheel as she listened intently to her mom. The traffic on the 405 was bumper to bumper.

"Wow, Mom. Maybe I should fly First Class more often. I wish my husband could turn into an angel. Right now, he's worse than the devil." Laney sighed.

"Honey, I'm sorry," Sophie soothed, coming back down to reality. She checked her face in the mirror. "Well, the senator said that everything happens for a reason."

Laney glared at her mom and slammed on the brakes before almost rear-ending another car. "What *senator*, Mom? Spill it?"

Sophie hunched over like a scolded child. She had let the cat of the bag. "Senator Rigby."

"I knew it," Laney hit the steering wheel with her fist. "So, did he mention Matt?"

Sophie looked out the window and gritted her teeth. She didn't dare tell her that Matt was in L.A. It was way too soon. "Uh…No…didn't mention him." And quickly changed the subject.

Twenty miles and forty minutes of small talk later, a disappointed Laney pulled into the circle drive of her 1960's ranch style home.

Sophie walked through the red Japanese-style door and felt a chill in the air. *The house feels sad and lonely*, she thought, as she placed her bag on the hardwood floor in the hallway. No one could read houses better than her. With her years of real estate experience, she could feel the emotions of a house the second she walked in. It was clear from the eeriness of the home that her daughter was indeed getting a divorce.

There was not a trace of Thomas around except for a hint of his cologne still lingering in the air. Laney pretended to be holding up just fine, but clearly she wasn't herself. Her confidence had diminished and she was definitely in a funk. Her usual positive attitude had turned negative, and she looked tired and drained. She just wasn't taking care of herself. All the way home, Sophie had held back commenting on Laney's formerly California blonde hair, which was now mousy and unkempt. Sophie felt almost embarrassed by her daughter's appearance.

"Honey, cut the bull. I know you're sad, but God forbid, don't let people know it," she declared, walking over to her, and running her finger through the bottom of Laney's hair. "Honey, your hair's a disaster. Go get it colored. It will make you feel better," she insisted, like a typical Southern mother. Image was everything to Sophie.

Laney rolled her eyes and shot back at her, "And when have I had time to do anything? I've been too busy dealing with my lawyer and Thomas's stupid demands to even think about my hair."

Without batting an eyelash, Sophie grabbed her cell phone out of her purse, and started dialing. "Honey, I'm calling your salon in Beverly Hills. Right now's the time to look your best, and to show that ole greedy English husband of yours what he's missing."

Laney knew that her mom wasn't going to take no for an answer and let her make the appointment. A new haircut and highlight always cheered her up. But this time, she wasn't so sure.

"Okay, it's done." Sophie ended the call and smiled. "You'll have beautiful blonde hair tomorrow. Now, let's open a bottle of wine."

Laney's spirits seemed to lift a little. "I've got a new bottle of Rombauer chilling in the fridge. It was almost five so it was officially happy hour.

With their Riedel crystal wine glasses in hand, Laney and Sophie walked out onto the expansive deck. The view of the Hollywood Hills had never looked more beautiful, yet both women were unable to appreciate it.

"Honey, I'm so sorry about this," Sophie said. "It's just not fair."

Laney placed her glass of wine on the table. "It's okay. I'll get through it. I've gotten through a lot of tough things in my life." She was sounding more like her confident self. Then, she put all of the bullshit aside and opened up to her mom. "I still love him and always will. I really wanted us to work this out, but obviously he didn't."

Sophie hated to see her daughter hurting like this. "Well, honey, I'm here for you. It's all going to be just fine, like you said. I promise."

"Thanks, Mom. And what about you? How are you really doing?" Laney said, putting her arm around Sophie.

Sophie thought for a moment and took a huge gulp of wine. "Oh, honey, you know. I'm just taking it one day at a time. And today was a good day," she said with a laugh. "Maybe one of the best in a long time."

"Looks like it," Laney said, waiting for her mother to say more. But nothing else was forthcoming, and she changed the subject. "Are you up for going to Mr. Chow tonight? I've made reservations for seven, and they were hard to get."

Laney was a regular at the upscale celebrity haunt that opened its doors in 1974. It was a Hollywood institution and had devoted clients from the world of art, fashion, music and entertainment.

"Honey, I'm always up for going out. But are you?" Sophie raised her eyebrows at Laney.

Without giving it another thought, Laney put her sorrows behind her, took another sip of wine and lifted her glass toward Sophie's. "Mom, you're not in Kansas anymore. The City of Angels awaits us."

"Great, honey. Mr. Chow sounds so exciting." Sophie had heard of the famous restaurant and knew that it was a celebrity hotspot. "But, honey, you'll have to do something with that hair. This can't wait until tomorrow." She made a sour face. "Do you have any root touch up?" Sophie showed zero diplomacy.

Laney wasn't going to argue with her mom. She placed her hand on her cheek and thought for a second. "Yep, I think so…under the sink in my bathroom."

With their wine in tow, they headed to the master bathroom. They talked and talked like best friends while Sophie worked her magic on Laney's hair. Within minutes, Laney's dark roots had vanished and she was a California blonde again. They got dressed and drove into Beverly Hills.

Laney pulled up to the valet attendant, standing on the curb at Mr. Chow on North Camden Drive. She collected her valet ticket, locked her arm in Sophie's, and they sauntered up to the understated, yet opulent entrance like two Hollywood stars. A friendly doorman acknowledged their arrival, and pulled open the elegant glass door for them.

As they entered, a piece of smoked glass shielded their view from the busy, jumping restaurant. A handsome maitre'd, dressed in a black Armani suit, quickly appeared from the dimly lit corner, where the hostess stood, and greeted Laney with a smile.

"Nice to have you back again, Ms. Montgomery," he said in his Italian accent, and escorted them past the intimate bar, and into the main room of the restaurant.

Heads turned as they walked past tables full of Hollywood elite. Sophie wore a black satin pantsuit, while Laney dazzled in her fuchsia, sequin mini dress.

"I have the perfect table for you and your beautiful sister." He pointed to a bistro table, lined with a crisp, white European tablecloth, in the corner of the all white, sophisticated room. It sat in front of a wall of mirrors.

Sophie blushed. "I'm her mom, not her sister."

The maitre'd pulled out Sophie's chair and placed a stark white napkin in her lap. "You are much too young to be her mother." He smiled a knowing smile as if he miraculously knew that she needed a boost of confidence after the death of her husband. "But, now I know where you get your stunning looks from, Ms. Montgomery," he said, glancing over at Laney.

Laney grinned from the other side of the table as a young, sexy Italian waiter, dressed in white tails, graciously slid out her chair and offered it to her.

The maitre'd smiled and whisked himself off to seat more of the rich and famous patrons, leaving them in the capable hands of yet another exotic waiter who handed them menus and took their drink orders.

Laney ordered a bottle of Dom while Sophie took in the sophisticated surroundings. She marveled at the black and white art deco kites that hung from the high ceilings and admired the beautiful fresh lilies that cascaded from tall white vases. She loved the contemporary art that hung on the walls. None of the restaurants in the South were like this, and she lavished in its eccentricity.

As they waited for their champagne to arrive, two L.A. starlets stopped by their table to tell Laney hello. Sophie beamed at her daughter's notoriety. She knew that Laney was an accomplished fashion designer, but she had never witnessed the effects of it firsthand.

Mr. Chow was pure eye candy, and Sophie was enjoying every minute. While Laney chatted with her A-list fans, Sophie picked up her menu and studied the overpriced Chinese cuisine; but her attention was soon diverted by a couple in the right hand corner of the room. Sophie put her menu down on the table, glanced over Laney's shoulder, and gasped. The man she thought she recognized was making out with a young woman in a booth. *Oh God*, she realized, *not Thomas. Laney doesn't need to see him on the night before their divorce.* Sophie had to somehow distract Laney from looking in his direction.

Laney said goodbye to her loyal Sparkelicious clients and turned to Sophie. "Mom… …your face is red. Is everything okay?"

Sophie picked up her chilled glass of bubbly and put it up to her face. "Honey, I'm just over stimulated by all of this Hollywood stuff. It's so much fun."

Within seconds, a busboy dashed by, and accidentally brushed himself up against their table. He quickly apologized and continued on his way. Laney's menu, which was hanging off the edge, fell onto the floor and slid behind her.

Before Laney could get up, Sophie jumped out of her chair to get it. "Honey, don't you get up," she said in a panic. Sophie snapped up the menu and placed it back on the table.

"Mom…what's going on? You're acting weird."

Sophie sat back down in her chair and took a couple of gulps of her champagne. Laney had come too close to seeing Thomas; she had to make sure and keep her attention away from him.

"Honey, you know, I've been thinking. Maybe I should move to L.A," she fibbed, knowing for a fact that she would never leave the South.

Laney squirmed in her seat. "Huh? Mom, you're not serious?"

Sophie frowned. "At least you could pretend that you might want me closer to you, couldn't you?" She now seemed to believe her own fictitious story. "Well, why not? What's in South Carolina for me now?"

Laney knew good and well that her mom wasn't cut out for L.A. But she wanted to let her down gently and get her off of the idea. "Well, Bridgett and Missy are there. And your friends…you have so many friends, Mom."

Sophie listened to Laney's reasoning as she discretely peered over her shoulder to see if Thomas was still sitting at the booth, but he was nowhere in sight. Relieved that Thomas had left the restaurant, she burst out laughing. "Oh, honey. I was just kidding. I would never…" And before she could finish her sentence, she heard an English accent finish it for her.

"Cramp your style?" Thomas quipped. He stood in front of them with a smirk on his face.

Sophie cringed. She would have liked to punch him in the mouth, but contained herself.

Laney shot him daggers.

"Oh, I'm sorry, ladies," Thomas mock – apologized, "am I now cramping the cougar's style too?"

Sophie bit her tongue like a good mother, but Laney couldn't.

"Don't give me that crap. I was obviously cramping your midlife crisis style," she snapped, glancing around the room. "So, where's your little tramp, anyway?"

"Wow, that's rough, considering you're the one that started this with that…*bartender*." Thomas said that last word as if it was synonymous with *loser*.

Laney stood up from the table and stuck her nose in Thomas's face. "Now, that's enough. You know that's not true. I never betrayed you. I think it's time for you to leave."

Sophie couldn't hold back her feelings any longer. She hopped to her feet and stood behind her daughter. "Thomas Morgan, you're full of shit. My daughter's too good for you…always has been."

Thomas held his hands up, as if to surrender, and backed away from the table. Out of nowhere, Kara appeared from behind him, and tapped him on the shoulder.

"I been waitin' for you, Tommy?" she said as if unaware he'd been talking to anyone. "Are we goin', or what?" She stood on her tiptoes and peered over his shoulder, and squealed. "Well, hey. Look who's here, honey?" Kara obviously, was still in awe of Laney.

Laney rolled her eyes and mimicked Kara's Valley girl accent. "Yes, honey. You better go, if you know what's good for you."

Thomas let out a sigh. He had told Kara to meet him outside at the valet stand, but she obviously didn't listen. He was busted. Thomas scowled at Kara, grabbed her by the arm and dragged her out of the restaurant.

"See ya tomorrow in court," Laney yelled out to Thomas as he headed for the door.

Now, that's my girl, Sophie thought, as she watched her son-in-law disappear out the door.

Chapter Eighteen

It was now "D" day, as Laney called it. She couldn't bring herself to say the word divorce. And she sure as hell never thought that this day would come for her and Thomas. They had so many great years together, but now it was all going down the toilet.

Laney felt like a failure and blamed herself. *Maybe it was the kid thing*, she thought. She was never ready to have children and Thomas probably did resent her for that. *Or maybe I was just too boring for him and that's why he had an affair?*

So many thoughts were spinning through her head. Laney pulled on her black Calvin Klein skirt, threw her tight black camisole over her head and pulled it down over her waist. She caught her tired refection in the mirror and sighed. *God, I look dreadful.* She added more concealer to hide the dark circles under her eyes.

She felt like someone had died and her mind, the Thomas that she loved had. But for some reason getting a divorce felt worse than death. This was the end of one of her most successful accomplishments in her life, and in Hollywood, a marriage that actually lasted more than a year was a milestone. It had been almost twelve years to the day that she had first laid eyes on Thomas.

She desperately tried to remember the good times that they'd had, but right now, Laney could only focus on the bad. But she had to be strong and get through this horrible day. She put on a brave face, added a hint of twinkle lip gloss to her lips, and gave herself a pep talk. "You can do this," she said to herself in the mirror. But she knew that she was just fooling herself. Losing Thomas was painful. Laney's slight smile quickly disappeared and her bottom lip began to quiver as tears filled her eyes.

Sophie knocked on the door; Laney grabbed a tissue and wiped her eyes.

"Honey, are you ready? It's time to go," Sophie called out softly.

Laney gave herself one last look in the mirror, took three deep breaths and tried to find her happy place. She wanted to smile but her lips just wouldn't curl up. This was the best she could do for now.

"I'm ready as I'll ever be," Laney said, opening the door, trying to hide her pain.

Sophie beamed with pride. "Honey, you look beautiful. Now, let's go get 'em."

The drive into Beverly Hills felt endless. Laney was a wreck on the inside, her stomach in knots. Sophie couldn't stand the silence and jump-started the conversation.

"Honey, I know that you want me to shut up while you think, but I just can't. I want you to take that English bastard to the cleaners," she proclaimed, sounding more like a biker-chick than a Southern Belle.

Laney frowned. "This is a no-fault divorce state, so I'll be lucky if I don't have to pay him spousal support."

"What in the hell are you talking about? That bastard walked out on you," Sophie seethed.

"It doesn't matter, Mom. The law's the law." Laney shrugged. But no matter what the law was she still couldn't help but feel a tiny remnant of love for her husband. At the same time, Thomas's betrayal was something that she couldn't forgive him for.

She began thinking about her discovery of Kara's earring in the sofa; and the text messages that Thomas had sent to her by mistake;

and finally, all of the lies that he had told her to try and cover up his affair. Her blood began to boil and her melancholy mood evaporated. Laney now wanted nothing but revenge. "Oh, don't worry, Mom. He'll get his due somehow. He'll be sorry that he ever asked for this divorce."

"That a girl, honey. Keep that fighting spirit." Sophie clapped her hands.

They arrived at 6565 Wilshire Boulevard, the Beverly Hills law offices of Alvin Siegler. Alvin was one of the most sought after divorce attorneys in Hollywood, and fortunately for her, Laney had the money to hire him.

A black leather briefcase on one arm, and the support of her mom on the other, Laney marched toward the office doors like a vixen.

Alvin and a female assistant greeted Laney and Sophie in the reception area and walked them to the small conference room where Thomas sat with his lawyer, Gerald Phillips, by his side. Thomas looked at Laney with a snarky expression on his face. But Laney didn't take any notice of him; she stayed focused, sat down beside Alvin, and opened her briefcase.

Sophie, on the other hand, was ready for a fight. She stared Thomas down and gave him her famous *go fuck yourself* look, which he had seen so many times before. He glared back at her, raised his middle finger, and slid his hair back with it to return the compliment.

Sophie slapped her hand down on the table. "I wouldn't do that if I were you."

But Thomas just released a cocky smile; while Laney ignored his little games.

Alvin felt the tension in the room and immediately stood up. "Shall we get started?" Laney and Thomas nodded for Alvin to continue.

Alvin cleared his throat and looked down at his notes. "After reviewing the case, here are some of the terms of the divorce. Ms. Montgomery will get the home in the Hollywood Hills, due to the fact that she bought the house before she married Mr. Morgan. It is considered separate property under California law.

Thomas groaned. Gerald kicked him under the table to shut up, then stood to speak on Thomas's behalf. "But we have a document stating that the home was purchased by both Ms. Montgomery *and* Mr. Morgan."

Alvin put his glasses on the tip of his nose and frowned at Laney.

"He's lying. I bought the house before I even knew him," Laney snapped.

"Can I please see the document?" Alvin asked. He held the piece of paper up to the light and inspected it. "It looks like his name was just added recently to the deed."

"W-Well, I sure didn't add it," Laney stammered. "He asked me to add his name to the deed years ago, but I never did."

"I can vouch for that. Her father and I stopped her from doing it," Sophie spoke up.

Thomas sneered. "Well, it looks like she did it anyway…Mom."

Sophie glared at Thomas like she could've killed him then and there.

Alvin put his hand over his mouth and whispered to his assistant, sitting beside him, taking notes. He handed her his copy of the deed and the one that Gerald had presented to him. She took them from him and walked out of the conference room.

"Let's talk about the money that Mr. Morgan spent from their joint account that only Ms. Montgomery contributed to …" Alvin started.

"Can I interject?" Gerald overrode him. "That was community property, so it was his to spend."

Thomas grinned at Laney. "See, I told you."

"That was my money, you bastard," Laney seethed.

Alvin jumped in. "Gerald, you're wrong again. This account was started when Ms. Montgomery was working as a buyer, and before she knew Mr. Morgan. Furthermore, all deposits were made by Ms. Montgomery. Mr. Morgan never contributed a dime."

Gerald squirmed in his chair. He was clearly not well prepared, and neither was Thomas. They were both unorganized as if they thought it was going to be a slam dunk.

"Is that correct, Thomas?" Alvin prompted.

Thomas crossed his arms and lowered his head in shame. "Okay. That's true. But I was added to the account." He was now regretting he hadn't brushed up on the California Divorce Laws.

Alvin smiled at Laney. "Yes, you were added years later. I have all of the deposit slips that show the amount of money that Ms. Montgomery deposited into the account before you were married and before she made it a joint account. So technically, Mr. Morgan, that money wasn't community property. So you will have to pay Ms. Montgomery back all of the money you took from her account."

Thomas moaned in his seat, knowing that he'd have to sell his precious car; while Laney felt a sense of relief after Alvin's cunning observation.

Within seconds, his assistant appeared with the two deeds in her hand. She leaned in and whispered something to her boss.

Laney sat anxiously in her chair while Thomas tapped his fingers on the table.

"Well, it looks like this deed is fake," Alvin said, glaring at Thomas, then Gerald.

Gerald threw up his hands in disgust and turned to Thomas. "Is there anything else you want to tell me…like the truth?"

Laney couldn't believe the crap that Thomas was trying to pull. She addressed his attorney. "Did he also forget to tell you about his personality change? His midlife crisis? And his mistress?"

"Mistress? You said that your wife was the one having the affair?" Gerald was now glaring at his client.

Alvin shot Laney a proud look. He loved her gusto.

Sophie had had it with all of Thomas's lies. She sprang up out of her chair and whistled like a football referee. "Wait just a damn minute here, mister. You can lie to your attorney, but you're not going to slander my daughter's name."

Thomas had way too much to lose. He wasn't getting the house, and now he owed Laney the Porsche money. That wasn't the way things were supposed to go. "Laney is the one who is lying," Thomas shouted, in his upper class British accent.

Laney tossed her hands in disbelief. "That's bullshit, you're the liar here. You've lied about everything."

Sophie noticed a young woman through the glass window of the conference room who seemed to be having an argument with the receptionist and realized, *My God, it's Kara.*

Sophie leaped out of her chair, sprinted into the other room, grabbed the young woman by the hand and dragged her into the conference room. "Well, if my daughter's lying, then who's this?"

Thomas scowled, his plan now sabotaged. This proved to his attorney that he was a blatant liar.

"Yeah, tell them who she is, honey," Laney added, sarcastically.

Thomas slumped down in his chair.

Kara stood dressed in a bright purple mini dress, white stilettos, and chewing on a piece of bubble gum, unaware of the consequences of her arrival.

"Hi, Tommy," she beamed, running over to him and jumping into his lap. "Thought I'd surprise you."

Laney cringed. "Awe, isn't that sweet."

"Well, aren't you going to ask about my alimony?" Thomas asked, looking at Gerald over Kara's shoulder.

Gerald rolled his eyes, with no response.

Alvin slammed down his hand like a gauntlet, closed his mountain of paper work and declared, "Ms. Montgomery gets the house free and clear, and she is to be paid back all the monies owed to her from Mr. Morgan. That means, the money from the joint account that Mr. Morgan selfishly spent on his new Porsche without her approval will be reimbursed, and lastly, he will pay back in full the advance that she gave him for his new film project. Based on the fact that Mr. Morgan created a fake deed, there could be other consequences for him. But that will be up to Ms. Montgomery. And as for alimony, Mr. Morgan, I wouldn't even go there, if I were you. This case is closed."

Sophie and Laney were elated. They leapt out of their seats and surrounded Alvin with endless hugs.

Thomas sunk miserably in his chair while Kara sat dumbfounded in his lap, wondering where his payout was. He'd had promised her that he would make out like a bandit in the divorce.

But right now Thomas was just a newly divorced, has-been film director without a penny to his name. He watched the two women exit the conference room, and yelled out, "It's not over yet, Laney, you'll see." Thomas wrapped his arms around Kara and thought about Plan B. *You better hide your Sparkelicious money, darling, because I'm coming to get it.*

It was barely five p.m., but Laney and Sophie were ready to revel in their victory.

"Let's go to the Peninsula Hotel for a glass of champagne," Laney sung, with relief. All of the pain Thomas had caused her, and the love that she had felt for him was beginning to dissipate. She was ready to start the next phase of her life. He was not the man that she had fallen in love with twelve years ago, and the outcome of her divorce had confirmed that.

Sophie happily agreed as they drove down Santa Monica Boulevard with the sunroof open to the glorious California sunshine.

Laney connected her iPod to the radio through the glove compartment, and cranked the volume up on her surround sound speakers. Adam Lambert's "Whole Lotta Love" screamed from console. They both sang along with the track at the top of their lungs to the American Idol star. Laney was obsessed with him after following him on the show, and Sophie had no choice but to love him too.

The circle drive at The Peninsula Beverly Hills was jam-packed with the most prestigious cars in the world. A Bugatti, a Rolls Royce, and a Bentley were parked safely to one side as Laney pulled her white Mercedes up to the entrance. Two valets greeted them with smiles and opened their doors.

Laney and Sophie sashayed through the double glass doors of the hotel, where they were welcomed by a doorman in a grey top hat and tails.

"Good afternoon, ladies. Shall I direct you to the bar, or to reception?"

"The bar, please," Laney replied as Sophie looked around in awe at the stunning surroundings of the famous hotel.

The doorman led them through the lavishly decorated entryway where a massive vase of fresh cut long stem roses and lilies hugged them with their freshness from the round glass topped table.

"I love that Beverly Hills smell." Laney sniffed the air and smiled.

"Me too, it's the best," Sophie giggled, feeling like a Hollywood movie star.

The doorman wished them well as he delivered them to the Club Bar. With its paneled walls of rich California birch and museum quality landscapes of Beverly Hills, the room oozed tradition and timeless elegance. A fireplace roared in the back of the dignified room.

Laney and Sophie found a small table for two in front of the windows that faced out onto Santa Monica Boulevard, and sat down. The light streamed in from behind the sheer green curtain while the glow from the fireplace added more stunning light in the legendary room. The table was perfect, allowing them a full view of the stunning bar.

A beautiful, leggy, dark haired waitress, dressed in all black sauntered in their direction with two full champagne flutes on a silver tray. Sophie and Laney were still getting settled into the green velveteen chairs when she surprised them by stopping by their table and placing one flute each down in front of them.

"These are for you," she said mischievously. "And the two, shall I say, gorgeous men, want to remain anonymous."

Laney and Sophie were both stunned, yet flattered. They glanced subtlety around the bar, hoping to catch a glimpse of the men who sent over the champagne, but they didn't see anyone who fit that 'gorgeous' description. There were just lots of pudgy old men with gold digger-type young women hanging on their arms.

"Oh well, I'll drink to that," Sophie cheerfully announced, giving up the search for the two mystery men; ready to take a sip of her expensive bubbly.

Laney chimed in, "Here's to us, and to the smart men who bought us the fab Cristal."

They toasted each other and then raised their glasses to Laney's victory. They were genuinely enjoying themselves for the first time in a long time. They both felt so liberated. Laney was now free of Thomas's cheating ways while Sophie was no longer Charles's caretaker. Even though she missed him terribly, his constant poor health had been a huge strain on her. Sophie's face now looked relaxed and happy.

"Mom, thank you for being here," Laney sweetly declared. "You were amazing today."

Sophie beamed and put her hand on Laney's. "No, honey. You were amazing, so strong, so in control."

Laney squeezed her mom's hand and smiled. "I couldn't have done it without you."

Sophie's eyes filled with tears as she took another sip of her champagne. She was so happy to be with her daughter, and to be able to offer her support.

Within seconds, the model-like waitress appeared again at their table with a grin on her face. "Ladies, you have now been invited to join the two gorgeous men for dinner." She turned and pointed to the entrance of the award-winning restaurant that was right outside of the bar.

Sophie was game, but she waited for Laney to respond.

"Well, why not? I'm single now." Laney quipped.

"Me too, honey. God bless you, my dear Charles," Sophie declared, tilting her head up to the ceiling as if she was talking to him up in heaven; then turned to the waitress. "So, where are these mystery men anyway?"

The waitress picked up their flutes and smiled. "Follow me, ladies, right this way."

She led them through the Club Bar and opened the glass door to Belvedere, The Peninsula's signature restaurant. They walked through the gracious surroundings and out onto the garden where a European water fountain flowed. The waitress escorted them past the fountain to a private table where the two men sat with their backs to them.

Sophie's heart raced. *It couldn't be,* she thought. But she knew that beautiful thick head of hair anywhere. Laney still wasn't sure what they were getting themselves into as they inched closer to the mystery men.

"Ladies. Well, here they are…the generous men who bought you the glasses of champagne." the waitress declared, leaving Laney and Sophie at the table.

And there sat the senator and his son, Matt, both looking as dashing as ever. Matt stood up in his black Armani suit and winked at Laney.

"Fancy meeting you in L.A," he beamed, pulling out a chair for her.

Laney was flabbergasted to see Matt's smiling face and stood frozen by the table. L.A. was the City of Angels, but right now, her angel may have arrived too soon.

"Wow…yeah, this is crazy," she stammered, looking around for a hidden camera. *This must be a set up.*

Sophie, on the other hand, was unabashedly elated to see the senator. She felt like she had won the lottery all over again. And he looked to be feeling the same way.

The water fountain danced behind them as the conversation and the champagne began to flow.

"Well, aren't you going to sit down?" Matt pointed to the empty chair next to him with a confused expression on his face.

Laney was guarded. She had only been divorced for a couple of hours, and in her mind, she was still off the market. But not wanting to seem rude, Laney took Matt up on his offer. "Sure. Thanks."

"Don't act so excited," Matt joked, trying to lighten her mood.

Laney raised a faint smile as she settled into her chair. She was conflicted about seeing Matt. The timing didn't feel right. It had been several months since they had seen each other, and right now it almost felt like they were meeting for the first time. She felt awkwardly shy around him. Laney placed her purse on the table and opened her mouth to speak, but Matt nervously interrupted her.

"Laney…uh…no, you go ahead. I'm sorry. What were you going to say?"

Laney was tongue-tied; still overwhelmed to be in Matt's presence in L.A., of all places. "Oh, nothing," Laney managed, sounding like a pubescent school kid.

Sophie tired of their ridiculous conversation broke the ice. "I have an announcement to make…" She clinked her baccarat champagne flute with a knife. "My beautiful daughter is now officially single."

Laney cringed. She didn't like the sound of the word "single". Nor did she appreciate her mom airing her dirty laundry.

Matt wasn't sure if this was good or bad news for Laney and wanted her to acknowledge Sophie's announcement before he commented. But Laney just stewed in her chair.

"Well, I believe that calls for a toast," the senator announced in a celebratory tone with his glass in the air. "Laney, to your new life adventures."

Laney winced. She thought that she'd be happy to be free of Thomas, but now the thought of starting all over again scared her. The single life was her new reality. Matt gave her a hopeful look, and Laney wiped the frown off of her face.

"Yes, to new adventures," they both broadcasted at the same time.

Sophie couldn't help but throw more fuel onto the fire. "And to new romance."

Matt locked his eyes onto Laney's, but she turned away and glared at her mom.

"Here, here," the senator agreed. But Laney and Matt didn't toast on that one.

Laney felt a sudden rush of heat sweep over her body. She

panicked and leapt out of her chair.

"Excuse me. I need to get some air," she declared and rushed toward the exit sign.

Matt jumped up and ran after her. He grabbed her arm as she reached the door of the restaurant. "California girl, are you okay?"

Laney stopped in her tracks. The anxiety that she was feeling began to leave her body. Matt's gentle touch made her feel calm and safe. "I just need some fresh air," she said, walking slowly down the hall that led to the front of the hotel.

Matt followed until he was close enough to touch her again. He softly moved his hand down her back, grasping her hand in his, and pulling Laney closer to him. "This isn't a date, California girl, don't worry," he said smiled. "We're friends, nothing else. Let's just enjoy the moment."

Laney breathed a sigh of relief and smiled in agreement. "You're right. I'm sorry. Let's go back to the table."

They walked back to the restaurant patio. Matt poured Laney another glass of champagne and she happily accepted it.

Sophie and the senator were engulfed in conversation. Except for a brief glance of acknowledgement; they were pretty much oblivious to their children's return to the table and were now practically sitting in each other's lap. Laney and Matt where a little shocked. They felt like the adults, chaperoning their children.

"Don't worry," Matt whispered to Laney. "My parents have been fighting for years, and my mom's the one who wanted the separation."

"What?" Laney put her hand to her mouth. "I had no idea they were separated. Are you okay with it?"

"Well, they're *adults.*" Matt responded diplomatically. "It's their life. I just want them both to be happy. And my mom seems ready for her own life. It's very hard being a senator's wife."

"And my mom looks like a kid all over again," Laney said, sipping her champagne. She didn't want to sound judgmental. She was just worried about her mom getting hurt. The senator seemed to be such a ladies' man. And then she laughed. "Good for her," she whispered to Matt, giving her mom and the senator her approval.

Matt had seen this kind of behavior from his dad a hundred times. He shook his head wearily and whispered back, "Your mom's cool. She's had a tough time. They'll be fine."

Matt's warm breath on her neck was making her crazy. *God, he's so tempting.*

"So, what about you, California girl?" he said in his normal voice. "How are you really doing?"

Laney's heart was now melting. Her guard was coming down. It had been months since she'd had sex, and Matt was turning her on more than ever. But this time it was different. *Even though I'm now single, we're just friends*, she reminded herself. She had to stay in control of the situation.

"You know, I'm sick of talking about me. What about you? What brings you to L.A.?" Laney sat back up in her chair and ran her finger around the rim of her flute.

Matt rested his arm on the back of Laney's high backed chair and gently caressed the top of her shoulders. A shiver ran down her spine as she waited intently for his answer.

"I've been meeting with some architectural firms here…as well, as other places," he said, wanting her to know that this wasn't about her and the fact that she lived here.

Laney played it cool too, even though she loved the thought of him moving here. "Oh really, that would be great. But is L.A. your kind of town?"

"I would like it to be," he shrugged. "But maybe New York is more my style. I'm going there in a couple of days."

Laney's heart sank. *Matt can't live in New York. He must know he isn't the New York type. L.A. is more his style.* But she replied with diplomacy. "Well, you should definitely check it out, and then make a decision."

The glow from the votive on the table was an up light on Laney's face.

Matt offered, "You know, L.A. girl. You look more beautiful than ever." He leaned in to kiss her on the cheek.

Laney blushed. The strain of the divorce had left her feeling old and worn out. It had also taken a toll on her self-confidence. She reminded herself that Matt was about eleven years her junior.

Matt couldn't resist. At the last second, instead of kissing her cheek, he moved his mouth to hers and gently kissed her on the lips.

Laney allowed the kiss, though she wondered if she would ever see him again.

Chapter Nineteen

The next morning Laney woke to the bright California sun streaming through the chocolate brown linen curtains. It was only 7:30, but she was wide awake and raring to go. She flung back the comforter, sprung out of bed, threw on her Victoria's Secret robe, tiptoed down the hall, so she wouldn't wake up her mom, into the kitchen to make a cappuccino. To her surprise, Sophie, was sipping coffee at the kitchen island, in her leopard print pajamas, taking in the view of the canyon.

"It's beautiful, isn't it, mom?" Laney whispered, approaching her mom from behind and placing her hand gently on her shoulder.

"It sure is. I can now see why you love it here," Sophie declared as a ray of sun highlighted her strong bone structure on her make-up free face. "Your father and I didn't understand it for so many years, but now I do. It's breathtaking."

"I know. Dad never understood why I had to be in L.A., but he let me live my dreams and I loved him for that."

"He was so proud of you, honey," Sophie placed her hand on Laney's and gave it a gentle squeeze.

It was one of the first honest conversations they had had about her father since he died, and it was refreshing. Laney missed him terribly and so did Sophie. Life had been so different without him.

"I know he was. He gave me the courage to move here. Both of you did. Thank you." Laney felt so blessed to have such supportive parents.

"You're welcome, honey." Sophie smiled up at her.

Laney took in the special moment and then walked over to the sliding glass doors in the den and threw them open. A slight breeze rustled through the trees. "Why don't we have some cappuccinos and go sit on the deck. Shall I make them?" She asked, making her way back into the kitchen to the Italian coffeemaker.

"Nope…this time, I'm in charge of the cappuccinos. I think I've finally figured out this fancy machine of yours," Sophie replied, from the coffee bar. The noise of the fancy machine echoed in the kitchen.

Laney obliged her mom's efforts and parked herself in the modern lounge chair on the deck and breathed in the fresh California air.

Soon, Sophie arrived on the deck with two ceramic mugs in hand. "Ta-da," she sang, "one cappuccino for you and one for me." She placed the mugs on the table. They sipped their coffee and took in the scenery.

But Sophie couldn't hold back her news any longer. "So, honey. I did it," she cheered like a teenager.

Laney sat up in her chair and tasted her cappuccino. "Yes, you did. I'm proud of you. You finally made a real cappuccino."

"Oh, honey, I'm not talking about the coffee," she laughed.

"Now, I'm afraid to ask." Laney sighed.

"I told the senator that I wouldn't be his mistress."

Laney breathed a sigh of relief. "Well, that's good to hear."

Sophie proudly touched her blonde hair and took a sip of her cappuccino. "Now, what about you and Matt? Spill it, honey."

Laney blushed. "Mom! Nothing happened." She hadn't talked about sex with her mom in years.

But Sophie wasn't buying it. "Oh, come on. Matt's crazy about you, and I know that you kissed him. I saw that big kiss, honey."

"You know, I don't trust men right now," Laney proclaimed. A moment later she giggled. "Yeah, I did kiss him, and it was amazing."

"Good for you, honey…" Sophie growled, "I mean cougar."

Laney made a cat-like face, curved her fingernails into claws and they couldn't stop laughing.

Laney loved having her mom around. She hated to admit to herself that it was nice having her mom all to herself. Charles was gone, which was terrible, but for the first time in years, she had her mom back. It may have been a selfish thought but the feeling was fantastic.

Laney's mood turned serious. "Do you really think that Matt's crazy about me?"

Sophie grasped Laney's hands and held them tight. "Honey, there's one thing that a mom's got and that's mother's intuition. The boy's in love with you."

Laney was flattered yet unsettled. "I'm not ready for this yet, Mom."

"Well, I think that Matt knows that, honey, but he won't wait forever."

The doorbell echoed through the house. "Hmmm…Who could that be so early in the morning?" Laney questioned, heading to the front door. "Probably the UPS guy."

Laney was expecting to see the man in brown, holding a package. She gasped as the door swung open.

"Surprise!" Missy and Bridgett yelled.

Her sisters had only visited her one time since she moved to L.A. She was shell shocked to see them.

"Well, aren't you going to let us in?" Bridgett asked, peeking into the house. Laney noticed a newspaper tucked under her arm. Missy stood patiently behind Bridgett, waiting to be invited in. She looked a combination of exhausted and worried.

"Of course," Laney beamed and opened her arms to them for a group hug. But she was suspicious. She knew that something had to be up. Her sisters wouldn't fly three thousand miles just for the heck of it. "Love you…mean it," Missy said to Laney with a forced smile.

Bridgett was her no-holds-barred self. "Now, where's Senator

Rigby's mistress?" She put her sunglasses on top of her head and stormed through the house like a private detective, in search of her mom.

Missy shot Bridgett her big sister look and yelled from the hall, "Cut the crap, Bridge."

Sophie heard her daughters' voices and got up to greet them.

"Did someone say mistress?" she asked sexily, imitating May West. She strutted through the sliding glass doors into the den. Sophie actually liked the thought of being the "other woman".

The girls laughed at their mom's pantomime.

"Now, what's the big deal?" Sophie said, walking over to her girls to say hello. "Are you both here to protect me?"

Laney thought for a second. "How would you two know about Mom meeting the senator here anyway? Wait…don't tell me?" Laney snatched the paper out of Bridgett's hand.

And there was the headline, splashed across the cover of the early morning edition of *The Greenville Times*. "Senator Rigby's New Choice: Sophie" with a picture of the two of them drinking wine together on the plane.

"Let me see that?" Sophie peered over Laney's shoulder. "I love it," she smiled proudly. "Your old mother isn't dead yet, girls."

"Mom? Are you serious? This doesn't bother you?" Laney gasped.

Bridgett added her usual two cents. "Like daughter, like mother."

"Like you can talk?" Missy interjected. "You're the biggest hypocrite of all. At least Mom isn't married. You were."

And the slinging match began. Bridgett couldn't resist. "You thought that Brody was the perfect man…and look how he's behaved!"

Sophie raised her eyebrow and put two and two together. Her "happy to be a tramp" mood at age seventy plus, turned motherly. "So, that's why you're really here, isn't Missy? That damn Brody." Sophie scowled.

Missy sniffled and reached for a tissue in her pocket. Sophie went over to Missy and put her arms around her. "Honey, I can take care of myself. But if another man hurts my girls, they better watch out."

Missy never cried. She was always so strong. But this time, she couldn't help it. "It's all my fault…"

Sophie put her hands on Missy's shoulders and glared at her. "Honey, you listen to me right now. His affair is not your fault. You get that crazy thought out of your head right now."

"Yeah, Missy, come on. You've been working your butt off and supporting him for years. You're the best thing that's ever happened to him," Laney added, trying to reassure her sister.

Bridgett tossed her things down on a leather chair. "Well, apparently he didn't think so," she said under her breath walking toward the open kitchen. "Can I get some caffeine?"

"Throw some Bailey's in mine, if Laney has any," Missy called after her.

Laney joined Bridgett in the kitchen and made Bailey's and coffee for everyone. She led everyone to the deck to finish the discussion.

After discussing Brody's affair at length, they all agreed that he was a major jerk, and that Missy would change the locks on her doors when she got back to South Carolina. Then, the conversation turned back to Sophie and the senator.

"So, spill it, Mom," Bridgett demanded. "We wanna know everything."

"Can I see that picture again?" Sophie asked, taking the paper from Laney. "I look pretty good, don't I?" She puckered her lips like a cover girl. "You know, no one takes notice of old people anymore, but all of a sudden now they seem to be really interested." Sophie reveled in the attention.

"So, whaddya we call you now? The Senstress?" Bridgett chuckled. "Get it? I put senator and mistress together."

Sophie shot daggers at her middle daughter.

"Bridge, the senator is separated from his wife. See, it says it right there in black and white." Missy pointed to the second paragraph of the article.

Sophie grabbed her readers out of her robe pocket and put them on the tip of her nose. "He is? He never told me that," she said, holding the paper up to her face.

Laney remembered Matt saying that his parents were having trouble, but she didn't know that they were officially separated. So she breathed a sigh of relief. "Well, isn't that a good thing, Mom?"

"Well, no, not really. I don't want to marry the guy and I sure don't want a commitment after one dinner," Sophie declared, playing hard to get. "I still miss your father and Charles way too much to get involved with anyone else right now."

The girls sat there in silence. It sounded like their mother liked the idea of being a woman on the side, and they were baffled. She had always been a one-man woman; but it was her life.

Missy savored the last drop of her warm Bailey's and coffee. Feeling a little tipsy, she reached into her purse and pulled out an envelope. "And this is for you, Mom. It's from Lake."

Sophie frowned. "I'll open it later. We're having too much fun talking about my escapades." She stared at the letter on the table and cried, "Damn it. Can't they just let poor Charles rest in peace?" She picked up the letter, sighed and decided to open it. "Oh, what the hell."

The girls anxiously waited for Sophie to open it. She tore the letter open, read it and held it close to her chest. "Lake's such a bastard," she seethed. "Can't they just let this go?"

"What's it say, Mom?" Laney politely prodded. But Sophie was too upset to speak. She threw the letter on the table and ran inside the house in a panic.

Missy spoke up. "Laney, you and Bridgett go check on Mom, and I'll take a look at the letter."

But Laney thought two "legal" heads were better than one. She sent Bridgett to console Sophie and reviewed the contents of the letter with Missy.

It read: "We happen to know that our father never loved you. He only loved one woman and that was our mother. We are contesting the will and will be expecting anything that is our father's to be turned over to us ASAP. He was our father and want what is due to us."

Within ten minutes, Sophie reappeared with Bridgett at the sliding glass doors looking radiant again. She had powdered her face and wiped away her tears. "You know, Charles did love me very much and I loved him, and if they can't handle it, then screw them. Those boys aren't getting a damn thing. Not even an empty picture frame."

The girls cheered and Laney announced, "Now, that's the mom that we know and adore."

"And she's making quite a name for herself too," Sophie grinned. She propped herself up sexily against the doors. "No one's going to mess with Sophie!"

"So, when do we get to formally meet the senator?" Bridgett cooed. "Is he still in L.A.?"

Sophie motioned for Laney to top up her coffee with more Bailey's and cream. "Oh, honey, he's a busy man. He's probably back in South Carolina by now."

Sophie's cell phone screamed from her robe pocket.

"That's probably your man now," Bridgett sang. "Answer it."

"Nah, let it go to voicemail. I don't feel like talking to anyone right now," she coolly replied.

The girls laughed. Sophie was still playing hard to get and they loved it.

Sophie pulled the phone out of her pajama pocket and delicately placed it on the table. She reclined back in her chair and still refused to check the message on her phone, even though she was dying to know who had called. She would give it a few more minutes.

"So, what about you, L.A. Laney?" Missy winked. "I hear Matt's here too?"

"Yeah, you're holding back some info. Inquiring minds want to know," Bridgett quipped.

Laney smiled slyly at her sister's question. Before she could answer, her iPhone chimed from the table, with an incoming text message.

Bridgett grabbed the phone and read the text message out loud: "Meet us at The Hollywood Roosevelt tonight. I may even tickle the ivories. Luv MTB," She frowned. "Who's MTB?"

Laney's face turned bright red, knowing exactly who it was.

"It's *Matt the bartender*, Bridge, you idiot." Missy shook her head.

Bridgett smirked. "Yeah. I know…What about you Mom? Who called?"

Sophie couldn't stand the suspense any longer. She grabbed her phone and pressed the voicemail button.

"Turn the speakerphone on, so we can all hear," Bridgett chirped.

Sophie touched the "speaker" button and out came the senator's deep, sexy voice, loud and clear: Hello my beautiful Sophie. I hope you're free tonight so I can buy you a drink at The Hollywood Roosevelt. And I will try to obey by your wishes, even thought it will be difficult.

Chapter Twenty

The Hollywood Roosevelt Hotel stood like a tall, glamorous lady on Hollywood Boulevard. The Spanish landmark, once a playground for such luminaries as Clark Gable and Marilyn Monroe, had become the place for the young Hollywood stars to see and be seen. And it still hadn't lost any of its old world charm.

The girls entered the 1927 mahogany doors and were welcomed by a handsome, aspiring actor-type doorman, dressed in black. He pointed them to the Cinegrille bar. They walked through the elaborate lobby of antiques and the preserved Spanish fountain, turned right past the front desk and the elevators, into the famous piano bar.

Elegant, sexy and dripping in rich fabrics of red and gold, the room was a decorative throwback to an era gone by. You could feel the ghosts of old Hollywood's past still floating in the air. Candle votives lit the tables and the smooth sounds of jazz standards purred from the baby grand piano in the corner of the room.

The girls were greeted with a smile, by a gorgeous, supermodel-type hostess. She showed them to a cozy booth, dressed with red velveteen cushions, by a window with a view of the famous Hollywood strip. They settled into the plush, decorative space as the hostess placed drink menus on the table for them to peruse. Missy and Bridgett scanned the menus, while Laney and Sophie anxiously glanced around the bar for Matt and the senator. To their dismay, there was no sign of either of them around. Within minutes, a dapper waiter stopped by their table and took their drink orders. While the girls waited for their wine, they chatted and admired the dramatic and famous room. It was definitely a Hollywood moment that they would never get to experience in the South.

The waiter promptly returned, holding a silver tray with four glasses of chardonnay. He placed the glasses down in front of the girls, reached into his pant pocket, pulled out a white piece of paper and handed it to Laney. "I was told to give this to the beautiful blonde in the pink dress," he winked.

"Oh?" Laney replied, perking up. She took the folded up piece of paper and clenched it in her hands.

"Well, aren't you going to open it, honey?" Sophie urged.

"Yeah, we're waiting." Bridgett added.

Laney squirmed in her seat. "Okay, okay." She carefully unfolded the paper and read it silently to herself.

"Honey, come on, already." Sophie tapped her fingernails on her wine glass impatiently.

Laney held the paper out in front of her and moved it closer to the candlelight. "I'm dedicating this song to you," she cooed, pulling the private note close to her heart.

A frustrated Bridgett grabbed the note out of her hand. "Is that it? Is that all it says?" *Maybe he'll man up and tell her about the girl I saw him kissing at the Goat, so I don't have to*, she thought.

And within seconds, the methodic sounds of the baby grand danced through the air. Laney blushed. She couldn't believe her ears. One of her favorite songs, *Home* by Michael Buble, filled the room. Overcome with joy, she became teary-eyed. She glanced over at the piano, in the corner of the bar, where Matt tickled the ivories like a seasoned pro. He began to sing and his velvet voice was emotional and strong.

The girls giggled with excitement; all were swept away by Matt's talent. Matt caught Laney's eye and smiled sweetly as he continued to serenade her from the baby grand.

Sophie reveled in Laney's exuberance, leaned back in the booth, and coolly combed the room with her eyes in search of the senator. *He has to be here somewhere.* She sipped her glass of chardonnay and resigned herself to the fact that he wasn't going to show up.

As the wine glass touched her lips, Sophie felt a warm breath kiss her neck and move to her ear. "He's quite talented, isn't he, for a senator's son?" the senator whispered sexily in her ear; then squeezed her hand.

Sophie smiled up at the senator, then looked him confidently in the eye. She was so intoxicated by him. *I'm way too old to feel like this,* she thought. *But then again, what the hell? I've lost the two loves of my life, what's wrong with possibly falling in love a third time…or just having fun?*

She squeezed his hand and whispered back, "I'm not surprised at all. He obviously takes after his father."

The senator escorted Sophie to the middle of the floor and they began to dance. For a moment, Sophie felt like a girl again; she didn't want this feeling to end. *Oh, what would Charles think? I'm sure he'd disapprove. But it's just a dance,* she kept telling herself, *nothing else.* The senator at least owed her that after the embarrassing headline in the *Greenville Times.* Either way, the senator couldn't take no for an answer and Sophie couldn't refuse him.

Matt played the piano flamboyantly with his right hand and with his left, then gestured for Laney to come over to see him. Laney felt a rush of embarrassment as she made her way over to the piano in the dark corner. Everyone in the dimly lit bar turned to catch a glimpse of the lucky girl who was being romanced by the piano man.

Bridgett was just plain jealous now. She sat in the booth with a long face and pouted. "Chase has never been that romantic, ever…and 'the first one', what she now called her ex-husband, well, that's the reason I left him. He never paid me *any* attention."

But Missy was happy for Laney and felt like she deserved this moment. "You know what, Bridge? Let's toast to romance, to L.A., and to Lane and Matt." She held up her glass.

With zero enthusiasm, Bridgett lifted her's too. "Well, if you insist. Cheers to them," she grumbled. "And while we're at it, here's to mom and the senator."

Bridgett and Missy toasted as they watched their mom and Cary dance cheek to cheek in front of their table.

Laney shyly gripped the hem of her pink mini dress as she sat down next to Matt on the red velvet bench. He flashed a smile, kissed her softly on the lips, and then began to play *Get Here* by Oleta Adams. It was another of Laney's favorite songs; always made her emotional, and this time was no exception. Her eyes welled up with tears and she did her best to hold them back. She didn't know if she was melancholy because she missed Thomas, or her father, or if she could possibly be falling in love with Matt. Right now she was just confused.

Matt leaned over and whispered in her ear, "It's your chance to show me what you're made of, California Girl." He moved the microphone toward her mouth and grinned. "You said that you wanted to sing again when we were at The Poinsett in Greenville, so here's your chance."

*I couldn't possibly…*Laney thought, *but singing has always been my therapy, and right now I could really use some.* She took in a deep breath, cleared her throat, and opened her mouth and sang. Soon her nerves vanished and her old confidence came back. She sounded incredible. Her vocals were silky, smoky and smooth. Matt was blown away. Laney was better than she had led on. All those years in a band had indeed given her amazing stage presence.

And the Hollywood crowd was also smitten. They showed their love with a hearty round of applause for the duo. Not something that very often happens in Hollywood, with so many amazing singers and musicians in town. Even the club manager had poked his head in for a moment to listen. He knew that Matt was one hell of a piano player when he heard his demo and booked him for the gig, but he was even better in person. He was curious about the female singer who'd dropped in. He loved her voice and thought they clicked very well together.

Matt finished the song and wiped away a tear that cascaded down Laney's face. The manager smiled, pointed to his watch and gestured at Matt from the bar to take his break. He grabbed Laney's hand and led her out of the room.

"Was my playing that bad?" he quipped, hoping to make Laney smile.

They sat on the green velveteen sofa in the lobby and Matt glazed into Laney's big blue eyes, waiting for her response.

"No," Laney sniffled. "I'm just so happy! Singing again feels good. I've obviously missed it more than I thought." Her fond memories of having her own band when she first moved to L.A. were rushing back to her.

"It was a magical time in my life." Laney frowned. "But I'm older, I have a mortgage to pay, and a fashion business with employees that rely on me."

"Well, you have an incredible voice," Matt said sincerely. "You never told me you could sing like that. I seriously think you should start singing again."

"Yeah, right. I was pretty good back in the day," Laney conceded. "But I couldn't abandon my company to focus on that."

"Well if you ever want a piano man, I'm yours," he grinned, holding his gaze on hers. Matt then became pensive. "It's been great seeing you again." He leaned in to kiss her on the lips.

Laney, caught up in the moment, kissed him back; then quickly retreated. "I'm sorry. I can't do this. We should go back into the bar."

Matt nodded. "I understand. I'm sure you need some time on your own after the divorce, and I don't want to put any pressure on you...He hesitated. "You're right. They'll wonder where we are." Matt stood up and Laney solemnly followed.

In her heart, she knew that the timing wasn't right for them, but deep down, she had hoped Matt would've told her that she was wrong. And she wondered why he didn't.

They arrived back at the booth where the girls were listening intently to one of the senator's many political anecdotes. Everyone briefly acknowledged the couple's return as the senator wrapped up with his punch line. They all erupted with laugher, except for Matt and Laney, who were both too upset to raise a smile. Bridgett, who'd had way too many, sloppily jumped up to make a toast.

"To new love, I mean, loves, sorry, Mom, almost left you out…and a shout out to all of the cougars of the world." She grinned and clumsily fell back down into the booth.

Matt rose stoically from the end of the booth. "Well, I guess now's as good a time as any." He glared at Laney and then at his father.

Laney nervously sipped her chardonnay. Her mind went to the extreme. *Don't tell me. He's going to pop the question to me in front of everyone? I'm sure not ready for another commitment.* She kept telling herself. *But God he does look gorgeous and extremely tempting standing there.*

And, Laney wasn't kidding. Matt was a sight for sore eyes. He was way too slick and dashing to be a musician. His hair was gelled back away from his handsome face, and the cuffs on the sleeves of his pressed white button-down shirt were turned slightly up. His hip skinny jeans were a little worn, but besides that he resembled a GQ model, not a man pursuing an architectural career. Everyone was captivated by his self-assured demeanor, especially Laney. With a renewed brightness in his eyes, Matt rubbed his hands together and sighed. "Dad, you don't even know about this yet..."

The senator perked up in his seat, as did Laney.

"I've decided to take a job…" he declared.

But before he could finish, Bridgett blurted out, then raised her glass to her mouth and mumbled. "Oh, you're probably staying in South Carolina now."

Laney and Matt both shot her a puzzled look.

Missy kicked Bridgett under the table and whispered, "Shut up! Let him finish."

Matt stood patiently at the table until satisfied Bridgett was done. "No, Bridgett, sorry, wrong coast. And I'm not staying in South Carolina either. The job's in New York."

A hush came over the entire table and everyone looked stunned.

The senator had hoped his son would stay in South Carolina, until he met Laney. Now he was in favor of Matt going to L.A. Laney was hoping Matt would opt to move to L.A. as well, to give their relationship a try, once she'd sufficiently recovered from the Thomas debacle. Sophie and Missy were wishing he was moving to the West Coast for Laney's sake too. For sure, he was heading to the wrong coast in all of their minds.

Bridgett just couldn't figure Matt out. *He's got that girlfriend in Greenville...What the hell's with this guy? Is he planning on stringing TWO women along now?* In either case, she had to stir the pot even more. She hoped if she played dumb and asked him more questions, then maybe he would admit the truth.

"What?" Bridgett cried. "I thought you loved my sister?"

Usually Sophie or Missy would have shut Bridgett up by now, but this time, they also wanted to hear what Matt had to say for himself.

Laney held her wine glass up to her face, hoping to hide from the embarrassment. She hoped her hand that was holding the wine glass wouldn't start shaking as she stood up to make a toast. "You know, I think New York is a great city, and you'll love it there. Here's to your new ventures," she said, trying to raise a smile, even though she wanted to burst into tears.

But Bridgett wasn't going to stand for all of this *skirting around the real issue crap*. "I'm still waiting, Matt." She tapped her fingers on the side of her wine glass and glared at him. "Do you love my sister?"

All eyes were on Matt. Everyone wanted an answer. Even Laney wanted to know how he really felt about her, because right now, he seemed to be moving on with his life.

He is probably moving there for a girl, Laney thought, torturing herself with so many *what ifs*.

"Wow, this a tough crowd." Matt laughed nervously and ran a

hand through his hair. "But I think this is between your sister and I."

Laney's heart sank.

"Well, this family shares everything, so spill it," Bridgett demanded. She was on the verge of blabbing everything she'd seen then and there.

Matt looked over at his father, hoping he would bail him out of this awkward situation.

"Son, she's right. Now spill it," the senator quipped instead, sounding like one of the girls.

Laney had never felt this vulnerable. Her face was red with embarrassment, but she wanted to know right now, too.

"Okay, okay," Matt replied, pushing back a lock of hair that had fallen across his face. "Are you ready for this, California Girl?" He looked deep into her eyes.

Laney's heart raced.

"I do care very much for your sister," Matt said sweetly, "I think that Laney already knows that. But I'm doing what's best for her. And she knows that, too."

Laney was crushed. Matt was obeying her request and setting her free. For the first time in twelve years, she would be on her own. She was petrified.

Bridgett was pissed at Matt's answer. Mr. Perfect wasn't so flawless anymore. She would have to tell Laney the truth sooner or later. But, she rationalized, *if Matt moves to New York, maybe Laney will get on with her life, and the problem will solve itself.*

Chapter Twenty One

Since Matt's departure to New York, Laney had completely immersed herself into her Sparkelicious clothing line. She felt rejuvenated and upbeat about her new, "single" life. Actually, she was semi-single. Her divorce would be final in three months.

Laney's brain had been overflowing with creativity. She was working tirelessly around the clock, designing two new "hoodie" looks a month, and her calendar was jam packed with meetings with buyers at trendy boutiques and high-end departments. They were all clamoring for her new hoodie designs, which reflected her youthful spirit and independent mood.

She had spoken to Matt several times over the last few months and received e-mails from him on a daily basis. But they had resolved, for the time being, to be just friends. Matt seemed happy in New York and extremely preoccupied with his new job and new life. Laney didn't pry into his personal life, she just felt that whatever was meant to be would be. Though Laney missed him terribly, she was determined to live her life without it revolving around a man, and she was succeeding. But she did wonder how she would feel about Matt if ever she saw him again. And deep down she hoped that he hadn't met anyone else. But c'mon, he was young, gorgeous, and single, so how could she blame him if he had? Why would he want to be with her anyway? She was soon to be a divorced, over the hill, woman with way too much baggage, and with far too many wrinkles for a hot young stud like him.

Her fashion line was to thank for her invigorated spirit. Laney's Sparkelicious brand was growing by leaps and bounds. She had moved the company headquarters out of her home office and into a funky space on Melrose; and she loved it. She wasn't so isolated anymore, which made her much happier. Laney had also hired another assistant and added two more sales reps. She just hoped she wasn't growing too fast. The fashion business was extremely volatile; she had to use her financial brain too, and not let her creative brain run the entire show.

The L.A. sunshine beamed through the sunroof of Laney's SUV as she pulled into The Coffee Bean and Tea Leaf at the corner of Ventura and Laurel Canyon. Today Laney was dressed in her famous Sparkelicious baby pink hoodie outfit; she ordered her usual non-fat cappuccino at the counter, then moved over to the "pick up" sign.

While Laney waited for her gourmet coffee, she scanned her personal and work e-mails on her iPhone. As she text-messaged a response to one of her sales reps, she heard her name called from across the café. Laney glanced up from her iPhone and cringed. *Oh, God! Not Kara!* she thought. That was the last person she wanted to see on a beautiful Monday morning. But it was indeed Kara, and she was waddling toward Laney like a duck. Laney's eyes darted back down to her iPhone. *I'll pretend I didn't see her, and maybe she'll go away*, Laney told herself. But Kara was full waddle ahead. She didn't care who she disturbed in the serene coffee house.

Kara grinned as she approached her, soon standing a little too close for Laney's liking, invading her personal space. "I thought it was you."

Laney had nowhere to hide. With a fake surprise expression on her face, she glanced up from her phone. "Oh…h-hi," Laney stuttered unenthusiastically, hoping her ex-husband's mistress would take the hint and go away.

"You look amazing," Kara cooed, still oblivious to the fact that maybe Laney didn't want to see the woman who stole her husband. She looked tired, overweight, and like she had aged about ten years since Laney last saw her. Laney couldn't help but feel extremely confident as she stared at Kara's puffy face. The barista called Laney's name and placed her cappuccino on the counter. *Perfect timing,* Laney thought, as she grabbed her coffee and turned to go.

Kara stood there patiently, blocking Laney's exit.

"Well…I need to get to the office," Laney announced, stepping past Kara.

But Kara wanted to talk and followed Laney to the exit. "Well, aren't you going to congratulate me?" she shouted out to Laney, pointing first to her belly and then to the huge rock on her finger.

Laney's heart sank. *First of all, where in the hell did Thomas get the money to buy Kara a ring like that? And second, Kara isn't fat, she's pregnant.*

Laney turned, a few feet from the door, and looked back at Kara, her bottom lip quivered as she spoke. "That's just great. Good for you and Thomas." Just as Laney was thinking, *what could be worse?* she heard Thomas's English accent ricochet off of the wall, from the other end of the coffee shop.

"My dear, your coffee's here," he announced to Kara and the rest of the Starbuck's customers. The room started to spin and Laney couldn't catch her breath. She wanted to die, then and there.

"Don't you want to come and say hello?" Kara asked, obliviously, rubbing her pregnant belly.

Laney just couldn't face her ex-husband. She was hurt and humiliated. Over the course of their marriage, Thomas had told her that he never really cared about having kids.

Laney flung the door open and rushed out of the café in a panic. "I'm sorry, I have a meeting to get to…I have to go." She called over her shoulder. Laney raced to her SUV, hurried inside and sobbed uncontrollably. She now realized that Thomas left her for a younger woman because he felt she was too old to have kids.

In a giant gasp of hyperventilation, Laney turned on the ignition and the sound of Vonda Shepard's *100 Tears Away* boomed from the surround sound speakers. She drove down the canyon, grabbed a tissue from her purse, wiped her eyes and began to sing along with the track, "The only way to feel your joy, is first to feel your sadness."

Laney sang at the top of her lungs and her mood began to brighten. Singing was still therapeutic for her. *Maybe Matt was right about my music?* So many thoughts were racing through her head. The dreams that she once had to become a singer now seemed possible again. *I'm in L.A. I could call all of my old band mates and get the band back together.* But then she became fearful. *It's been about ten years since I've performed with my band, and I'm just beginning to reap the financial rewards of my clothing line.* So she buried her dream of singing once again and forced herself back to reality.

She turned right off of Melrose onto Orange Avenue and into the parking lot behind her office. Laney reached for the key to turn the engine off, but with the Bluetooth still connected, the phone rang through the car speakers. She glanced down at the navigation board, which read, incoming call, "Missy." She pressed the phone button on her tan leather steering wheel and frowned. "Hey, sis, is everything okay?"

"Hey, L.A. Laney," Missy cheerfully replied, ignoring her question. "How's everything with you?"

Laney hesitated. She didn't want to dump all of her crap onto her sister. Missy had her own issues. "Oh, ya know, another sunny day in L.A. What did you do about Brody?"

"I changed the locks, but Brody is begging me to take him back."

"Did you tell him to take a hike?" Laney quipped, sipping on her cappuccino.

"No," Missy sighed, "he brought me flowers the other day to work…but that's not why I called."

As smart as Missy was in other areas, she was stupid when it came to men. And Laney knew that she was fighting a losing battle with her anyway. Brody had had affairs before and Missy always took him back, so there was no point in offering her sister any more advice.

"I'm calling about Mom." Missy continued.

Laney placed her cappuccino back into the cup holder and moved in closer to the speakerphone. "Oh, no! Is she okay?"

"She's just having a hard time. She stopped seeing the senator cold turkey and just isn't herself."

Laney perked up with an idea. "Mom's birthday is next month. I'll come home and we'll throw her a surprise party. I'll organize it. What do you think?"

"I love it!" Missy cheered.

"Okay, then it's a plan. I'll start organizing it." Laney replied. She said goodbye to her sister, and headed into her office to start planning the party and her trip home to South Carolina.

She gathered her things and headed into her bright and sunny Sparkelicious office on Melrose. The walls were painted a pale yellow, and the space felt creative and alive. Laney sat down at the long glass-topped table in front of the windows that faced out onto the famous, hip street. One of her assistants greeted her with mail and phone messages; the other was busy updating the Sparkelicious website with Laney's new hoodie design, Queen E; while her salespeople were out calling on Nordstrom's and Macy's.

Sequin fabric swatches, yards of chenille and velveteen squares lined her desk. Laney moved the clutter and found her laptop hiding underneath. She answered countless e-mails, made a first class reservation to South Carolina on Delta Airlines for her mom's birthday, and then called The Lazy Goat. The outdoor patio at The Goat would be the perfect place to have her mom's surprise party.

She sent party invitations via Facebook to her aunt, uncle and cousins. Her thoughts turned to Matt. She missed him more than she allowed herself to admit. *This would be the perfect excuse to see him*, she thought. She typed in his e-mail address and was attaching the invitation when Janie, her assistant, yelled out to her, and Laney jumped.

"Wait one second," she replied. But Janie said it couldn't wait. She had a *huge* celebrity on the phone who wanted to endorse the Queen

E line, and she had to take the call NOW.

Laney stood up from her chair, but she was determined to get her e-mail off to Matt, and leaned back down and squinted at the keyboard, searching for the "send" button.

Janie called out to her again from her desk. "She can't hold any longer, Lane, hurry up." Laney unknowingly put her finger on the "delete" button and the e-mail disappeared into cyberspace.

With that supposedly taken care of, Laney quickly took the phone call from the celebrity starlet. As they discussed promotional ideas, Janie ran over to her desk in a panic. "It's the bank. There's a problem with the account."

Laney put her hand over the receiver. "I'll have to call them back," she whispered.

Janie's face turned pale. "They said that the Sparkelicious account is empty!"

"What?" Laney shouted, then apologized to the actress over the phone. "I'll have to call you back." She hung up the phone, quickly went to her computer, and pulled up her Sparkelicious bank account. "I just made an $18,000 deposit the other day. There should be at least $100,000 of working capital in there."

"Well, the bank said that you had to make a deposit today because there was nothing in it," Janie insisted.

Within seconds the account appeared on the screen. Laney peered at a debit of $100,000 and screamed, "That damn bastard! So, that's where he got the money for that rock!"

Jamie frowned. "Who are you talking about?"

"Thomas!" Laney yelled, calling the bank in hysteria. "If he's manipulated that little wannabe actress at the bank again, I'll kill him."

The phone rang and a receptionist answered.

"I need to speak to the manager, immediately." Laney barked.

Within seconds, a Mr. Brown picked up and soon answered and verified that Mr. Morgan had withdrawn money from the Sparkelicious account from one of his tellers.

"Mr. Brown…Thomas Morgan has no rights to my money," Laney yelled.

"I'm sorry, Ms. Montgomery, but he is your husband, and he has withdrawn money from the account before."

Laney was infuriated. "Well, he's not my husband anymore. I want all of this money put back into my account immediately."

Mr. Brown sighed. "Ms. Montgomery, I'm so sorry about this. His name is on the account, you know?"

"Since when?" she snapped. "I never added it."

There was a slight pause, followed by the tapping of computer keys. "It says his name was added last year."

Laney huffed. "Well, you need to fire that little tart. She had no right to add his name to my account, or to let him walk out with my money!" Laney slammed down the phone. "This is a disaster," she shouted to Janie.

Laney picked her iPhone up and called Thomas. The phone rang and rang and finally went to voicemail. "I knew he wouldn't pick up the phone when he saw it was me," she fumed. She listened impatiently to his voice massage, waiting for the beep. "If you know what's good for you, you'll return MY MONEY!" She ended the call, grabbed her purse and threw it over her shoulder.

"Where are you going?" Janie cried.

"I'm going to see Alvin." Laney flew out the door. Like a racecar driver, she jumped in her car and sped to Beverly Hills. She called Alvin on the way there so he would be expecting her.

Laney arrived at Alvin's office and the receptionist immediately escorted her in to see him.

Alvin greeted Laney with a frown.

"Why are you looking at me like that?" she demanded. "Thomas stole my money, I didn't steal his."

"Well, technically he didn't steal your money," Alvin said, sitting uncomfortably in his chair. "Why didn't you tell me about this account before?"

"Because it was my private business account." Laney threw up her hands. "Thomas had his, I had mine, and we never mixed the two... like Thomas could have...he always operated in the red."

Alvin put his glasses on the tip of his nose. "But, didn't you acquire this money during your marriage?"

Laney scowled. "Yes, but this was all *my* hard earned money. Thomas didn't do a damn thing!"

"It doesn't matter, Laney." Alvin sighed. "The money is community property. He is entitled to half of the money made by Sparkelicious while you were married."

"This is bullshit," Laney cried. "I've worked my ass off for my company. So, now he just gets to reap *my* rewards?"

"I know, I don't make the laws, but I have to inform you what they are."

Laney's eyes filled with tears. "So, what are you saying?"

"I'm saying whether you've made a million dollars or a hundred dollars from Sparkelicious during your marriage he gets half. I'm sorry." Alvin shook his head sadly.

Laney couldn't believe what she was hearing. Sparkelicious was now in financial trouble and she may have to shut it down for good.

Chapter Twenty Two

The Delta Flight from LAX to Atlanta to GSP landed at The Greenville Spartanburg Airport at 3 p.m. sharp.

"Welcome to the South. It's a perfect 82 degrees in Greenville. I hope y'all enjoyed your flight. And we hope ta see y'all again soon," the pilot's Southern twang streamed over the intercom. Laney grinned. She hadn't heard a heavy Southern accent like that in so long. It was refreshing. Her troubles in L.A. seemed millions of miles away. She hadn't told her family about her financial problems, and she didn't plan.

This trip was about celebrating her mom, not about wallowing in her legal dilemmas. Laney had way too much pride, and was way too independent. She would go this alone, for now. She opened the overhead bin and grabbed her carry-on bag from above her first class seat.

With her hot pink Mercedes Benz baseball cap disguising her unwashed blonde hair, she added some twinkle lip gloss to her dry lips before she exited the plane.

Hot, humid air engulfed her body as she walked through the corridor. She took a right toward baggage claim and glided down the escalator to the automatic glass doors that led to the curbside pickup.

As Laney waited at the curb, keeping an eye out for Missy's car, she caught the attention of every traveler who passed by. Laney looked every inch a Hollywood movie star, in her fuchsia Sparkelicious, Queen E hoodie outfit, baseball cap and Chanel sunglasses.

Three cars down, in the queue, Laney finally spotted Missy's 1988 silver Lexus sedan, and gave her a wave. She wheeled her black bag to the car, threw her luggage in the trunk, opened the passenger door, jumped in, and gave Missy a hug.

"The eagle has landed," Laney laughed, fixing her baseball cap firmly on her head. "Thanks for picking me up," she added, settling back into the worn leather seat. "Where's Bridge? I thought she was coming?"

Missy put both hands firmly on the steering wheel and moaned. "Oh, don't get me started. They have Chase's kids today, so he wouldn't let her come."

Laney shook her head in disbelief. She now found it hard to sympathize with Bridgett. "You know, be careful with what you wish for…" she preached, referring to her sister's affair with Chase, and to her recent divorce. "I just hope Bridge is happy…" She hesitated. "but Bridge will never be happy. She will always be the victim."

Missy nodded in agreement. They had all tried to tell Bridgett that the grass wasn't always greener, but Bridgett didn't listen; and now she was stuck with a possessive, jealous man, and had zero freedom.

They drove down Highway 85, took Exit 5 to Pelham Road, then turned left into Pelham Heights.

Laney was so excited about the party, and hoped that her mom was still oblivious about the surprise. "So, Mom still doesn't know about the party, does she?"

"No, she thinks that we're taking her to a movie tonight," Missy reassured her. "Brody and I are picking her up at seven, so you can drive Dad's truck to The Goat and surprise her."

Missy had taken possession of their father's beloved Chevy truck after he died, and it pretty much sat idle in her garage, so she was happy for Laney to drive it.

The thought of her deceased father made Laney sad, although she loved the opportunity to drive his treasured truck.

"Perfect…" Laney said, then paused and frowned at Missy. "Brody?" she asked, like a protective mother, "Don't tell me he's back?"

"Yep, he is," Missy shrugged. "Plus, he cooks for me and takes care of Pixy and the house when I travel."

God, Laney thought, *Missy will never change*. To think that she was keeping Brody around just because he cooked and dog-sat for her was ridiculous. But who was she to judge? She had let Matt walk away while her ex was having a child with his soon-to-be-wife.

Laney knew that she was fighting a loosing battle with Missy. "If you're happy, that's all that I care about." She glanced down at the e-mails on her iPhone and scowled.

Everyone had confirmed the party but Matt. The fact that she hadn't heard from him was odd. He usually replied back to her with lightening speed; she hoped that he was okay.

They pulled into the driveway marked 1423 Pelham Road and Brody's Black SUV sat in eye view. Laney tensed up. She dreaded seeing him and hearing him. Brody had the voice of a foghorn, the mouth of sailor, and terrible cigarette breath. He had cheated on Missy so many times that Laney wanted to tell him to go to hell. But she was grateful to Brody for helping her with drunken Thomas when he got out of hand after Charles's funeral. For that one reason, and for Missy's sake, she would at least offer a fake smile and be civil to him.

Laney walked into the back door from the garage and Brody went for her with an obnoxious bear hug with a rum and Coke in hand. Before she could defend herself, he had wrapped his strong arms around her, squashed her boobs into his chest, and gave her a little pat on the butt.

Laney pulled away from his grip and flashed him a pageant smile. "Good to see you too," She wanted desperately to wash her body of his germs. Laney was just thankful that the party was less than two hours away, and she wouldn't have to be around him much longer. She was only stopping at Missy's house to freshen up, and then she would stay with her mom after the surprise party was over.

Brody topped up his drink, poured Missy a glass of white Zinfandel, and offered Laney a choice of wine. "What'll it be, La-La Land Laney?" He snorted, puffing on a Marlboro.

Laney leaned away from the billowing smoke and fanned the remaining fumes that lingered in the air. No one smoked in L.A. and this was killing her. "I'll take a chardonnay, if you have one," she coughed, opening the glass door in the breakfast room that led out to the backyard. "I'll be outside with Pixy," Laney said over her shoulder to Missy in the kitchen, as she hurried out the door for some fresh air. "Missy, aren't you coming out?" Laney yelled from outside as she patted Pixy on the head.

Missy soon followed her out to the patio with two cheap crystal glasses in her hand, passing the chardonnay to her sister. "Sorry, L.A. Lane." She sat down next to Laney on the lounge chair under the cabana. "He's supposed to smoke outside, but he never does."

Laney already reeked of smoke and her new hoodie outfit was ruined. "I don't know how you stand it. And poor Pixy." Laney glanced down at the small black mutt and frowned. "This secondhand smoke isn't good for her either."

"I know," Missy moaned. "But Brody will be Brody."

Missy accepted him the way that he was, and Laney knew that any of her words of wisdom would be wasted on her.

It was almost time for the party. Laney jumped in the shower and scrubbed the smell of cigarette smoke out of her hair. She packed her smoke-filled hoodie in the front compartment of her suitcase, away from the rest of her clean clothes, and got out her BCGB leopard print dress. She dried her hair and pulled it into a high ponytail on her head. It was way too humid outside to wear her hair down, so her cute "I Dream of Jeannie" signature updo would be perfect.

She dusted her face with a powder foundation, a plum blush, and a hint of bronzer and she finished off her look with a touch of shimmering lip gloss. Laney checked herself in the mirror one more time and headed down the stairs to the garage. As she reached the bottom stair, Pixy greeted her with a squeaky toy, wagging her tail at Laney.

"Sorry, I can't play right now. Bye, sweet girl. See ya later," Laney said to Pixy in a baby voice. She leaned down and kissed her on the top of her head. Pixy reciprocated with a wet kiss but lowered her head sadly as Laney walked toward the door.

Laney got in to her dad's beloved truck and drove the small two-seater Chevy down Highway 85 toward downtown. She thought about her father and how much she missed him as she passed the local mall and headed toward the exit that read "Downtown Greenville."

Rarely a day went by that she didn't think about her father, and right now, she felt closer to him than ever. The truck was still so pristine, the way that her father had left it. She could still smell the leather cleaner that he used religiously on the seats. It was almost as if he was in the truck with her.

She made a left onto Main Street, and Laney consciously made a promise to herself to visit her father's grave while she was in town. Charles was buried in the same cemetery, so she would ask her mom to go with her. But since it hadn't even been a year since Charles died, Laney wasn't sure her mom would be mentally ready to go to his grave. Sophie had only been to Clayton's grave twice in five years, and those visits were with Laney. She would broach the delicate subject at the appropriate time.

Three minutes later, Laney arrived at 110 Main Street. She drove the truck under the overpass that connected The Drake Hotel to The Lazy Goat. The valet stand was open at The Goat; she put the truck in park, and left the engine running. She grabbed the valet ticket from the young parking attendant and veered left toward the cobblestone steps that led down to the patio. She stopped at the first step, and sent Missy a text on her iPhone: "I'M HERE…WHERE ARE YOU NOW?" She wanted to make sure they hadn't arrived yet.

Her phone dinged within seconds with Missy's reply: "We're about ten minutes away. Meet us on the patio."

Laney continued down the steps, admiring the stunning backdrop of the Reedy River, and thought about Matt. This was where it all began for them. She hated to admit it to herself but she had missed him terribly. With luck, he would be one of the first people to greet her at The Goat.

From a table on the patio, Laney heard her name being called. Bridgett, with a drink in one hand, was waving her other hand frantically in the air. "Hurry, Lane, they're almost here!" she yelled over the waterfall.

"Okay, I'm coming." Laney sprinted across the patio toward Bridgett.

Bridgett opened the glass doors to the inside bar area. "We're all hiding in here and then we're going to run out and surprise mom when she enters the patio."

Eddie, her favorite uncle and her mom's younger brother greeted Laney with a jolly grin, and a near-empty drink in hand. "Hey, darlin'. Glad you could make it here from Hollyweird." He gave her a big wink. The rest of her relatives, including her cousins, nieces, nephews and Joyce, Uncle Eddie's wife, stood up from their assigned hiding places, and welcomed Laney home.

"Hey, everybody." Laney smiled and waved to her family. Before taking her position under the table beside Bridgett, she scanned the bar area, then scowled. Matt was AWOL. A loud ding came from Laney's iPhone.

"It's from Missy. They're here," she announced with a giggle, rushing over to the table in front of the door where Sophie would enter.

"Everyone take your places," Bridgett shouted, putting her finger to her lips to shush her talkative family. Then she slouched down under the wooden table and waited anxiously for her mom to arrive.

Within seconds, Sophie appeared on the patio, wearing a cold shoulder black satin top and black leopard print Capri's. She looked like a Southern Sophia Loren.

Only my mom would wear leopard print pants to 'the movies', Laney thought as she watched Sophie from under the table and through the windows.

"I thought we were going to the movies?" Sophie said, glancing around suspiciously. "This sure doesn't look like a movie theater to me."

Brody and Missy assured her they had plenty of time, and suggested a quick birthday drink. Sophie wasn't about to turn that invitation down.

Missy nodded to Brody to open the door.

"It's hot out here, why don't we all go in and get one," Missy said, taking her mom by the arm and leading her into The Goat.

Sophie fanned herself in agreement.

Brody held the door open to the downstairs bar. "Birthday girl…after you," he said, in his smoker's voice with Missy escorting Sophie into the large bar area.

As Sophie entered, Laney, Uncle Eddie, Bridgett and the rest of the family jumped out from under the tables and shouted, "Surprise!"

Sophie gasped and threw her hand up to her mouth. "My God, what are y'all tryin' to do? Kill me, on my birthday?" And then she screamed with delight at the sight of Laney, standing in front of her.

"Oh my God, honey, you're here. You're really here. All the way from L.A.?" Sophie ran to Laney and wrapped her arms around her. She then took a step back and analyzed her daughter's appearance. "And your hair, honey, it's freshly highlighted. You look beautiful."

Oh, God, here she goes again, Laney thought. But Laney just bit her tongue and grinned. It was her mom's birthday after all, and she didn't want to argue. "Happy Birthday, Mom," she said, hugging her mom back. "I wouldn't miss your party for the world."

Missy and Bridgett joined Laney and surrounded their mom in a group hug. "We love you, Mom," they cheered.

Sophie beamed from her daughters' affection. She was so happy to have everyone all together for her birthday.

The Goat staff had prepared the tables on the patio for the party. Bottles of wine were placed in silver wine buckets on each of the five adjoining tables that overlooked the river. Uncle Eddie led the group out to the patio. He was always the life of the party and tonight was no exception.

Corks were popped and wine was flowing as Eddie stood to toast to Sophie.

"To my older and much wiser sister," he announced, and winked at Sophie. "May this be the best birthday yet!" Eddie cupped his vodka tonic in his hand and continued. "Love ya, Soph, cheers." He raised his glass to her and everyone followed.

Sophie relished all of the attention. After all of the birthday toasts had been made, she got up from the table and tapped the side of her wine glass with a butter knife.

The grandkids giggled at Sophie's Queen of England like theatrics. "I want to thank everyone for coming tonight," she dramatically announced. She gave Laney a proud glance. "And especially to my Laney, for flying in, all the way from Hollywood."

Bridgett sunk down in her chair and shot Laney a jealous look.

"To family," Sophie sweetly smiled and raised her glass in a toast. The sound of crystal echoed in the air as a tall figure appeared at the top of the stairs. Matt stood like a god, and looked down on them with a wide grin. Missy winked at Bridgett when she saw Matt appear. Missy was so glad that he had responded to her text and booked a flight out of New York to South Carolina. She hoped that Laney would be pleased.

Laney sipped her chardonnay and gasped, catching Matt's visage out of the corner of her eye.

Bridgett flinched at the sight of Matt's arrival and whispered in Missy's ear, "We have to tell her."

"Tell her what?" Missy said distractedly.

"About the girl I saw him with at The Goat last night…Same one I saw him with her tongue practically down his throat, a few months ago, just as Laney was leaving town." Bridgett replied in a rasping whisper.

"Last night?" Missy frowned, trying to keep her voice down. "I thought he just got in today."

"Exactly…sounds a little too suspicious," Bridgett said, keeping an eye on Laney, making sure she couldn't overhear their conversation.

"Why didn't you tell me about this earlier?"

Bridgett covered her mouth with her hand. "I tried to, but you've been a little busy today. Plus, I didn't think she'd ever see Matt again. Especially today."

Missy thought about Bridgett's allegations for a second and then dismissed them. Her sister was always trying to meddle in everyone's business and gossiping about nonsense; this was probably all a mistake. "Let Laney enjoy her moment. Keep all of this quiet. I'm sure you're blowing things out of proportion…as usual."

Bridgett sighed, "Alright, big sis, sounds like an order." She remained tight-lipped but her face tensed as Matt approached the table.

"Surprise! I heard that someone was having a birthday," he announced with a smile, walking over to Sophie, bending down and giving her a big hug.

Sophie peered over Matt's shoulder and winked at Laney. With her mother's intuition, she wasn't surprised to see him at all. She knew that if Laney was in town, Matt wouldn't be far behind. He seemed to be turning up whenever her daughter was around. And Sophie believed this man loved her daughter. Sophie just hoped for Laney's sake that she was right about Matt's affections.

Laney sat speechless in her chair. She had given up all hope on Matt's arrival, resigning herself to the probability that he'd met someone else in New York. She was somewhat miffed at him for not RSVP-ing to her party invitation, and remained reticent.

Matt walked passed Sophie, leaned down and kissed Laney on the cheek. "So, are you surprised to see me?" he whispered in her ear, giving it a little nibble. He briefly imagined what it would be like to ravish her body.

Laney felt a tingle down her spine and giggled, quickly dismissing the fact that he had dissed her. *God, he's sexy*, she thought, *who cares if he never responded to the party invitation.* She had missed Matt more than she imagined.

Laney took her designer sunglasses off and locked eyes with Matt. "I'm so happy that you're here. I've missed you terribly."

He kneeled down in front of her chair and kissed her, and Laney kissed him back. It was a kiss that Laney never wanted to end. But it had to, because it was Sophie's birthday party, after all.

Bridgett glared at Matt from across the table with her arms folded. She still didn't trust him one bit. But she would do as her big sister said and keep her big mouth shut… for now. She had ruined enough lives by being impulsive, so she'd watch and wait for the right time, if ever, to divulge her secret to Laney.

Sophie rose from her seat at the head of the table, cleared her throat and tapped the side of her wine glass again. She glared down at Matt and Laney with a twinkle in her eye. "Listen up," Sophie announced with a smile in her voice. "Either you two love birds need to get a room, or join the rest of the party."

Everyone chuckled…except Bridgett.

"It seems my daughter has gotten her present, now what about mine?" Sophie faux-sulked. "I'm the birthday girl."

Laney went over to the table where Sophie's beautifully wrapped gifts sat and gestured for Missy and Bridgett to help her present them to their mom.

"This is from Uncle Eddie and Aunt Joyce," Missy said, handing a huge red package to Sophie.

"Here's one from all three of us," Laney smiled, placing the hot pink package on the table beside the others.

Laney reached for a smaller package wrapped in purple paper that was hidden under a pile of larger gifts. "And who's this pretty package from?" Laney sang, looking at the nametag on the present. She read the tag and frowned.

"Well, I'm waiting," Sophie said impatiently from the head of the table.

Laney remained silent, unable to speak. Missy rushed to her from the other side of the table and glanced down at the nametag and gasped.

"Give it to me," Bridgett said loudly, running over to Missy and snatching the tag out of her hand.

Missy shot Bridgett a warning with her eyes, hoping she wouldn't announce the name on the gift tag, but Bridgett didn't get the hint and blurted it out anyway.

"It's from Charles?" she declared with a dazed expression on her face.

The family that never stopped talking was now silenced. Sophie's face turned pale, like she had just seen a ghost. "What?" She reached across the table and grabbed the package out of Bridgett's hands.

She feverishly opened the small gift card. And there it was in black ink, "To my darling Sophie. Happy Birthday! Charles."

"This has to be a joke," Sophie cried, glaring suspiciously over at her brother. "Ed…is this one of your silly pranks?"

Eddie responded without hesitation, "No, Soph…I swear it's not from me."

Sophie held the small package in her hand and inspected it like the FBI. First she smelled it, and then she shook it.

Anxiety filled the air as the entire family waited for Sophie's inspection to reach its conclusion.

"Maybe you should open it, Mom?" Missy suggested.

Bridgett shook her head incredulously. "What if it's really from Charles?"

Sophie threw the purple box down on the table like it was poison. "But how did it get here?"

And then Missy remembered. "I saw it sitting on the small table in your kitchen when we picked you up, so I brought it along."

The waiter walked by to check on the party and Sophie yelled out for another bottle of chardonnay. Her party spirit had now turned melancholy. She picked up the tiny package again and held it with both of her hands. "Girls, I don't know what to do?" She squirmed in her seat. "This is spooky and fabulous at the same time."

Laney put her arm around her mom from the next chair and said, "I always told you that Dad and Charles were both around you. I guess I was right. Charles's spirit is here right now."

"Oh, this is so crazy." Sophie held the package up to her mouth and whispered. "Charles, you were always surprising me."

She tore into the purple box like an eager child. "OK, this is freaky." Sophie's hands shook as she reached in to pick up the two-carat diamond that she had lost from her wedding ring a few months earlier. "I've been looking all over the place for you," she said in awe, cupping the sparkling diamond in her hand.

"What is it, Mom?" Bridgett crowded in to try and see.

Everyone stood from their chairs and gathered around Sophie.

"I think I'm going to faint," she declared, holding up the brilliant diamond.

The girls gasped. They now knew that this wasn't a joke. Sophie had indeed lost her diamond and had been heartbroken about it at the time.

Laney handed her mom a glass of water and fanned her with a food menu. Missy asked the waiter for a cold wet cloth to wipe her mom's face.

Sophie sipped on the ice water and then grasped Laney's hand as the air from the menu caressed her face. "I've never believed in ghosts," she solemnly announced. "But I sure as hell do now." And at that moment, Sophie wasn't spooked anymore. She now felt calm and at peace.

"This has been an amazing birthday." Sophie clenched the diamond tighter in her hand. "I'm so glad that everyone could come to my birthday party, including my beloved husband. Now, let's keep the party going with another round of drinks." Sophie now felt a closure with Charles's death. She'd often declared that life after death was hogwash, but she was a believer now.

The girls stayed close to their mom's side while Matt mingled with the rest of the family. As the party went on, Sophie looked happier than ever. But Laney and Missy knew that this strange chain of events had to be taking a toll on her.

"Go have fun, you two," Sophie said, shoeing them away like flies. "Matt and Brody are waiting for you. Now go on."

Eddie pulled up a chair beside Sophie and gave them the signal that it was okay to leave.

Matt smiled at Laney as she approached him from the other end of the patio.

He had been away from her for only about thirty minutes, but to Laney it felt like years "I missed you," Matt said, taking Laney in his arms and planting his lips to hers. "How's your mom?"

Laney giggled and kissed him back. This time around she wasn't going to shun his affections. "My mom seems fine, but I know that she isn't," she replied, keeping one eye on her mom. Laney fell back into Matt's arms and cooed.

It was after eleven and Uncle Eddie and Aunt Joyce said their goodbyes to Sophie and the girls and walked up the stairs to their car. They were the last of the family to leave. The girls packed up the birthday gifts while Sophie tucked the infamous box and purple wrapping paper that her diamond came in, into her purse. Matt loaded the packages into the back of Brody's SUV.

Sophie stood by the passenger door and yelled out to Laney who was handing the gifts off to Matt. "Honey, I'll have Missy and Brody take me home. You two go and have fun." She flashed Laney a devilish smile. "You come home when you feel like it. I'll leave a key out for you under the doormat."

Bridgett couldn't hold in the secret any longer. "Lane, I don't think…"

Missy grabbed Bridgett's arm and shoved her into the backseat of the car before she could finish her sentence.

Laney was too worried about her mom to give her sister's comment a second thought.

She walked over to Sophie, now sitting in the back seat of the SUV and frowned. "Mom, I can't let you go home and spend the rest of the evening alone."

Sophie brushed Laney's cheek with her hand. "Honey, I'm fine. Go have some fun." She closed the door and rolled down the window. "I'll see you later tonight, but be a good girl."

Laney blushed. "Mom!"

Sophie winked. "And Matthew, please tell your father I said hello."

"I will," Matt nodded, glued to Laney's side. "Oh, he just sent me a text telling me to wish you happy birthday."

She blew them both a kiss as the electronic window began to close. "See ya later, honey," she chirped through the small gap of the glass, as the car pulled away.

Matt and Laney waved to Sophie watching the car drive off into the night. They were finally alone. The Drake Hotel stood invitingly in front of them. Matt took Laney in his arms. The heat was rising off of their bodies. They were like two pubescent teenagers, ready to rip each other's clothes off.

"I've already gotten us a room," Matt whispered to Laney in between kisses.

"You didn't?" Laney gazed up at Matt, at first suspiciously, then smiled.

Matt reached into his jean pocket, pulled out The Drake room key, and waved it like a tantalizer in front of Laney. She blushed, but when she didn't object to his offer, Matt grabbed her hand and led Laney through the lobby.

The elevator doors couldn't open fast enough. Once inside, they began to devour each other's body. They prayed that no one else would get on before they reached the eighth floor. As they kissed, a loud ding rang out.

Laney peeled her lips away from Matt's and glanced up. "We're here. I guess we should get off."

"Yeah, good idea," Matt laughed, realizing that Laney wasn't aware of her inadvertent pun.

The doors opened. Matt picked Laney up and carried her down the hall. Room 833 was the last door on the right.

"Here we are!" Matt said, balancing Laney while fitting the card key into the door.

They smothered each other in more kisses as he threw the door open. He placed Laney gently down on the plush tan carpet and they began tearing off their clothes; without even making it to the bedroom, they fell onto the floor.

"God, I've been waiting for this for so long." Matt panted, running his hand slowly over Laney's body.

"Me too," Laney whispered.

They made love, and Laney forgot about her divorce, their age difference, and the rest of the world. She felt alive again. Being with Matt made her feel whole.

Matt looked deep into Laney's eyes. "This is the best night of my life…not counting the first night that I met you."

Laney responded with another kiss as a tear fell from her eye. This was the best night of her life too, bringing up a feeling that was possibly love. But she wasn't ready to tell Matt that just yet. She wondered how he spent his nights in New York, and whether or not she was the only woman in his life.

Chapter Twenty Three

Matt slowly opened his eyes as the sun pierced through the light and airy white linen curtains. He gazed down at Laney still sleeping soundly in his arms, and smiled. He squeezed her tightly and kissed her forehead. Laney stirred as she felt Matt's soft lips touch her skin, but she quickly settled back into his arms and fell fast asleep.

Matt closed his eyes, caressed Laney's arm as she slept, and thought about their magical night of lovemaking. He reached for his iPhone on the bedside table to check the time. He glanced at it and frowned. *Shit*, he thought to himself as he read a text message from his boss. He turned his phone over and sighed, kissing Laney on the forehead again to comfort her and himself. It was almost nine and he had to meet his dad for coffee soon. He also knew that Sophie was probably worried about Laney. He would have to wake his *sleeping be*auty soon.

"California Girl," Matt kissed Laney on the top of her head and whispered.

Laney squirmed and slightly opened one eye. "The sun's so bright," she moaned, putting her hand over her eyes. "I'm not a morning person," she frowned. "What time is it?" Her blonde hair was matted down and stuck to her head. "I don't wanna get up," she whimpered like a baby.

Matt laughed. He was quite the opposite. He loved the mornings, especially this one.

"Wow. You West Coast people do like to sleep, don't you?" he teased.

"See, us Yankees 're up oy-ley and ready ta seize da day," he declared, in his best *Tony Soprano* accent.

Laney giggled and nudged her elbow into his side. "Are you saying that Californians are lazy?"

Matt sat up and gazed into Laney's tired eyes. "Yes, but thank God you make up for your laziness with your beauty."

She gazed up at Matt's chiseled face. His dark wavy hair was perfectly in place, and he looked meticulous after only a few hours of sleep. *It isn't fair*, Laney thought, *but I am ten years older.* And she sure felt it, staring at his youthful face.

He leaned down and kissed her with vigor.

She kissed him back, but soon pulled away from him and looked toward the window with worry. "So, what do we do now?" She knew that Matt would have to return to New York very soon.

Laney's long bangs fell across her eyes and Matt gently brushed them away from her face. He tilted her face up to his, leaned in and pressed his lips to hers. "We can do whatever we want to do."

She frowned and unlocked her lips from his. "I know, but what do you want to do about us?" Laney didn't want to play any more games. "Please be straight with me, Matt."

Matt sighed. He wanted so badly to tell Laney what she wanted to hear, "You know that I wanna be with you, but the city is calling," he whispered in her ear, running his fingers down her arm. "And I have to leave, tonight."

"What?" Laney cried, sitting up in the bed. "I thought you were leaving tomorrow."

"I did too." Matt sat up and put his arms around Laney, hoping to comfort her. "But I got a text while you were sleeping from my boss, and I have a meeting first thing in the morning."

Laney felt like a woman who just had a one-night stand. *Maybe he has to get back to his REAL girlfriend in New York?* she thought. *But I'm not going to ask him about it. I'll be damned if I'm going to look desperate and jealous.* She grabbed the robe from the end of the bed, put it on, and said evenly, "I should really get dressed and go."

Matt sprung out of bed and walked to the foot of the bed, where Laney was standing. He took Laney's hand. "No, don't go. We still have an hour before I have to meet my dad."

But Laney didn't respond. She needed to hear more.

Matt squeezed her hand. "This is not a game to me. I'm crazy about you," he said, gazing into her eyes. "I love you, California Girl. I've loved you since the day I met you."

Laney's heart couldn't help but to believe what Matt was saying, even though her head was telling her differently. Her eyes filled with tears. "Then why can't you stay? I don't want you to go…or for this to end."

Matt gently removed Laney's robe. "It doesn't have to, and it won't." He lifted Laney's naked body onto the bed, falling on top of her. They made love over and over again. His father would have to wait, and so would Sophie.

After an hour of lovemaking, they sat up against the headboard, both exhausted. Laney knew that she had to cherish every last second that they had together. They would soon be on opposite coasts again.

Matt laid his head against Laney's. She tingled with the feeling of his sweat on her forehead.

"I'll call you every week," Matt announced.

Laney scowled. "Just every week?" She said, kissing him passionately on the lips.

The sound of another text message sang from Matt's phone. He reached over to the bedside table and turned it over to check it. He shrieked with a twinkle in his eye, peering down to read the message. "Okay, every day." He replied, kissing Laney in between sentences and turning his phone back over. "I wish I could wake up like this every morning."

"Me, too." Laney cooed, trying to sneak a peek at his text

message, but he had it angled the other way. *He obviously doesn't want me to see it*, she thought. Thomas's affair had left her so paranoid. She hated feeling this insecure. She knew she had to stop being suspicious. She didn't want to scare Matt off with her childish ways when she was supposed to be the more mature one in the relationship. She also knew she had to learn to enjoy the moment. She would love to see him every day, but right now, that was impossible.

"Well, I guess we better get going." Matt sighed, reluctantly releasing Laney from his grasp and slowly getting out of bed.

"I know. I hate it. But my mom's probably wondering where I am."

Matt grinned. "I'm sure she is."

They got dressed and kissed each other passionately goodbye. Laney drove back to her mom's house, while Matt walked down to Starbuck's to meet his dad for coffee.

As Laney drove away from downtown Greenville to her mom's home in the burbs, Laney cranked up the 1986 stereo in her dad's Chevy and sang along to *A Thing Called Love* by Bonnie Raitt. She hadn't been this happy in years. Of course, Matt was one of the reasons for that, but as she bended the notes perfectly in key, Laney realized even more how much joy music also brought to her life. *I wonder if there's a way that I could start singing again*? she thought, as she flew down the freeway.

Exiting I-85, she turned right onto Ridge Road, and then left on to Chatham Road, and drove through the enormous iron gates that led into Hampton Hills. Her mom's upscale French provincial home sat quietly in the cul-de-sac, at the end of the street. Laney pulled into the driveway, parked and walked through the garage into the back door. Sophie had seen Laney pull in the drive through the window, and had raised the electronic garage door for her.

Laney opened the back door and shouted from the kitchen, "Hello? Mom?" The house was strangely quiet, with only the sound of the television blaring from the den.

Sophie soon appeared from the dining room dressed in black jeggings, a black top, high-heeled leather boots with her face fully made up. She placed her hands on her hips like May West and declared. "Hi, honey. So, I guess someone had a pretty good time last night."

Startled by her mom's abrupt entrance, Laney jerked her head around.

"Mom, stop!" she blushed. "But my night was pretty amazing."

"That's my girl," Sophie said, sounding like a proud madam. "Not that I fully approve. I just would have preferred that you let me know if you weren't planning on coming home last night. But you're an adult."

Laney pouted. "I did leave you a message."

Sophie walked into the kitchen and plugged in the coffee maker. "You did?" She frowned, staring down at her incoming messages on her cellphone. "Oh...here it is. This phone is so darn irritating." She threw it down on the counter and smiled. "You're off the hook now." She peered into Laney's tired eyes. "I think we need some caffeine, don't we?"

Laney nodded and yawned as Sophie put on a fresh pot of coffee, and then relaxed on the stool at the kitchen island. Sophie put the lid down on the coffee pot and sat down on the stool next to her.

"I hope you had fun, honey." Sophie smiled, wanting to hear more about Laney's little adventure.

Laney's tired eyes perked up. "I did, mom. Matt's so amazing." She was giddy with love and Sophie knew it. She desperately wanted her daughter to be happy and she hoped that Matt might be the one for Laney; but inside she was sad and lonely. She desperately missed Charles. It was getting harder without him, not easier as everyone said that it would.

Laney went on gleefully about her newfound happiness until she was practically blinded by Sophie's big diamond ring.

"Wow! That's some bling!" Laney picked up Sophie's left hand

and examined the newly reset diamond.

Sophie's next door neighbor was a jeweler. He had secured the diamond for her in the 18k gold mounting first thing that morning.

"Charles sure knew his diamonds, didn't he?" Laney shook her head in admiration.

"He loved giving me diamonds and I loved getting them from him." Sophie tried desperately to smile as tears filled her eyes instead. "I know he's here somewhere with me. I just wish that I could see him."

Laney put her arm around Sophie. "Charles is here, Mom, and so is Dad. I know that they're both in this room right now…" She thought for a second. "Mom, would you want to go to the cemetery and visit Dad and Charles?"

Without hesitation, Sophie smiled. "I would love to honey. I've been so wanting to, but I've been too sad to go by myself."

"Okay, let's finish our coffee, get dressed and go." Laney agreed.

They finished their morning routine and drove to the cemetery to see the only two men that Sophie had ever loved, knowing it would be therapeutic for them both. They called Missy and Bridgett on the way, to see if they wanted to meet them at their father's grave; but they declined. Even though it had been five years since Clayton had died, they were still unable to deal with his death.

"It's sad," Laney said to Sophie as they drove through the cemetery gates, up the narrow paved drive, lined with flowers, "I wish they would meet us."

They reached the trio of adjoining mausoleums at the top of the hill. Sophie pulled her luxurious sedan up to the curb next to them and put her car in park. "At least we tried, honey." Then she frowned. "I always forget which mausoleum your father is in. It's all still a blur."

Laney pointed to the stone building in the middle. "It's that one." She remembered her father's service like it was yesterday. "I'll take the key and make sure it opens the door." She said, taking the key from her mom. She opened the car door, walked to the glass doors, placed the key in the lock and pushed the door open.

She waved at her mom to get out of the car and walked bravely into the silent, small churchlike room. She scanned the Italian marble crypts in the walls; each one, identified with a name and a date. Her eyes stopped on "Clayton Montgomery 1932-2000." She kneeled down and put her hands to the cold marble.

"I miss you so much, Daddy," she cried. "I wish that I could see you again and that you could hear me. There are so many things that I want to tell you and ask you." Laney sobbed, backing away from the crypt and sitting down on the wooden bench in the middle of the cold mausoleum.

So many emotions had been hidden deep inside of her for so long, and it felt good to let them out. She wiped her eyes, and decidedly walked back over to the marble slab and spoke to it as if she was talking directly to her father. She asked questions about her future and prayed that that her father was there, listening to her. She leaned in and pressed her lips gently on the cold tile. "I'll see you again soon, Dad. I love you."

She exited the mausoleum, and gazed up over the brow of the hill where her mom was standing, in front of Charles's grave. *Oh, no*, she thought, M*om shouldn't be alone.* Laney hiked past grave after grave decorated with vases of roses, sunflowers and tulips, joining Sophie at the top of the hill. She looked down at his placard: "Charles McKenzie Williams 1927-20011." Laney put her arm around Sophie and smiled.

"Mom…Charles and Dad can keep an eye on each other every day," she remarked, noticing how Charles's grave looked down on the mausoleum where her father lay. She thought it ironic that they had gone to the same high school and were friends for over 35 years.

"You're right, honey." Sophie replied, checking the eye line of both gravesites.

Laney wanted to be strong for her mom, but she was way too emotional. "I miss Dad so much."

Sophie grasped Laney's hand. "I know. I miss your father too, and my sweet Charles." They shed some more tears then walked down the hill, back to the car. They were thankful that they had each other to share this moment together.

"I'm just lucky that I had two great loves in my life," Sophie declared, with a sniffle. "Most people never have one."

Laney frowned. "I thought I had one, but I was wrong."

"But you may have found him now, honey, have faith."

In the distance, Laney spotted Missy's Lexus parked in front of the mausoleum.

"It's Missy and Bridge. I can't believe it," she cried.

"Me either, that's wonderful." Sophie too was surprised that after five years her other daughters had finally made an appearance at their father's gravesite.

Laney and Sophie approached them as Missy and Bridgett stepped out of the sedan.

"Where's Dad buried?" Bridgett queried without even saying hello. She wanted to get this over with and fast.

Missy was more diplomatic. "I don't think that I'm ready for this, but here I am." She looked like she'd already seen a ghost.

"Girls, I'm so happy that you're here," Sophie said, embracing them both.

"Me too," Laney added, joining in the group hug. "I know this isn't easy, but it will be good for the soul."

She led her sisters down to the mausoleum. Missy's face turned white and she stopped in her tracks, turning back toward the car. "I don't think that I can do this."

Bridgett wasn't going to let her chicken out. "If I'm going in there, then you are too."

She grabbed Missy by the arm and pulled her back toward the entrance. "We had a deal."

Laney opened the glass door with the key and Missy and Bridgett tentatively followed her to their father's crypt.

"I can't look." Bridgett covered her eyes and cringed.

"Me either," Missy cried, doing the same.

"Do it for Mom's sake," Laney whispered to them, with Sophie looking on. "She needs some support here." Although, Laney was the youngest child, at times like these, she felt like the oldest. "I'll walk up there with you." She took both of their hands and guided them to the marble tomb.

Sophie sat solemnly on the wooden bench in front of Clayton's crypt and sobbed.

"This is so weird," Bridgett said, staring morbidly at the grave. "I can't believe he's really in there."

Laney smiled and said, "His spirit left his body when he died. So, Dad's here right now, and around us every day."

Missy couldn't handle all the talk about death and sped out the door. Even her tough exterior couldn't get her through this.

"I miss him," Bridgett whispered.

"Me too," Laney nodded. "But we have to know that he's in a better place."

"Wow, that's deep," Bridgett replied in a hippie-style tone, still not sure of what Laney was talking about.

Sophie went out to check on Missy. She hoped that one day Missy would be able to go to her father's grave and have some closure with his death. But it looked like today wasn't gong to be the day.

Missy bolted for the car and Sophie hightailed it after her. "Honey. I'm right behind you, if you need me."

Missy spun around. "Mom…dammit, I should be here for you," she cried. "I need to do this for myself and for you." Missy sighed. "So…let's go see Dad."

Sophie and Missy marched back to the mausoleum, hand and hand, like two strong soldiers going into battle. They joined Laney and Bridgett in front of the crypt.

Not a word was spoken, only tears were shed. But for the first time, they were all together to grieve their father and the loving husband that Clayton had been to Sophie.

Chapter Twenty Four

It was a busy Saturday afternoon at The Goat. The girls had decided to celebrate their grieving time together over a nice glass of wine. There was one table left on the patio so they snagged it.

Laney glanced down at her iPhone and frowned. She anxiously scanned her e-mails and double-checked her voice mail. *Hmmm*, she thought, *not a word from Matt.* Since she wouldn't see him again before he left for New York, she at least wanted to tell him goodbye over the phone before he got on the plane. Also, there was no word from the bank. She was hoping to be approved for a line of credit that would allow her to retain all of her employees, and to keep her business afloat. Things weren't looking good. Not only was her Melrose office space expensive, but the costs of manufacturing overseas had also gone up. She was afraid that without the extra cash flow, Sparkelicious was doomed.

The waiter approached their table and Sophie ordered a bottle of California chardonnay before he could even hand out the lunch menus.

Missy checked her Blackberry for work emergencies while Bridgett fielded calls from the still very jealous Chase.

"Look everybody. Guess who?" she smirked, pointing to the screen on her phone that read "Chase, Accept or Decline."

"Decline?" Bridgett said, pretending to be torn with indecision; then casually pressed the red button. "I need a break. He'll have to get over it."

Sophie cheered from across the table. "Good for you, honey."

Laney squirmed in her chair, unable to relax. She cupped her phone in her hand, hoping that Matt would call or send her a text.

"Everything okay, L.A. Lane?" Missy asked, putting her Blackberry away.

Laney placed her iPhone down on the table in front of her. "Oh, just hoping to hear from Matt."

"Why? Isn't everything okay?" Missy shot back like she knew something that no one else did. But everyone ignored her tone.

Sophie butted in and winked at Missy. "Oh, I would say that everything is just peachy with them."

But Laney wasn't in the mood for jokes. The waiter arrived with a bottle of wine and four crystal glasses. He poured a glass for each of them.

Bridgett snatched the glass of wine from the waiter's hand and took two swigs. "You did it with him, didn't you, Lane?" she giggled. "I hope he hasn't already dumped you for…"

"Bridgett! Stop it!" Missy snapped. "You don't have any proof."

"No, Missy, it's okay," Laney said, perplexed. "What are you talking about, Bridgett? Dumped me for who?"

Bridgett swigged down more wine. "Well, I didn't want to tell you, but I saw him kiss another girl at The Goat."

Laney flinched. "What? When? Who was it?"

"A few days ago. Some cute blonde. About the same age as him. I don't know who she is. But I've seen them together a couple of times. Maybe, it's just me, but I've got the feelin' it's an old girlfriend?" she suggested. "Seemed to have that kinda "energy."

"An old girlfriend?" Laney raised her voice. "Why didn't you tell me? You seem to want to tell me everything else?"

"I wanted to, but Missy told me not to," Bridgett pouted, shooting Missy an *I told you so!* look.

Missy sighed and kicked Bridgett under the table. "I'm sure it's nothing, Lane, don't worry."

"That bastard," Laney seethed. She couldn't believe what she was hearing. *I knew he was too good to be true.*

Laney's iPhone sang from the table.

"It's him," she announced, glaring at the phone. "I'm not going to pick it up."

"I think you should talk to him. He's innocent until proven guilty," Sophie said, handing her the phone.

Laney held the receiver to her ear and looked out toward the river. She was distant as she spoke to Matt. "Glad that you could finally find the time to call."

Matt held the phone to his ear but the engine noise of the plane was making it hard for him to hear Laney. He turned up the volume on his iPhone.

"I'm sorry. I was dealing with emergencies at work," he said loudly. "I wanted to tell you…" his voice broke up from the bad connection.

Laney shook the phone as if it would help. "What?" she asked. Laney had hoped he would tell her about the girl that Bridgett saw him kiss without her having to ask.

"…sorry…I have to go. The stewardess is giving me the eye. I'll tell you lat…" Matt said, in a barely audible tone, his voice trailing off into the distance, without a goodbye.

Laney disconnected her phone and sat there in stunned silence.

Missy touched Laney's arm. "What's going on? What did he say?"

"He's already on the plane, about to take off. The stewardess made him hang up. He wanted to tell me something but he had to go," she said sadly, still clutching the phone in her hand. "Maybe you're right, Bridge. Maybe he used me? Maybe I was just a conquest to him?"

Sophie glared at Bridgett, "Oh honey, I don't think Matt's that kind of guy. There must be an explanation…" But Sophie couldn't come up with any.

Laney didn't know what to think. But she couldn't get any answers right now; Matt was on the plane, and Bridgett didn't have any more pertinent information. She'd thought Thomas would never stray either. "You know, Kara's pregnant." Laney blurted out, raising her glass to her mouth.

"What?" Sophie gasped in a high-pitched voice. "Thomas and Kara are having a baby?"

Laney gulped down her wine. She was starting to feel a little tipsy and it felt good. "Yep. The man who never wanted kids is having a child."

"I knew it," Bridgett declared. But before she could say anything else, Missy kicked her leg under the table to shut up.

"And it gets better," Laney quipped. "I just wrote him a big fat check for $526,000 from my Sparkelicious account because it's deemed as community property. It was money earned while we were married and before he filed for divorce. All thanks to the State of California," she moaned. "I may have to kiss Sparkelicious goodbye."

They were hushed by Laney's bad news.

"Honey," Sophie broke the silence, "I thought that something was wrong when I talked to you a few weeks ago."

"I didn't want to worry you. This is my problem…" Laney trailed off, "maybe it's for the best."

"For the best?" Sophie squealed. "You love what you do, and you've worked your can off. Plus, you're a damn good designer."

Missy and Bridgett voiced their agreement.

"Everything happens for a reason," Laney sighed. "Maybe God's trying to tell me something."

"Well, honey, he sure does work in mysterious ways." Sophie said, reaching into her purse and pulling out another box wrapped in purple paper. "Speaking of spirits, I'm still being haunted with mysterious gifts." She placed the package on the table.

The girls went silent. This was now getting a little eerie. "Another box from Charles?" Bridgett winced.

Sophie picked the box back up and put it to her ear. "Yep…found this one beside the bed when I woke up this morning."

Laney scratched her head and put her problems aside. "This is now getting weird. Aren't you going to open it?"

Sophie sat the box back down in the middle of the table. "I'm going to let him sweat a little bit this time," she said with a wicked grin on her face. "Honey, you made me crazy enough when you were alive. Now, stop it," she exclaimed, looking skyward. She threw her hands up in the air. "Oh, what the hell." Sophie picked up the box and ripped it open.

The girls watched with anticipation. "Hurry, Mom," Bridgett yelled, biting her nails.

Sophie pulled the top off of the 3"x2"x5" box and reached inside. "Oh, he's such the jokester," she sneered, holding up a rolled up piece of light green paper. "It's nothing."

Laney raised her eyebrows as she looked more closely. "No, Mom, I think it's a check."

Missy chimed in. "I think you should unroll it."

Sophie took their advice. "Looks like you're right," she declared, placing her leopard print readers on the tip of her nose and inspecting the check. "Yep, it's a cashier's check written out to me, 'Sophie Williams'." She held the check six inches from her face. "No, it can't be!"

Bridgett grabbed the check out of Sophie's hands. "It's for $500,000," she said nonchalantly…then starred at the check again and screamed, "Oh my God, I've never seen that many zeros!"

"Let me see it." Missy snatched the check out of Bridgett's hands and held it up for Laney and her to take a peek. Laney stared up at Charles's handwriting and smiled. "It looks authentic to me."

Bridgett sipped on her wine. "Now, I finally know why you married him, Mom."

"Shut up, Bridgett," Laney and Missy said together.

While the daughters were excited about their mom's newfound fortune, Sophie wasn't so thrilled. That only meant that Charles's sons would come after her if they found out about her windfall, demanding their share…if not all. Sophie was miffed. She wondered why she didn't know about this extra stash of money while Charles was alive. Even though they relished in an extremely comfortable lifestyle while he was alive, she would have preferred to enjoy this money with him when he was healthy and still on the planet. They could have done so many other things together with this money.

"God does work in mysterious ways," Sophie said as her eyes suddenly lit up. She looked at the girls and beamed. "I know! I'll give the money to you girls. I'll split it three ways…she did the mental math, "about $165,000 each. Then Laney, honey, you can keep your business running."

Missy and Laney looked at each other and shook their heads in disagreement while Bridgett clapped her hands with excitement. "That's the best idea I've ever heard."

"I think it's the worst," Laney said, and Missy seconded.

"Mom, Charles left this for you, not us," Laney said sweetly. "I don't want your money, Mom. "

"Me neither, mom." Missy declared.

"Well, I could sure use it. I could do some real damage with it," Bridgett said with a wicked grin. "But, no…you keep it, Mom."

Sophie folded up the check and put it away in her wallet for safekeeping, "You're good girls."

She stared calmly out at the Reedy River and smiled. Her face was radiant and relaxed. It was almost as if the spirit of her beloved Charles was near by, smiling at her. She was more at peace with his passing than ever. These gifts that he'd left for her were indeed therapeutic.

"Well, now. I think it's time for a little champagne," Sophie said, waving the waiter over to the table and ordering a bottle of Dom. "Charles is paying for this one," she giggled.

The girls were impressed with their mom's champagne selection, and couldn't help but get lost in Sophie's upbeat mood.

Bridgett fidgeted in her chair and chomped on a piece of gum. "So, Mom, what happened with the senator?"

Without missing a beat, Sophie cocked her head back and replied, "I dumped him. Told him to go back to his wife and make it work."

"You didn't?" Laney's mouth flew open in disbelief.

Bridgett frowned and rolled her eyes at Sophie. "Mommm…but he's so hot, and so powerful."

Missy just sat there passively and listened as her sisters gave their mom advice. She was still getting over Brody's affair. *What do I know about men*? Her sisters both thought she was an idiot for taking Brody back. *So who am I to give advice on love?*

Sophie sipped her champagne. "Well, it was fun, but way too much too soon." She put her flute down and turned to Laney. "Honey, good Lord, I'm being so selfish. I'm so sorry to hear Thomas's baby news."

"Me too, Lane," Missy added.

Laney twirled her champagne flute in her hand. "You know, Mom, Thomas took my money and broke my heart, but it's okay because at least I've learned something from it. No man is ever going to hurt me again," she said in a tipsy tone. "I thought that I was falling in love with Matt and that I'd finally found a decent, honest guy. But now, look what's happened. If he's a player, he's damn good at it. Anyway, I don't need a man to make me happy."

"Honey, like I said, it's not for sure. You need to find out for yourself," Sophie urged.

"Yeah, L.A. Laney, Mom's right," Missy chimed in.

Bridgett didn't say a word. She'd said enough already.

Laney continued to stare at her flute, as if it somehow contained the answer. *Bridgett isn't the most reliable source*, she thought. *Yes, mom's right. I need to find out the truth from Matt for myself.*

Chapter Twenty Five

Early Monday morning, the sun was just starting to peek over the horizon. Sophie sat at the table in the sunroom, overlooking the expansive backyard. She held the check from Charles in her hand and thought about how she would spend it. She was deeply worried about Laney's financial problems and really wanted to help her out, but she knew her daughter too well.

Laney will never take any money from me, Sophie thought, *she's way too stubborn, but I have to find a way to get her through her crisis.* Her mind then drifted to exotic locales. *Maybe I'll go to Europe for the first time? Or buy a house on the beach?* Sophie daydreamed, but with those thoughts, she began to miss Charles even more. She didn't want to do these things alone, she wanted to do them with him.

Was I just plain stupid to dump the senator? she contemplated. *At least I wouldn't be alone in the world.* She shook it off and stopped feeling sorry for herself, realizing how lucky she was to have been loved by two amazing men in her life. Sophie got up from the table, poured herself a cup of fresh coffee, when she heard a knock at the back door.

"God, is it already nine o'clock?" she mumbled, glancing at the kitchen clock. It was only 8:30, so Sophie wasn't losing it, like she thought.

She opened the door and Hallie, Charles's housekeeper of twenty years, stood at the door. "You're a little early this morning, aren't you Hallie?" Sophie said pointing down at her gold diamond watch that Charles had given her when they got married.

"Just thought I'd get an early start today, Ms. Sophie." Hallie replied grumpily, walking past Sophie, into the kitchen, without further explanation.

"Well, okay, whatever you have to do. I'll get out of you way." Sophie frantically cleared up the pile of papers that she had placed on the kitchen counter and tossed some magazines in the trash. Every time Hallie came over to clean, it seemed like Sophie was working for Hallie and today was no exception.

Hallie placed her cardigan and hat in the laundry room and gathered her cleaning supplies while Sophie organized her mess. The two women had never cared for each other very much and it was obvious by the silence. They had just tolerated one another for Charles's sake. Hallie's loyalty had always been to her boss, Charles, and never to Sophie. And when Charles married Sophie, she resented another woman being in "her home."

Hallie missed her boss desperately. They had a great working relationship. Charles had been very good to her over the years, paying for her health insurance, giving her Christmas bonuses, and paying her dearly for her less than adequate housekeeping services.

The two women continued to danced around each other without saying a word until Sophie finally broke the awkward silence. "My daughter's in the blue guestroom asleep, so please wait until she wakes up to go in there," Sophie said, picking up her tennis shoes off of the floor.

Hallie ran her rag across the kitchen counter and looked up. "Oh, don't worry, Miss Sophie. I'll do that room last."

"Perfect." Sophie replied, putting on another pot of coffee, hoping that Laney would smell the fresh aroma, wake up from her slumber and have breakfast with her.

From the bedroom, Laney heard voices coming from the kitchen and the smell of caffeine lingering in the air. She turned over in her bed, with her eyes barely focused, and peered over at her iPhone, on the bedside table. She reached for it and saw a text from Matt. She immediately perked up as she read it. "Made it to NY. I'll call you soon." That was it. No "I miss you," or "I love you," or "about that hot sexy blonde I was with…"

Hmmm, she thought. *Well, I can't wait any longer. I have to find out about this girl.* She grasped the phone in her hand, sat up in bed and wiped her bloodshot eyes, hoping to get a little clarity. *Okay, I'm ready*, and she typed in her reply, "Maybe you might want to tell me about the blonde you were with the other night?"

She read back her words, pressed "send" and waited anxiously for Matt's response. But after five minutes, he still hadn't responded to her question. Laney glared at the phone and frowned. *Well then, he must be guilty*, she thought, *but I really should give him a chance to explain.* Laney desperately wanted to send him another text but she stopped herself. *I'm a grown woman, not a teenager. Even though I'm now acting like one.* She clutched her phone in her hand, staggered out of bed, and grabbed her robe from the end of the bed. She made her way, slowly, down the hall toward the kitchen.

Hallie dusted the top of the coffee table in the den and greeted Laney with a soft-spoken hello. Sophie smiled at Laney as she walked sleepily toward her in the kitchen. "Here, honey. This should help." She held a white china cup in her hand. Sophie knew that Laney wasn't a morning person and hoped the caffeine would give her a boost.

Laney groggily took the cup from her mom's hand and walked into the sunroom. Sophie followed and offered her cereal, juice, and a bagel.

Laney shook her head and moaned, "Mom, I can't eat yet. Let me drink my coffee first."

"Okay, I'm sorry." Sophie tiptoed around Laney's "morning mood," sat down at the table with the Greenville Times, and silently read the paper. She placed her readers on her nose and peered over at Laney, slouched on the sofa, applying Visine to her eyes. Her mother's intuition kicked in. She knew there was something else wrong with her daughter besides just being tired. "Honey? Did you hear from Matt?" she gently asked. "Did he make it to New York okay?"

Laney sipped on her coffee, and leaned her head back on the sofa, and yawned. "Yeah, just got a text from him. He's safe and sound."

Sophie put the paper down on the table. " Did you ask him about that mystery girl?"

"Yep. But he didn't respond." Laney sighed. "What a bastard. Guess Bridgett's right after all."

"Oh, honey, stop it. You still don't know what's true until you hear it from him. He's probably in a meeting or something, or his phone has lost reception. I'm tellin' you that boy's crazy about you," Sophie declared, walking over to the sofa to console her.

Laney's mood turned philosophical. "You know…whatever will be will be. I can't control what's going to happen or not happen. I never thought I'd get a divorce, or possibly loose my business either, but look what's happened. And, now Matt? What was I thinking, getting involved with him? I should have known that a younger guy wouldn't stick around for long." She raised her coffee cup to her lips, and over the rim she watched Hallie surreptitiously put a purple box in the cabinet drawer in the den. *Now it all makes sense*, Laney thought. Hallie was the one placing the gifts strategically around the house.

"Honey, I really want to give you some money," Sophie insisted.

"Mom, thanks…don't worry, I'll be fine," Laney replied, keeping one eye on Hallie.

Sophie sighed her frustration.

"I need to go to the bathroom," Laney abruptly announced. She excused herself and scurried down the hall. Sophie was oblivious to what was going on and went back to her reading.

Laney peeked her head into the guestroom where Hallie was dusting. "Excuse me, Hallie. Can I talk to you for a second?"

Hallie put her cloth down and raised her eyebrows with concern. "Is everything okay, Miss Laney?"

"Everything's fine," Laney smiled. "I just noticed that you had a purple box in your hand a few minutes ago."

Hallie sat down on the bed. "I did, Miss Laney," she whispered. Laney sat down beside her and waited patiently for Hallie to go on.

"It's from Mr. Charles for Ms. Sophie," Hallie finally admitted. Hallie turned to her left and winked as if to someone who was standing there. But clearly, there was no one, Laney noted. "He wants me to give all them gifts to her."

"My mom thinks the gifts are really from Charles," Laney said. She needed Hallie to understand the emotional ramifications these gifts were having on her mom.

Hallie took Laney's hand and stared her directly in the eye. "They are, Ms. Laney. Mr. Charles is right here…aren't you, sir?" she said, looking to her left. "See…he just shook his head."

Laney believed in a lot of things, including spirits, but she wasn't sure what to think right now…until she felt a cold breeze sweep through the room. "I-I think you're right…he is here," she shivered.

"That's right, Miss Laney. You have to believe," Hallie smiled, handing her a blanket.

"So, what do we tell my mom?" Laney asked, wrapping the throw around her.

Hallie looked to her left again like she was staring straight at Charles. "We tell her that the gifts are from Mr. Charles, because it's true."

Laney had no more questions for Hallie. It was clear that she believed that Charles's spirit was alive, in his home, so why try to tell her otherwise. Plus, her mom seemed happier than ever knowing that Charles was still floating through her life, so to speak.

In the next instant, Sophie, glowing like a light bulb, walked into the bedroom, holding the purple box in her hand. "Look! Another gift from Charles."

Hallie winked at Laney, as if to say, there's nothing wrong with telling a little white lie. Laney's phone chimed in her hand. She looked down and it was a text from Matt: "Sorry, just got out of a meeting. And heading into another one." And that was it. Laney doubled checked his text again to make sure he didn't say anything about the "girl" that she'd questioned him about. She wanted desperately to believe that he was innocent, but the evidence was mounting against him. Laney closed the text and didn't reply.

Chapter Twenty Six

The flight from Atlanta to L.A. seemed longer than it's usual four hours, but it gave Laney time to reflect on her life. As the First Class flight attendant refilled her glass with chardonnay, she thought about her career and her love life. *I have worked way too hard to see my fashion line fall from grace, but maybe filling for bankruptcy is my best option after all?*

While she hated to give Thomas half of the Sparkelicious money, and putting her company into dire straights, Laney was philosophical about it. *Like I always say, 'Everything happens for a reason.'* She did like designing, but her company had become something of a burden in the last few years, making her more and more overworked. And dealing with the celebrities who promoted her line, and their contractual demands, was exhausting.

Her love for the business was waning fast, but she did have her employees to think about, so she would do whatever she could to keep them employed. As of now, she had exhausted all of her investment connections, and so far, she didn't have any takers. Even though her line was well known, the advertising, celebrity endorsements and the cost of manufacturing overseas was going up every day. And her daily operation costs had doubled since moving to Melrose Avenue.

The trip back to South Carolina had gotten her thinking about her mortality. Her life was going by way too fast, and she felt so unfulfilled. *Is it because I didn't have a child? Or the fact that I am now divorced, and feel more alone than ever? Or because Matt has possibly moved on with his ex?* she wondered; her imagination getting the best of her.

The plane landed at LAX, and Laney caught a cab back to her Hollywood Hills home.

The traffic on the 405 was running at its usual snail's pace even at seven o'clock on a Tuesday evening. After almost an hour, the yellow cab finally reached Laurel Canyon.

The driver took a right into Laney's drive and pulled up in front of her dark empty home. Laney got out of the cab and collected her luggage from the driver. She walked toward the door feeling sad. It was now hitting her that she was alone, and that no one would be there to welcome her home for the first time in twelve years. The usually confident Laney Montgomery was now deflated.

She rolled her suitcase into the entryway, walked into the kitchen and turned on the pendant lights that hung above the island. She glanced around her beautiful modern kitchen and the rest of her luxurious home and sighed. *Not bad*, she thought, mentally patting herself on the back. And she began to put all of those negative thoughts out of her head.

The night was still young; Laney opened the wine cooler and pulled out a bottle of Rombauer, one of her favorite, buttery, Napa Valley chardonnays. She poured herself a glass and began sifting through the mail at the kitchen island. As Laney sipped her wine, the light beside the sofa clicked on and she nearly jumped out of her skin. She grabbed a filet knife from the knife rack with one hand, and the phone to call 911 with the other, when she realized it was Thomas sitting on the sofa. He looked worn out and tired. His beard was full, his eyes sad.

"God…what in the hell are you doing here?" Laney cried. "And how did you get in? You scared the shit out of me."

Thomas tried to raise a smile. "I had to see you," he said, holding up a black key box for her to see. "You should get a new hiding place for this."

Laney rolled her eyes, walked over, and snatched the box out of his hands. "What's so urgent that you have to break into my house? Do you need more money for your new baby?"

Thomas reached for her hand but Laney pulled away. "There isn't a baby," he sighed. "Or rather, it wasn't *my* baby."

Laney crossed her arms and straightened up. "What are you talking about?

Thomas stood up and let out a deep sigh. "Like I said, the baby isn't mine. I found out Kara's been fooling around with practically every director in Hollywood…hedging her bet. I was such a stupid fool. I don't know what I was thinking. *I* was the baby…I mean I was acting like one. I know you deserve better, but Lane, I promise, if you give me another chance, I will do *anything* to make it up to you. Can you please forgive me?" Thomas pleaded.

Laney sat down in the chair, rubbed her brow, trying to break the magical spell he'd always seemed to cast on her. She was so torn. The man she once believed to be the love of her life, then betrayed her, was begging her forgiveness. And the man that she was still deep down in love with had also quite possibly betrayed her with his ex-girlfriend, and was on a different coast, and still hadn't explained himself to her. *As a matter of fact, he got the hell out of Dodge after we made love*, she thought. *And he never responded to my text.* Laney was thoroughly confused. *Maybe Bridgett's right about the ex-girlfriend? Or Matt finally realized that I was just too old for him?*

"Well, aren't you going to say something, Lane?" Thomas kneeled down at the foot of the chair and gazed up at her with big doe eyes.

"You broke my heart, and you left me almost bankrupt, and now you want me to take you back?" she said with tears in her eyes.

Thomas squeezed her hand. And then leaned toward her with an endearing British smile. "I'll pay you back the money. And I promise I'll never break your heart again. I love you," he whispered, moving in to kiss her.

Laney felt his tender lips on hers. She breathed in the smell of his familiar breath. She remembered their passionate kisses, their amazing nights of endless sex and she began to kiss him back. Thomas French kissed Laney and they both moaned.

Laney didn't know why, perhaps purely on instinct, but she opened one eye and peered down. She noticed what appeared to be a small tattoo on the inside of Thomas's left arm. It took a couple of seconds before what she was looking at came clearly into focus: KARA in bold black letters. She broke off the kiss and jumped to her feet, pushing Thomas away.

"I can't do this," Laney said, marching toward the door.

"Where are you going?" Thomas sprinted after her like an abandoned puppy.

"To let you out," she said evenly. "It's over. I want you to leave."

"What?" He reached out for her, but she brushed him off. What's wrong with you Lane?"

"This!" Laney grabbed Thomas's left arm and positioned the KARA tattoo in front of his face.

"Uh..." Thomas struggled, "I can explain..."

"Explain it to your next wannabe actress girlfriend."

"Huh? Are you serious," he said in his rich brogue accent.

Laney opened the door and pointed to the outdoors. "I've never been more serious in my life."

Thomas clearly read the look in Laney's fiery eyes, and he knew he didn't have a chance. He hung his head and walked slowly out the door. "If it's any consolation," he said, turning back to her, "I'm really sorry, Lane. I do hope that one day you will forgive me."

"Maybe one day, but not today." Laney replied and slammed the door.

Laney walked back into the kitchen, picked up her glass of wine on the granite island and took a sip, mentally patting herself on the back for what she had just done. She pictured Thomas walking defeated, down the block to where he must have parked his car so he could "surprise" her. *Nice try, Thomas*, she thought. *You will never be good enough for me.* Then Laney's mood shifted and she became melancholy. *Am I going to end up an old washed up woman with a houseful of cats? I was so hoping Matt might be the one, and now I can't tell if he's a player, or is he's for real?*

Laney was savoring her wine and trying to put the negative thoughts out of her mind, when her iPhone began to ding from her purse. She removed it from the side pocket and read the text messages coming in. There was one from her assistant, welcoming her back to L.A., another from Missy and… she tensed up and her heart began to race…a message from Matt. *I shouldn't even give him the time of day*, she thought, but she couldn't help herself. She had to see what he had said. She nervously twirled a strand of her hair in her hand and read the message aloud: "I need you to do me a favor." She paused, reread the text and frowned. *Still no I love you, I'm sorry, or I miss you?* she thought. *And still no response to my text about the girl in question*? "I'm not doing any favors for you until I know the truth," she said as if he could hear her.

Laney angrily texted him back. "So, are you ever going to tell me the truth? Who was that girl Bridgett saw you with?"

She stared at her phone and another text came in from him. "I told you in the text yesterday, she was just an old friend. Nothing more, she's my past, you're my future."

Laney rolled her eyes. *Yeah right*, she thought, *I've heard that before. And what text is he talking about*? She quickly scrolled through her texts from Matt. *I never got…*It was a day late, but there it was, the text from Matt briefly explaining about the girl. Laney desperately wanted to believe him.

Before she could text Matt back, another text came in from him. "If you believe me, please do me a big favor. A dear friend of mine is playing tonight at the Cinegrill. He needs a good turnout for his first show. Can you please go see him? For me? Please! Gotta go."

Laney shrugged her shoulders. She had to hear Matt's voice. She wanted to hear him say the things he had texted to her about his ex-girlfriend over the phone. She went to her favorites list on her iPhone and touched "Matt" with her finger. The phone rang four times and then went to voicemail.

She sipped on her glass of wine and thought about Matt's strange message over and over again. After over an hour of debating with herself on whether or not to go to The Cinegrill, Laney shrugged and decided to arrive L.A. style--fashionably late. She went back to the master bedroom and spruced herself up.

She then threw on a simple, black mini dress, black, metallic wedge sandals, put her hair up in a high ponytail, grabbed her Gucci purse, and was out the door.

The L.A. rush hour traffic had now subsided. She made her way from Highland to Hollywood Boulevard in about twenty minutes. She arrived at The Hollywood Roosevelt and parked her SUV at the valet stand in front of the hotel. Laney handed the keys to the valet attendant.

"Are you here to see the new act at the Cinegrill?" the young man asked, tagging her keys.

Laney smiled. "Yes. He's a friend of a friend."

The valet smiled back. "Well, he's great. You'll love him."

The bellman opened the door to the hotel for Laney. The sounds of a baby grand piano filled the air as she walked through the lobby toward the Cinegrill. There was an overflow of couples, standing outside of the famous listening room, waiting eagerly to get a seat. *Wow, this guy's popular*, Laney thought as she squeezed herself through the Hollywood crowd.

Laney found the one and only empty stool at the far end of the bar. She plopped down and immediately felt claustrophobic, squashed within the hip L.A. music crowd. She used the bar for leverage, raised herself up, and peered over several tall patrons in front of her, trying to catch a glimpse of the musician on the stage.

As Laney peeped through a small gap, with a bird's eye view to the piano, she gasped. It was Matt playing his heart out on the baby grand. She flung her purse back over her shoulder, muscled her way through the crowd, and stood in front of the piano so he could see her.

Matt finished the song and raised his head up from the mike. The light streamed across Laney's face. He beamed as his eyes met hers. "I would like to introduce my new duet partner…California Girl," Matt announced into the microphone.

Laney blushed, her knees began to shake, and she felt a rush of panic come over her as she mouthed the words to him, *I can't get up there and sing right now.*

Matt moved the microphone away from his face, got up from the baby grand, walked over to Laney and took her hand. Laney melted from his touch. Without any reservations, they began to kiss, forgetting about the Hollywood onlookers.

The creative throng cheered. For this, was better than renting a Hollywood romantic comedy. Matt led Laney over to the piano, gave her a hand-held mike, and they sang three songs together. They struggled a little through the first song, *Cry Me A River*, trying to find their range and match their harmony. On the second song, *Feeling Good*, they were better able to feel out what stanzas to sing separately, and when to blend their voices together. By the third song, *Get There*, their instincts kicked in and it was like they'd been performing together for years.

And the L.A. pack thought so too. They erupted in a round of applause after their last song. Matt and Laney stood up from the velveteen stool and basked in the glory of their admirers. Matt thanked the crowd for coming, took Laney's hand, and led her over to the bar.

"I wasn't kidding. I want you to be my duet partner." Matt stared deeply in to Laney's eyes.

Laney stammered, "A-Are you serious? What about your old girlfriend? What about our age difference? Plus, you live in New York."

He smiled at Laney in the candlelight. "I told you, I want you… and only you. There never has been anyone else. And I couldn't care less about our age difference."

Laney raised her eyebrows. "I want to trust you and believe you. But Bridgett said that she saw you with her twice."

Matt looked at her and sighed. "I texted you the short explanation…here's the long version. Yes, I met with Jill twice. The first time, we sat at The Goat and kicked around old times. We were each other's first love and we once thought that we'd have a future together. Jill was an amazing violinist and won a scholarship to Berklee, which she couldn't pass up, so we said our tearful goodbyes. She caught me by surprise when she showed up at The Goat that night…straight from the airport. I thought she'd moved on and had long forgotten about me. As it turned out, she wasn't over me, and after Berklee things didn't go so well, so she came back because she wanted to give us a second chance." Matt paused and took a sip of wine.

"And what did *you* say?" Laney prompted nervously.

"I told her that I'd met you and was falling in love. She was sad, but seemed to understand and left. Then, I moved to New York, Jill stayed in South Carolina and we didn't see each other for months until the night before your mom's party. She found out that I was in town, having a drink at The Goat, and showed up unannounced, again. She had a few too many Chablis and got a little too 'friendly' with me…which is what Bridgett probably saw. But after I walked Jill to her car, she suddenly turned on me…she always had a fiery temper…and she tried to guilt-trip me into taking her back." Matt paused for another sip.

"And *you* said?" Laney echoed herself.

"I told her that I was deeply in love with you, wished her a wonderful life, then turned around and left," Matt said with finality.

"That was it? Nothing else? Because from what Bridgett claims she saw of you two, she thought for sure…"

Matt smiled as he unlocked his iPhone and tapped on the green text message sign. He scrolled down, found what he was looking for, and passed his phone to Laney. "I almost deleted this."

"What is it?" Laney's brow furrowed.

"My last text from Jill."

Laney hesitated and then grasped the phone and started reading:

Jill: *What happened to all of the hot sex you promised when we got back together? Liar!*

Matt: *First off, I didn't "promise" you anything, and second, all of that talk was long ago – and before I met the woman I'm going to spend the rest of my life with.*

Jill: *GO TO HELL! NO…GO FUCK YOURSELF ASSHOLE!*

Laney looked up from the phone and shook her head. "Why didn't you just forward her text to me? That would have explained everything."

"Because I thought you'd get mad," Matt said, taking his phone back.

"How could I get mad at that?"

Matt gave it some thought; then scrolled farther down Jill's text: *P.S. Have a "wonderful life" yourself…with your old shriveled up MILF!*

"Ouch! Yeah, that hurts." Laney frowned. "But not as bad after reading what you texted to her."

Matt squeezed Laney's hand. "You will always be able to trust me. Do you believe me when I say that?"

Laney nodded her head. "Yes. I believe you.

Matt lifted Laney's hand to his mouth and gently kissed it. "Good." He then caressed her face with his hand and gazed into her eyes. "And finally, I *used* to live in New York."

"So, are you saying that you've moving here?"

"Yep, after the hotel manager heard my demo reel…and it probably didn't hurt that I'm the son of a controversial senator," Matt admitted. "He offered me a gig that I couldn't refuse. I quit my job and hopped on the next plane." He kissed her on the lips.

"Plus, I missed you, and I can't live without you."

"You do?" Laney wanted to burst. She was so happy that she had finally found out the truth from Matt. He had restored her faith in love again. She loved his confidence and exuberance for life. His positive energy was so contagious. Laney giggled and replied, "Yes."

“Yes?” Matt crinkled his brow.

“Yes, I’ll be your duet partner.” Laney smiled.

Matt grinned like a little boy. “What about…for life?” he asked, sitting on the edge of his seat.

Laney kissed him on the lips and raised an eyebrow. “Well, that’ll cost you more than a song.”

Matt pulled out a dollar from his jeans pocket and handed it to Laney. “Well, I’ve got the money.” He kissed her madly.

When they finally came up for air, Laney’s eyes were filled with tears. “Well, that’s good because Thomas took most of mine.”

“What?” Matt blinked in disbelief.

“I didn’t want to tell you about this now, but I’m going to have to say goodbye to Sparkelicious,” she said softly. “But you know, it’s okay. It was time.”

Matt pulled Laney closer. “Everything will be okay, I promise.” He looked deep into her eyes. “I love you, California Girl, and ever since I first saw you, I’ve always known I wanted to spend the rest of my life with you. And, you’ll never have to worry about anything because I’ll always take of you.” He assured her. “And, besides, who needs money, when we’ve got this kind of love?”

“You’re right. I love you too, Matt, the bar…I mean, Matt, my piano man,” Laney replied, planting another kiss on his lips.

As they celebrated their love and Laney’s iPhone rang loudly from her purse.

“Shouldn’t you get that?” Matt asked, pulling his lips from hers.

“No, it’s probably Thomas wanting more money from me.” Laney reached for her phone to turn it off.

“No wait. It’s Alvin.” Matt said, peering down at her phone. “I think you should take the call.”

Laney held the phone to her ear and frowned at Matt as she answered it. She listened to Alvin, and soon perked up with interest. “Really? Are you serious?” she laughed. “This is amazing. I can’t believe it.”

Matt sipped his champagne and caressed Laney’s hand. After a couple more minutes, Laney hung up the phone and shrieked, "Someone has offered to buy Sparkelicious."

"That's fantastic!" Matt replied, giving her a kiss, "Who is it?"

Laney was shell-shocked. She couldn't believe the news and was overcome with a huge sense of relief. "Alvin said they're a solid buyer, a conglomerate. They already own a few successful clothing lines and are willing to pay top dollar for mine. Even after I give Thomas half, I'll still have plenty of money left over to pay off my debts and to put some money towards our music. Plus, they're willing to keep all of my employees on the payroll and I'll have the option to be on retainer for two years as a consultant—which, after the divorce, Thomas won't get any of."

"Well, this night deserves some major toasts," Matt said, holding his glass to hers.

"To you, to me, to Alvin, and..."

Laney jumped in, clinging her glass to his, "…and to us making beautiful music together for the rest of our lives."

At that moment, Laney knew that her life was finally on the right path. She would now be able to resurrect her dream of being a singer. *Better late, than never*, she thought. And she would also take this journey with someone she loved and someone who believed in her. *Life really does begin at forty*, Laney thought. She felt like the luckiest girl in the world. Her life was now, truly, Sparkelicious!

ABOUT THE AUTHOR

Libby has been a national on-air television personality for over 15 years with appearances on ShopNBC, Shop-At-Home and The Food Network. She was the youngest ever nominee for Poet Laureate of South Carolina following the release of her poetry book *A Winning Heart.* Libby is a graduate of the University of South Carolina and was a contestant in the Miss America and Miss USA programs.

Chardonnay Press is a Limited Liability Company

www.ingramcontent.com/pod-product-compliance
Lightning Source LLC
LaVergne TN
LVHW020712110826
845149LV00012B/2219

* 9 7 8 0 9 8 5 8 4 7 6 3 0 *